IN THE SHADOW OF THE PROPHET

A. AFAF

CONTENTS

Historic Note   vii

Prologue   1

PART ONE
1. NOOR: Hassan   5
2. NOOR: Fatima   10
3. NOOR: Journey   18
4. NOOR: Sheikh Ruhi   29
5. NOOR: Hallah   36
6. NOOR: Sawdah   41
7. NOOR: Mecca   50
8. NOOR: Beloved   58
9. NOOR: Home   65

PART TWO
10. SAWDAH: Sheikh Ruhi   75
11. NOOR: Amira   82
12. SAWDAH: Hallah   88
13. NOOR: Leila   95
14. SAWDAH: Nadia   103
15. NOOR: Priestess Stone   111
16. SAWDAH: Allah   118
17. NOOR: Abdullah   126
18. Sawdah: Al-Islam   135
19. NOOR: Al-Islam   141
20. SAWDAH: Ahmed   148
21. NOOR: Amr   158
22. SAWDAH: Mecca   167
23. NOOR: Hajj   175

PART THREE
24. SAWDAH: Hajj   187
25. SAWDAH: Home   196
26. SAWDAH: Ali   203
27. SAWDAH: Noor   213
28. SAWDAH: Hassan   219

Epilogue   223

Acknowledgments   225
About the Author   227

*This story is for Victor,
who taught me to love history,
for Afifi, who taught me to dream,
and for Lulu, who taught me to believe.*

In The Shadow of the Prophet
Copyright © 2023 by VK Publishing

Interior Book Formatting: AuthorTree

All rights reserved under the International and Pan-American Copyright Conventions. No part of this book may be reproduced or transmitted in any form or by any means, electronic or mechanical, including photocopying, recording, or by any information storage and retrieval system, without permission in writing from the publisher.

This is a work of fiction. Names, places, characters and incidents are either the product of the author's imagination or are used fictitiously, and any resemblance to any actual persons, living or dead, organizations, events or locales is entirely coincidental.

Warning: the unauthorized reproduction or distribution of this copyrighted work is illegal. Criminal copyright infringement, including infringement without monetary gain, is investigated by the FBI and is punishable by up to 5 years in prison and a fine of $250,000.

HISTORIC NOTE

Many of the lines of poetry that introduce each chapter herein come from the Mu'Allaqat, the Hanging Verses of Mecca, a group of seven pre-Islamic poems, which legend says hung on the walls of the Kaaba in Mecca and remained even after the pagan idols and other pre-Islamic relics were removed.

Also included in this work is the poetry of Al-Khansa, a seventh century female poet whose elegies for the dead are among the greatest works of pre-Islamic and early Islamic poetry.

There are several wonderful scholarly translations of the Mu'Allaqat poems and those of Al-Khansa, and the author encourages her readers to seek them out. The simple translations in this novel were created for this work alone and would not have been possible without the loving guidance of the author's mother, an extraordinary scholar, teacher, and mentor, who does not know how truly exceptional she is. The Arabic script for each poem is written in her hand.

CONTENT WARNING

This book includes themes of Domestic Violence, Infertility, and Miscarriage. Please be aware of these sensitive topics while reading.

هَلْ غَادَرَ الشُّعَرَاءُ مِنْ مُتَرَدَّمِ
أَمْ هَلْ عَرَفْتَ الدَّارَ بَعْدَ تَوَهُّمِ

Have the poets left a place in need of patching?
-Antarah

PROLOGUE

In the name of *Allah*, the most merciful, the most compassionate, we bid you greetings, fellow traveler. We are Noor and Sawdah, the daughters of Sheikh Amr Ibn-Ghazi. We have come from a far land to tell the tale of our people. We pray you may see what we have seen, lest our history be lost forever. We live again in these words, and through these words, we live again in you.

PART ONE

كَأَنِّي غَدَاةَ البَيْنِ يَوْمَ تَحَمَّلُوا
لَدَى سَمُرَاتِ الحَيِّ نَاقِفُ حَنْظَلِ

*On the morning of parting, as they prepared to go,
By the acacia trees, my heart split bitter gourds.*
-Umr Ul Quais

CHAPTER 1
NOOR: HASSAN

There is a stillness to the air just before the first lights that herald the dawn, like a lover, pausing, her hand on the door, savoring the delicious ache that comes in that moment, knowing her beloved waits on the other side. That stillness, that breath of anticipation, stops my dreams and opens my eyes.

I breathed in the crisp air, the smell of the desert, of water, of life, and thanked the gods for another day. I moved silently out of the low bed, careful not to wake Hassan.

Wrapping myself in a blanket, I walked outside to the cooking stove, started a fire underneath and watched the flame curl the ends of the kindling. I marveled, as I did every morning, how one small fire could fill the land with light. I removed the cover from the pot of water I had prepared the night before and set it carefully atop the stove. As the flame grew beneath it, I collected spices and added them to my mortar. They called to me as I crushed them together. First, cardamom, whose sweet bite burned my nose as it released its pungent oils. Sweet cinnamon filled the air with the smell of promise and desire. Next came mint, fresh and clean as the day itself. All these I slid into the water.

While I waited for it to boil, I braided my hair. The plait fell to my waist, where I tied it with a leather cord. The water was rising now, and I stirred it back carefully as it boiled once, twice, three times. The scent of the spicy mixture filled the air. I used a cloth to lift the pot from the heat and set it on the ground.

From lidded baskets, I removed a bit of cheese and two long, flat sheets of bread. I rolled the cheese inside the bread and placed both rolls onto a wooden dish. I poured the hot herbal broth into a cup, carrying it and the dish back into our small house.

Setting the dish and cup at the side of the bed, I stroked my beloved's soft curls. The grey mist of the coming dawn gently illuminated his beautiful face. I loved to watch him sleep. "Hassan," I whispered, "it is time."

He sighed and rolled toward me. "Just a few minutes more," he said, eyes still closed.

I brushed my finger along his bottom lip. "Wouldn't you rather spend those minutes with me?"

He smiled and opened his eyes. In one quick motion, he gripped my waist and flipped me onto the bed at his side. I laughed. "Hassan, your drink will get cold."

He growled, nuzzling my neck with his lips. "Let it."

Desire coursed through my body at his touch. I had loved this man my whole life and had been his wife now four years. I knew every line of his skin, every expression on his face. By now, he should have been familiar, ordinary even. He was not. With each touch of his hand, each taste of his mouth, I wanted him more. Our bodies fit together as though the gods had fashioned us from one stone. The taste of his mouth was like a drink of cool water in mine. I loved him with every part of my being. Could I have pushed my soul through my fingers, I would have pressed it into him, to feel, even for a moment, the thrill of truly being one with my beloved.

He held and kissed me, our bodies melting into one another as our souls returned to the mundane earth. I reached over him to fetch the cup. He sat up and took a sip then set it down, shaking his head. "Still too warm," he said. His eyes twinkled as he moved toward me again.

I pushed him away, smiling as I got out of the bed. "Time for you to get ready." He sighed and shrugged. I handed him his food. "Eat this. Braheem and Sameer will be here soon."

"Where's yours?" he asked, watching me slip on my shift and simple cotton work dress.

"I'll eat something later," I said.

He knew me well enough to know I might well begin my day without stopping to eat. He shook his head. "Bring your drink at least and sit with me a little."

I went outside, poured the pungent liquid from the pot into another cup and walked back toward the door. As I stepped to cross the threshold, the cry of a hawk pierced the silence. I dropped the stone cup and watched it shatter as it hit the ground. My heart stopped in my throat, and I cried out.

Hassan was at my side in an instant. "What was that?" He looked at my face. "What's wrong?"

"I dropped the cup." I was shaking. "I'm sorry."

He put his arms around me. "It's nothing, Noor. It's just a cup. It means nothing." He stroked my hair, and my body relaxed into him. "Come on. I'll help you clean it up."

He picked up the larger shards, and I swept the rest into a pan. When we finished, he went back inside to collect his things while I watched the dark stain soak into the pale earth.

The sun's first rays peeked over the horizon as Hassan saddled his horse. I had collected the last of the food and clothing he would need for his journey. As I set the parcel into Shihab's saddlebag, I felt

Hassan's body behind me and turned to meet his embrace. I put my head on his chest and felt hot tears fill my eyes.

"I shall miss you, my beloved," he said softly. He pulled back and noticed the tears as they slid down my face. He wiped them away. "No need for tears. We will be together soon."

I nodded, but I could not speak. My heart raced. He would be gone a month, an eternity. We had sometimes been apart a few days at a time but never this long. His journey would take him east, to my mother's lands, then south with her people to our holiest of cities. We would not meet again until Mecca.

"Ride quickly, my love," I said, when at last I found my voice. "Ride with the gods."

We walked together to the eastern gate of the village. Shihab followed, his beautiful black mane glistening even in the dim light. Hassan's companions approached on horseback, and Hassan nodded toward them. "It is time," he said.

I patted his horse and whispered in his ear. "Keep him safe, Shihab. Bring him home to me."

Hassan mounted then leaned over to take my hand. He bent to kiss it. "Be well, Beloved." I opened the gate for the riders. Hassan took up his reins. "Let's go."

I watched him ride away into the desert until at last he disappeared into the rising sun. I felt a hand on my shoulder and turned to see my mother standing behind me. "May the sorrow sown at parting reap a joyful reunion." I smiled at the old words. "Come," she said, "let us give thanks."

Mother carried a basin of water, and we walked along the eastern wall to the small altar where rested our sacred stone, icon of the goddess Manat. Manat was the goddess of my ancestors, of my grandmother's family. When my grandfather married her, carrying her from her home in Yathrib, she brought with her the faith of her people, passed down by the women of her family. She had passed it to her daughter, and my mother had taught it to me.

Mother held out the basin. I dipped my hand in the cool water and shook some drops to the west. "We give thanks for what has passed." I sprinkled water to the east, saying, "We open our hearts to what will be." To the south, I said, "May our foundation bring us strength." Then, to the north, "May our lives be testaments to the gods we honor."

Mother set the basin down before the stone. "Manat, Daughter of Al-Lah, we ask your blessing on your people who love you and for the safety of those who journey forth in your name."

We stood together, looking out at the desert. I heard the sound of the village waking behind us. "I saw Fatima on my way to you this morning," Mother said. "She needs help making baskets."

I nodded. "I'll go to her now."

My mother slipped a stray strand of hair behind my ear. "Our work and the journey will help time pass more quickly."

We walked toward the village together. At the door of my brother's house, she stopped. "Give Rullah my love," I said, "and a kiss for the baby."

Mother nodded, and I could see in her eyes that she was still reeling from the thrill of having helped to birth her first grandchild. She knocked gently on the door, her features set again into the confident gaze of the healer.

I smiled and walked on.

مِنْ مَعْشَرٍ سَنَّتْ لَهُمْ آبَاؤُهُمْ
وَلِكُلِّ قَوْمٍ سُنَّةٌ وَإِمَامُهَا

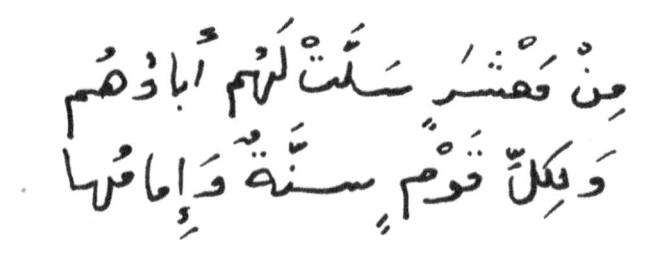

We come from a people whose ancestors have paved the way,
And of course, each has its customs and its captains.
-Labid

CHAPTER 2
NOOR: FATIMA

The village was awake now. My friends and family mingled around the well, the heart of the village. I waved good morning to Hassan's mother who was feeding her chickens. She smiled and waved back. I saw a touch of sadness in her eyes, but perhaps it was only a reflection of my own.

I found Fatima in her favorite spot, sitting on the ground at the foot of the enormous fig tree that stood near the village center. This tree had begun its life as three saplings, each with its roots only a few feet apart. Over time, the whims of fate had woven the branches of these three trees together. They grew into, around and through each other until the three became one. Its fruit could feed the entire village, and when my great-grandfather came to this spot, this tree had spoken to his heart, calling him to settle his Bedouin family in the valley between it and the little river that nurtured its roots.

Fatima looked up and smiled as I drew near. "Noor!" she called, "Come. Sit with me."

I bent to kiss her cheek. "Good morning, Auntie." She was not my mother's sister but might just as well have been. They had been friends from childhood. Fatima and her daughter, Rullah, had no other family but ours. When her husband died, Fatima left my grandfather's city, bringing her infant daughter, to live with us. Rullah and I had grown up together, cousins in spirit. When Rullah married my brother Ghazi, we became one family in every sense of the word.

Fatima moved a basket aside to make a place for me to sit. I reached into the pile of palm fronds and settled into the work. I enjoyed the simplicity of weaving. It busied my hands and left my mind free to wander.

"So, Noor," Fatima said, looking intently down at her work, "Your lover has left for *Bayt* Afhaz?" That was the name Fatima always gave the large, thriving city that my mother's ancestors had established along the route to Baghdad, *the house of Afhaz*.

I laughed. "If by *lover* you mean my husband, then yes, he left at dawn."

She looked up, smiling. "I have seen the way he looks at you. He is most certainly your lover." She looked away, and I saw an uncharacteristic cloud pass over her features. She put her hand on mine and gripped it gently. "Cherish this time, Noor. It will pass quickly and will not come again." She was silent and still, looking out at the horizon.

After a few moments of quiet reflection, she shook her head and smiled gently, then turned back to look at me with a wicked gleam in her eyes. "If the gods will, perhaps Hassan left his seed behind when he took leave of you." She grinned and quickly added, "Praise Hadad," naming one of our gods, the one whose province was fertility. She patted my hand before returning to her work.

I shook my head and giggled at her brashness. There was no topic off limits with my Auntie Fatima, but I was determined to change the subject. "Are you looking forward to Mecca?" I asked.

She nodded. "It has been too long since my last trip. It will be good to see old friends and visit the Kaaba once more."

I had been to Mecca only once. I was ten years old the last time we made a family pilgrimage. "I remember the noise of the marketplace," I said, "and the delicious smells. But the journey seemed to take longer than a month."

Fatima laughed, "You were a child," she said. "To a child, any journey is an eternity. And a month is a long time for any traveler."

We worked on in silence until my mother appeared. She sat with us and picked up one of Fatima's baskets, turning it over in her hands as though examining the handiwork. "You missed a turn here," she said, shaking her head sadly.

"Where? Show me!" Fatima snatched the bowl from my mother's hands and turned it over. "Liar," she snapped. "It's perfect."

"I didn't want you to get a big head," my mother said sternly. They melted in a fit of giggles that had them crying from laughter, and I saw for a moment the little girls inside them both.

Fatima wiped a tear from her eye and asked, "How is my grandson today, *Sitt* Leila?"

"*Our* grandson is happily napping in his mother's arms," my mother said, adding, "*Sitt* Fatima." Since the baby's birth, just two days ago, my mother and Fatima had taken every opportunity to call themselves by their new title, *Sitt*, from the word *Sittu*, meaning grandmother. They meant both to insult and praise one another. I shook my head and smiled. I loved to watch their joy.

I heard a fluttering sound and looked up from my work. My sister, Sawdah, came running toward us, her long black hair billowing behind her as she ran. She stopped at the tree and leaned against it, chest heaving. "Have you heard?" she said breathlessly. "We're going to meet a great sheikh!"

I looked at my mother. She shrugged and smiled.

Fatima spoke first, "What are you going on about, Sawdah? Your father is a sheikh. You see him all the time."

Sawdah scoffed. "I mean a *real* sheikh, one with servants and a great palace!" She gathered her hair and tied it casually atop her head while she spoke. Even messy, windblown, and breathless, she was easily the most beautiful woman I had ever seen.

Sawdah turned to me, speaking in her rapid, excited way. "I heard father talking about it. We're going to meet Sheikh Al-Azeem. His city is halfway between here and Mecca. We'll stop there for four whole days! Oh, I hope I get to stay in the palace! Can you imagine, Noor? Servants to cook for you and clean for you, wouldn't that be wonderful?"

Fatima laughed quietly. I knew she had little patience for my sister. "I think you already have that, child. When did you last cook a meal or beat a rug?"

Sawdah ignored her. "I'm going to ask Rullah if I can take her blue dress. If I'm going to meet a sheikh, I want to look my best. He might have a son good enough to marry. I better go ask her now. Do you think she's up? Of course she is. That baby of hers must have been up at dawn."

Without waiting for a response, she turned and ran back in the direction of Rullah's house. We watched as her hair came undone, whipping out behind her.

Fatima shook her head, exasperated, and nudged me with her elbow as she said wryly, "You see, Noor, you married too soon. You too might have married the son of a sheikh."

I smiled. "Auntie Fatima, I married a king."

"That you did, child," she said, and my mother nodded. "He is a treasure, your Hassan."

The pile of leaves dwindled as we worked. When we finished, I collected the baskets and delivered them to the large tent that served as my father's meeting place. For the moment, it had been converted to a warehouse for the supplies we would take with us to Mecca.

The tent was full of baskets and bags, weeks of work coming together for the journey we would undertake in a few days. I brought the baskets to Hassan's mother, Selma, who was helping to organize our provisions. She smiled and kissed my cheek. "Put them there," she said, pointing to the few empty spots along the wall. "The bakers will be here to collect them in a minute."

I set them down and looked around. I was overwhelmed by the sheer volume of supplies in that tent. Those of us traveling in the caravan to Mecca would be gone three months. It would take one to reach the city, and we planned to remain there one month to celebrate the feast of the gods. Another month to return home meant we would be gone an entire season. Some provisions we would find along the way, but the journey across the desert would be hard. We had to be prepared.

I spent the day helping Selma, running errands and helping bring order to the tent. We stopped for a quick meal, then worked on into the afternoon. Selma and I worked well together but did not talk much.

When at last we stopped for the day, I walked slowly, not wanting to return to an empty home. I thought of Rullah's infant son and stopped at her door. I knocked softly. Her gentle voice bid me enter.

Rullah smiled as I walked inside. She was lying on the bed with a shawl around her shoulders, holding her sleeping infant in her lap.

Still standing at the foot of her low bed I whispered, "I don't want to wake the baby."

"Don't worry. It's time for him to nurse anyway." She indicated some cushions at the side of the bed. I sat watching her as she stroked the baby's small, soft cheek. He stirred, and she brought his mouth to her breast. He gripped her fiercely as he took his fill.

"Does it hurt when he does that?" I asked, watching his whole body engage in the effort.

"Not at all," she said, touching his cheek again. "It seems the most natural thing in the world." She looked back at me. "You will see when it is your time."

Hassan and I had long been disappointed the gods had not seen fit to bless us with a child. Rullah knew I despaired of ever having a baby but never let me give up hope. I touched a tiny foot that stuck out from under his swaddling blanket. "He is so small and helpless."

She nodded. "And one day he will tower over me like his father does." We laughed together.

My mother appeared at the door. "I brought you some herbs you may find useful when we're away." She set some small packages on the table. "I marked them, so you know what they're for." She put a gentle hand on the baby's side. "How is he this evening?"

"He's wonderful," Rullah said. I could hear the joy in her voice. "He is a strong baby."

My mother nodded. "He is that. Just remember you must also be strong. Be sure to eat well to ensure your milk flows." She took a roll of bread and cheese from her basket and held it in front of Rullah. "Here. Take a bite." Rullah rolled her eyes but ate as instructed. I watched how she held the baby's body with one hand while supporting her breast with the other. It was no wonder she could not feed herself. Watching this, it seemed to me that women ought to grow extra arms to bear the many tasks of motherhood. I found a cup of water and offered that to Rullah. We all laughed at the effort it took to help her eat her dinner while the baby ate his.

Mother stroked the baby's head. He refused to release his hold. "I wish there was a way for you to come with us," she said, knowing the journey to Mecca would be too much for them. "These first few weeks with a new baby are very trying."

"We will be fine," Rullah said firmly. "Ghazi will be here."

Mother nodded. "Bassam's cousin, Shadia, is staying in the village. She is quite a good healer in her own right and has my leave to use any of the stores in the healing tent." Mother smiled. "And I know my son is a cautious one. He will not hesitate to send a rider to Damascus to bring help."

Although most of our village would be joining the caravan, many people were remaining behind. Shadia was another young mother whose children were older, but not old enough for the journey. Those too young, too sick, or too old to travel would stay in the village and greet other travelers who would pass through on their own journeys to Mecca.

This was the time of Hajj, when our people communed in Mecca to honor their gods and trade their wares. Travelers were protected by ancient oaths of peace. Warring tribes set aside their differences for three months, so caravans could travel unmolested to Mecca and back. Another holy month, later in the year, was similarly protected.

Tribes that otherwise were sworn enemies, jointed together in Mecca to feast and celebrate. When the time of peace was over, they might massacre one another, but for these holy days they would be united. It was not uncommon for a young couple to meet in Mecca only to discover their families belonged to warring tribes that would not accept their union after the days of feasting and pilgrimage had ended. These unlucky lovers would often choose to remain in the city to start anew.

Rullah had finished her dinner, and the baby was slipping back to sleep. Mother arranged Rullah's wrap over her shoulders and covered the baby with another blanket. "Just be sure to rest, Rullah. Let Ghazi show off his son in the village while you nap."

Rullah laughed, "I think he will be happy to do that."

My mother turned to me. "Noor, the moon is rising. We need to give our offering." She touched her hand to Rullah's cheek. "I'll see you again before I sleep tonight." She kissed Rullah's head, and we both stood to go.

At the altar of Manat, we ended the day as it had begun. We offered our thanks for the day and paused to watch the sky fill with stars. I thought of Hassan, unafraid to cross the desert in broad daylight. After traveling all day, he and his friends would rest only a few hours before continuing their journey by the light of the guiding stars.

When we walked back together and arrived at my house, Mother took my hand. "Why don't you stay with us tonight? We'll all be leaving in a few days. Stay with us until then."

My eyes filled with tears as she held me close. She followed me inside, and I looked around my empty house. She was right. I did not want to stay there alone. Hassan's absence was palpable when I stood in the space we shared. Mother helped me collect a few necessities then walked outside with me. Closing the door behind us, we walked down the road to the house my father had built for Mother so many years ago.

The next three days were filled with preparation and packing. My father was busy organizing the men. Despite the oath of peace, there were still bandits who refused to follow the law, and our men would have to be prepared to meet them.

The men would take the journey on horseback. Some would ride out in front to guide us, some would ride in back to watch us, and others would ride alongside to protect us. The women and children would ride in canopied seats atop the camels. Our remaining camels carried the provisions. The small herd of goats we were taking for milk and trade would walk among them.

As the sun met the horizon on the third day, I made an offering with my mother then joined the rest of the village at the well where the caravan was preparing to depart. We hugged and kissed Rullah and Ghazi and the others who were remaining behind.

Our camel knelt in the soft sand, and as the sun set, I took my seat with my mother, Fatima, and Selma in the howdah atop the beast's back. Sawdah sat on another camel with some of the younger women. I loved my sister but was relieved to be spared her chattering.

I felt the familiar swoop in my stomach as our camel rose to his feet, and our journey began.

سَتُبْدِي لَكَ الأَيَّامُ مَا كُنْتَ جَاهِلاً
وَيَأْتِيكَ بِالأَخْبَارِ مَنْ لَمْ تُزَوِّدِ

The days shall reveal things of which you knew nothing,
And the one for whom you did not provide will return with revelations.
-Tarafah

CHAPTER 3
NOOR: JOURNEY

Our village shrank into the distance as the caravan moved on into the desert. I moved aside the canopy to better see the stars emerge. I knew some astronomy, had learned the patterns of those beautiful lights. Still, as I gazed up at the glory above us, I wondered at how my father could distinguish in all the brilliance of that enormous sky, the stars that would guide our way.

After some hours, we stopped to rest the animals and eat. The moon had risen full in the sky and shone above us now. Our camel knelt, and Hassan's brother, Ali, stood at its side to help us down. He smiled and steadied me as I set a shaky foot on the ground. "It will take a moment to get your balance," he said. "Hold onto the camel. She will support you." I set my hand on the camel's strong, hard back as Ali helped our mothers and Fatima dismount.

When I regained my equilibrium, I helped the other women prepare food. We had a light meal of bread and cheese and sips of water from the sacks each of us carried. We would reach an oasis after two nights' travel but were careful to ration our water while we rode across an unforgiving sea of sand.

My father called the order to resume our journey. I was soon back in my seat, and we traveled on into the night. I slept fitfully as the camel rolled beneath me. When I woke, I looked up at the stars and thought of my beloved.

I opened my eyes to see the sun dawning over the horizon. Before it rose fully, the caravan stopped. We would make camp and rest in our tents during the heat of the day.

Mother and I completed our rituals early that afternoon. When we were done, she left to talk with Father. Fatima came to my side. "Let us walk a bit before we take our seats again."

It felt good to walk after a night spent sitting. We stopped to contemplate the desert that stretched out around us. No trees, no villages, nothing but sand and sky. "It is a wonder anything survives in this wasteland," she marveled.

I gazed at the barren sands. "Nothing does," I replied. I was accustomed to the green that surrounded us at home and never liked to stray too far outside the valley in which we lived.

"You aren't looking carefully enough," she said reprovingly. "The desert is full of life. Look there in the distance." She pointed north. "There is a hawk circling in the sky. Do you know what that means?"

I shook my head. "Life," she said, simply. "The hawk is circling his prey. Somewhere beneath him is a small animal or snake. He senses it, and he waits for it."

She turned to the west, the direction in which we traveled. "There is a blur on the horizon. Can you see it?" I strained my eyes and saw a hint of grey where the desert met the sky. "Trees," she said. "That is the oasis. The desert does not completely abandon her children." We walked on in silence until my father sent out the call to move and we rejoined my mother and Selma in our respective seats.

We reached the oasis at dawn. It was a small grove of palm trees and a pool of fresh cool water. I saw the tents which indicated other travelers. Some, like us, would stay only a day then move on. Others would stay for many days. Some made this place their home.

The men tethered the horses and camels while the women unpacked what little we would need to make camp. The men set up two large tents where the women and children would rest together. Another tent sheltered the men who would nap while their animals stood in the shade of the palms. As they did every day of our journey, they took turns keeping watch over us all.

While helping to clean up after our meal, I was surprised to find myself exhausted and ready for sleep. I had thought I would have difficulty sleeping in the daylight after sitting all night and said so to my mother.

"Riding a camel is hard work," she told me as we lay on our mats that morning. "We have another long night ahead of us. We would do well to rest while we can."

I closed my eyes for what seemed a moment and opened them to see my mother preparing for our afternoon blessing. I stretched and stood, carefully rolling my mat and collecting my things. We made our prayers, and our caravan set off again as the sun began to set.

We journeyed on like this for over a week. Each morning, as the sun emerged over the horizon, we stopped to rest and eat. When we could, we stopped at an oasis. When we could not, the men set the camels and horses in a circle around our tents lest bandits be out looking for easy prey. On those days, the men kept a keen watch, taking turns to sleep while others patrolled the perimeter.

My muscles ached from the constant movement. When we stopped, I wanted to sit on the ground or sleep immediately, but my mother and Fatima reminded me I needed to walk first. Tired as we all were, we needed to keep our legs moving when we could.

After many days of desert travel, we reached the rocky ridge separating the desert from the coast. We moved slowly over the rocks until at last Father stopped the caravan. I looked out and saw water stretching before us. It had a red sheen to it as it reflected the dawn's light. The smell of the sea filled the air. We made camp early and gave our animals a rest from their difficult climb.

"Noor, I want to show you something." My father held out his hand, and I walked with him to where the waves lapped against the shore. He dipped his hand in the water and brought it up to me. "Do you know what this is?" he asked, indicating a clump of white sand in his palm. I shook my head. "Taste it."

I touched my finger to the sand and put it gingerly to my tongue. I exclaimed at the taste. "Salt!"

He smiled. "The waves bring it up to the shore and the sun dries it. There is enough salt in this sea to last us all for centuries."

I saw a flash in the water and stepped back, surprised. Father laughed. "Just a fish, Noor," he said. He led me closer to the water. My feet were bare, and the water tickled my toes. We waded in until the water covered our ankles. He pointed to a rainbow of color beneath the waves. Fish of every description swam among colorful plants. I looked closer. The plants did not move. They must have been rocks, but of a sort I had never seen before.

Mother joined us at the water's edge. "The gods have given us a world of treasures," she said, looking out at the sea.

Father took her hand and kissed her. "I number you first among them all, my love," he said.

Father put his arm around her shoulder, and they looked out at the water together. They were lovers still after all these years. The love they shared emanated from them, blessing and comforting us all. I walked back to the camp to give them their moment alone.

Reaching the sea meant we had nearly reached the midpoint of our travels. We were planning one long stop in the grand city of Sheikh Al-Azeem, a wealthy and powerful man. His lands lay halfway between our village and Mecca. We would stop there for one week to rest and trade for what we would need to complete our journey.

Sawdah could not contain her excitement as we neared the city. Whenever she could, she regaled us with stories, both learned and imagined, about the city that awaited us.

"He sleeps on silk sheets," she sighed, longingly. "He has a hundred servants, and a palace covered in gold!" I smiled and nodded, but my head was a thousand miles away across the desert, thinking of my beloved Hassan. Every day of our journey brought me one day closer to him.

As we neared the city, Father kept us moving for several hours after the sun had already risen. At long last, I saw the gilded rooftops of a palace reflecting the morning sun. We approached the eastern gates, and three men on horseback rode out to meet us. They rode alongside my father, escorting us as our caravan wound its way through the gates and into a large campground.

This sheikh had made every accommodation for his guests. From my vantage point atop the camel, I could see he had set aside a large parcel of land for travelers. There was at least one well, though I thought I saw another in the distance. The aqueduct that fed his crops also ran into a pool at the edge of the campgrounds. My grandfather had built just such a pool in our own village to give visitors a convenient source of water for their animals, though ours was much smaller than this one.

A wall ran along the southern edge of the campgrounds, holding a variety of tables and troughs for guests and their animals. These were shaded by an awning that stretched the length of the wall. It was supported by beams and was high enough to easily accommodate a camel.

The winds blew from the West as we made camp. A storm was coming, and we wanted to be settled before it arrived. We would be here for many days and had no need for guards while we were within the walls of this city, so we put up all our tents and settled in for our stay.

This stop also coincided with our moon time, and I helped the women set up the tent we would use for that purpose. The older women who no longer experienced their moon cycles did not need to stay in the tent but would come and go for the gossip and camaraderie we all enjoyed when sharing that time together each month.

The tent had hardly been up a moment when Sawdah appeared. "Are you ready, Noor? Mother says we can go to the marketplace if we go together."

Smiling, I decided to indulge her. There was work to be done but enough hands to do it. I wiped my face and smoothed my clothes where they had been mussed by my labors. For her part, Sawdah looked fresh and beautiful as ever. "Let's go."

My sister beamed and took my hand as we walked out of the campgrounds into the bustling city.

We passed Ali and the other young men as they led the camels and horses to a large clear patch of earth and laughed as we watched these enormous beasts flip their bodies over and roll like children in the cool, dry sand. Ali bowed to us and called out a greeting. I smiled and waved to him as we passed.

The fragrances of the marketplace assailed our senses before it even came into view. From every corner, rich, sweet jasmine blended with the fragrant bite of spice. I took a deep breath, intoxicated by the beauty around me.

Sawdah rushed toward a clothing stand. She ran her hands through the piles of rich fabrics. "Oh, Noor," she sighed, holding out a cloth that seemed to have been woven from water itself. "Feel how soft."

I ran the back of my hand over the surface of the cloth, barely believing what I felt. It was so delicate I was afraid to touch it with my fingers lest the calluses snag the tender fibers. I had felt silk before. Bedouin traders sometimes brought it with them as they passed through our village, but I had never felt a cloth so thick and rich. The colors were breathtaking.

The woman running the stall anticipated our questions before we opened our mouths. "It is silk," she said, presuming our ignorance. "It was brought from China, woven there to the specifications of Sheikh Ruhi himself." It was clear she did not think us worthy to buy her wares.

I urged Sawdah to return the cloth to its place. "No doubt only Sheikh Ruhi can afford such a treasure."

The woman bowed her head and turned to attend a more promising customer.

We walked to another stall where a man was selling herbs and perfumes. Sawdah sighed over the exotic fragrances. I bought a small pouch of thyme, and we moved on. As we turned a corner, Sawdah gasped. Before us lay row upon row of exquisite jewelry.

Sawdah ran to see the precious gold, her enthusiasm more fascinating to me than the riches which inspired it. Laughing as she modeled necklaces and trinkets, we wound through the row of stalls until she stopped, mesmerized.

I followed her gaze and beheld a magnificent object of art. A small cage, of finest gold, held a tiny sapphire bird with diamond eyes and jeweled wings tipped with gold. The work was exquisite. He was so real I half expected him to sing.

Sawdah touched it gently. "Isn't it wonderful?"

A voice echoed behind us. "It is indeed." The deep voice startled me, and I turned to find its source.

A tall, slender man stood behind us. He wore rich red robes and carried a regal air. He bowed to Sawdah. "It is a treasure that would honor a queen." He looked at her for a moment, his deep black eyes boring into hers, but said nothing more. He bowed and turned, disappearing into the marketplace.

I looked at Sawdah. Her eyes wide with excitement, she spoke in a low whisper. "Who was that?"

The shopkeeper smiled. "That was Sheikh Ruhi Al-Azeem, the master of this land."

"But he's so young," she said. "I thought the master of this land was an old man."

"He was," the shopkeeper sighed. "Our beloved Sheikh went to our ancestors but three months ago. He left his only son to rule us in his stead." He shook his head. "It is a heavy burden for one so young, but he has his father's strength. He will manage."

Sawdah said very little the rest of the morning. She h
at the stalls we passed. I showed her a dress I thought she
She gazed upon it dreamily, but I knew she was not real
smiled and knew that my sister's thoughts were cons   by a
different kind of treasure.

When we returned to camp, we joined our family in Father's tent. Sawdah sat silently. She seemed not to notice any of us nor to taste the food we shared. Mother and Fatima talked quietly together, and I sat with my father and older brother, Jibran.

I had not spoken much with my father or brother during the journey. They had been busy guarding the tribe and managing our travels. It was wonderful to sit with them again. Father asked me what I had seen in the city, and I told him what the shopkeeper had said about the old Sheikh leaving his lands to his son.

Father was saddened by the news. He had been to this city many times and knew its former ruler. "I will miss him," he said. "If his son has half the wisdom his father had, he will rule with honor."

That night, the winds howled outside, but we were protected by the walls of the city and the strong fabric of our tents. I heard rain and thanked the gods for the water that brought with it life.

The next morning, Mother and I woke before the sun and left our tents to prepare for our morning prayers. I was surprised to see that a few members of our party had already risen. They nodded to us and smiled as we passed. Everyone seemed excited to be in a new city and anxious to visit the marketplace. We walked on to the well where we found fresh water had already been drawn. We poured some into a small stone bowl. I carried it in two hands, as my mother had taught me, and we walked away from our camp to begin the thanksgiving.

We stopped at the eastern wall, where the city met the desert. Mother had with her the rock of Manat that accompanied us to Mecca. She set it along the wall as I raised the bowl to the heavens, asking the gods to bless my people. Our ritual honored the days that passed with the setting moon and the future that comes with the rising sun. We remembered our ancestors and asked blessings on our descendants.

. AFAF

As we finished the ceremony, Sawdah ran to us, her face flushed with excitement.

"Mother!" she cried, catching her breath from her run. "Noor! You must return now!"

We looked at her. "What is it, Sawdah?" Mother asked.

"An emissary is coming!" She breathed rather than spoke the words. "From the palace. Come on! Let's go!"

She grabbed my hand and pulled at me. The small bowl of water flew from my grasp and fell to the ground. I watched, helpless, as the desert ground consumed its contents. We would not now be able to bring that water to Selma. She had not been well the night before, tired from our long journey. We had hoped the waters of the morning blessing might bring her some comfort.

I shook my head. "You must learn to take care, Sawdah! Look what you made me do! That water," my words trailed off as I saw her fallen face. I looked at my mother who stood watching us in silence.

I sighed. "It is alright, Sawdah. It was only a little water. Just please be more careful next time."

She nodded quickly. "I promise, Noor. I am sorry. Now can we go?"

I stooped to retrieve the bowl. Mother took it from me. "I'll put it away for you. You go on ahead. See this emissary." She kissed each of us on the cheek. "I'll be there after I check on Selma. I'm sure the rest has done her a world of good."

I turned to my sister. "Then let us go." She took my hand and hurried me toward my father's tent.

We arrived to see a well-dressed man bowing low before my father who had just emerged through the door of his tent. "Sheikh Amr, I am Youssuf Bin Mustafa. My master, Sheikh Ruhi Al-Azeem, bids you welcome to his lands and asks that you accept these tokens of his esteem." The man produced a large package wrapped in red silk more beautiful than any I had seen in the market. This he gave to my father. I looked at Sawdah. Her eyes were wide, and she seemed transfixed.

Father accepted the gift with a bow. "Will you join us for a meal?"

"Thank you, Say'yed. But I must return. Sheikh Ruhi invites your family to dine with him at sundown."

"Please, give Sheikh Ruhi my greatest thanks. We are blessed by his generosity and honored to accept this invitation."

The man bowed low and took his leave.

When he was barely out of sight, Sawdah rushed to Father's side. "What is it? What has he brought us?" She grabbed at the package, eager to reveal its contents.

"Patience Sawdah," Father said quietly. "Let us wait for your mother." Sawdah followed him into the tent, her eyes fixed on the gift in his hands. He set the package aside and spoke with my brother who had entered with us.

When Mother returned, Father invited Sawdah to sit with him. "Let's see what this Sheikh Ruhi has sent us," he said, as he undid a golden cord and spread open the rich, red cloth. His eyes met my mothers' as he reached inside.

From the depths of the sack, he drew a length of rich, blue silk. It was the sort I had touched in the market. He gave it to my mother. She caressed the fabric between her fingers, "This cost him dearly." She wound it about her hair and face, and her eyes reflected the blue in the beautiful cloth. My father smiled at her, his eyes shining with love. Sawdah said nothing.

Father reached in again and pulled out an inlaid chess board. He set this on the table along with a small, blue bag that contained the game pieces carved from onyx and ivory. My brother was thrilled at this gift and smiled broadly. He loved the game, and we played it often. Again, Sawdah made no remark.

Once again, Father reached into the depths and brought out a carved wooden box. He opened it carefully, and this time Sawdah gasped, covering her mouth with both hands. In his hand, Father held the small gold cage we had seen in the marketplace. The brilliant blue sapphire bird rested on a perch, his diamond eyes glittering.

"This is a generous gift," said my father, turning it over in his hands as he examined the fine detail of this precious object.

Sawdah's stared as she looked at the miniature treasure. Father held it out to her, and she touched it gently, running her finger along the jewels which encrusted its base.

My mother shook her head. "I have never seen anything so beautiful," she said in a low voice.

My father leaned forward. He stroked Mother's cheek gently and smiled. "I have."

كَرِيمٌ يَرْوِى نَفْسَهُ فِى حَيَاتِهِ
سَتَعْلَمُ إِنْ مُتْنَا غَدًا أَيُّنَا الصَّدِى

A generous man drinks his fill while he lives.
If we die tomorrow, we will know who thirsts.
-Tarafah

CHAPTER 4
NOOR: SHEIKH RUHI

Mother and I made our sunset blessings early before joining the rest of the family in the walk up to the palace. Sawdah had spent the afternoon dressing and preparing for this evening. I saw that she had applied kohl around her beautiful black eyes and could not help but think she was wasting her time. Beauty such as hers needed no improvement.

Jibran walked with me some little ways behind Sawdah, leading the pair of goats that Father would present as a token of respect. Jibran would have preferred to stay behind with Ali and the other young men, but he knew his place was at our father's side. Ali's father, Bassam, was taking charge of the camp in our father's absence, and

Selma was with him. Although Mother had asked Fatima to join us, she had declined, preferring instead to remain with Selma who was still suffering some effects of our long travel.

We turned along a major street that lay just beyond the marketplace and approached the grand courtyard. I saw the palace fully for the first time, and it was an impressive sight. The palace faced west, and its gilded rooftops reflected the beautiful light of dusk. The courtyard itself was enormous, stretching back between the walls of two front rooms. The walls of the palace were supported by tall, red columns. Palm trees lined the walkways that led to two large entrances. To the right, I saw the gate of an outer wall that ran along the southern side of the palace grounds. To the left, a covered path separated the palace from stables and grazing lands. The servant, Youssuf, waited for us before the northernmost door, and we walked along the path toward him.

As we approached, Youssuf made a low bow and spoke to my father. "Welcome, Sheikh Amr. His Eminence, Sheikh Ruhi Al-Azeem Ibn-Adel Ibn-Ruhi Al-Azeem welcomes you to his humble home." The man stepped aside, retreating back into the shadows as the towering figure of his master filled the entryway.

Sheikh Ruhi bowed to my father. "I pray you enjoy your stay in our lands."

Father returned the bow. "You honor us with your hospitality. Please accept these goats as a small token of our appreciation. May they bear many young in your care."

Sheikh Ruhi made a sign to Youssuf who emerged from the doorway to take the goats from my brother. He led them back down along the northern wall toward the path that led to the stables.

"Please, come in. My home is yours," Sheikh Ruhi said, moving aside to let us pass.

I had never before seen such a dwelling. The entryway alone was larger than the home I shared with Hassan. The floors were lined with exquisite rugs whose crimson and emerald pattern brought the room alive with color. The walls were draped with luxurious fabrics. Cushions and low tables ran along the walls.

The fabric parted on the north wall, and a woman entered. "Permit me to present my uncle's daughter, Hallah," Sheikh Ruhi said, taking her by the hand. "She is Priestess and Healer of these lands and honors us by making her home in this palace." Hallah was tall, with striking features and ebony eyes like those of her cousin.

Hallah greeted my mother first. "I am told you also are a healer and priestess," she said in a rich smooth voice. "I would enjoy sharing what little I know."

"That would be lovely," my mother said. She turned to me. "My daughter is my acolyte. She too knows much of the healing arts."

Hallah smiled at me. "Then we will have much to discuss." She turned to the rest of the family, and her cousin introduced her to my father. "Welcome, Sheikh Amr," she said, bowing low.

Father turned to Jibran and Sawdah and introduced them in turn. "Sawdah," the Sheikh said, rolling the name along his tongue as though it were a ripe fruit. "What a curious and lovely name."

Sawdah smiled, and Father addressed Sheikh Ruhi. "We named her for the beautiful still darkness that covered the earth at her birth. My daughter was born in an hour when the moon eclipsed the sun."

Sheikh Ruhi nodded. "And now her beauty eclipses both." I saw Sawdah smile and blush at the compliment.

Servants opened two large doors, and Sheikh Ruhi invited us into a second room, even larger than the first. Plump cushions of red and blue silk surrounded a low, rectangular table of beautifully carved wood, the design of which ran the length of the table. The table was grand yet seemed small for this enormous room. When I sat and could examine it more closely, I could just make out seams that indicated this was in fact several smaller tables pushed together. Along the walls, I saw matching tables and marveled at the skill of carvers whose work would fit together no matter how its owner chose to arrange its parts. From the number of pieces that lined the walls, I guessed this table could be made large enough to fill the room.

Sheikh Ruhi invited us all to sit, first helping Mother to a seat at his right. Father sat opposite her, alongside Jibran. Hallah took her place next to my mother, and I sat on her other side. Sheikh Ruhi and

Sawdah were both still standing. He gestured to the seat at the foot of the table, opposite him. "Please," he said, "do me the honor of sitting at my table."

Sawdah walked slowly to her place and sat in one graceful movement. I looked at Sheikh Ruhi who was watching her. At last, he took his seat.

As soon as he sat, servants approached the table with large platters of bread, cheese, and olives. Sheikh Ruhi reached for a piece of bread and handed it to my mother. "Let us eat," he said, smiling.

While we helped ourselves to these appetizers, the servants began serving the main meal. I stared at the feast before me, amazed at the bounty. The bread and cheese alone would have made a meal for our entire family, yet servants brought in an enormous fish, beautifully prepared with lemons and vegetables nestled around it, soaking up its fragrant juices. They set out bowls of sea salt with which we seasoned our food. Figs and dates and the blood-red juice of pomegranates completed the meal.

Sheikh Ruhi served wine with dinner. "It is made from the grapes of my own vineyard," he said, offering a crystal goblet to my father who sipped the crimson liquid and smiled in appreciation.

The food was delicious, and my senses delighted in the new flavors. Hallah talked with Mother about some of the recipes and spices. The servants attended to our every need, serving food onto our plates that we scooped up with the flat, tender bread.

As we ate, I observed our host. He was a young man, about Hassan's age, clad as he had been in the marketplace, in robes of deep red silk. He seemed very much at home in this palace and very much at ease in the position of power he had so recently inherited. He spoke elegantly and laughed freely. He had a strong, handsome face with black eyes. They were the color of Sawdah's, but while hers shone and sparkled like an ebony pool reflecting starlight, his eyes were the deep black of night, and I could understand how easily my sister had been drawn into their mesmerizing depths.

"I was saddened to hear of your father's passing," I heard Father say.

Sheikh Ruhi smiled sadly, "He was a good man, my father. It has not been easy to fill his place."

Father nodded, "He ruled this city well for many years. I'm certain you will carry on well in his stead."

They continued talking, discussing our travels. Sheikh Ruhi would not be attending the festivities in Mecca this year. He had to remain in his city to establish himself as the true leader of the land. "There are some who wait for me to fail," he said to my father and Jibran. "They think because I am young that I will not have the strength of will necessary to uphold order." His face turned stern and serious. "They are wrong."

While the men continued their discussions of trade and government, I turned my attention to Hallah and my mother who were discussing various herbs that could be used to promote good health. Hallah told Mother about a plant she was newly cultivating in the palace gardens. "It comes from the lands of Egypt," she said. "When made into a tea, it eases sleep and quells nightmares. I will send some with you. Keep the roots moist while you travel, and keep it well watered and shaded upon your return. It will grow well."

Mother thanked her. "Tell me, Hallah, have you found that this flower," she paused, "Chamomile, did you call it?" Hallah nodded. "Does Chamomile also ease sorrows?"

Hallah thought a moment. "It can," she said, "but I have found something much better. Do you grow oats in your lands?" Mother nodded. "Gather the seeds in late summer, when the pods are milky white, and use them with the Chamomile. I think you will find the combination quite soothing."

I turned to speak to Sawdah, but her eyes were fixed on our host.

Sawdah had never seemed happy with our simple life. Even as a young girl, she often lingered over the fine cloths that merchants brought to our small marketplace, running them through her fingers, her eyes wistful. She had no patience for weaving, no love of cooking. She preferred the more delicate arts of sewing and embroidery. She could sit for hours with a cloth, embroidering upon it beautiful designs, or take a simple garment and alter it to be more flattering.

Sawdah walked among us yet was not one of us. She rebuffed the advances of our young men, scoffing at their soiled clothes and dirty hands. I knew Ali adored her, but he did not dare let his heart speak. He too knew she was waiting for her chance to escape the mundane life to which she had been born.

I watched her now as she looked upon Sheikh Ruhi. Her garments were not unlike my own, yet her simple alterations fitted them to her body as if held there, captivated by her every movement. My sister was indeed beautiful. There was a magic about her as though she did not quite belong to this world. I looked at the room around us. She fit this place. She belonged here, surrounded by beautiful things.

After dinner, servants entertained us with music and dancing. I sat with my mother and Hallah, fascinated by their discussions of healing and mysticism. At Hallah's encouragement, Sawdah danced for us. Here was another art at which she excelled. Her body was her instrument, one she played beautifully. Her movements told stories and captivated her audience. Sheikh Ruhi's eyes never left her.

At last, Father and Sheikh Ruhi stood, bringing the evening to an end. "Say'yed Amr, I would be honored if you and your family would remain in the palace as my guests this evening. The view of the gardens at sunrise is truly a sight to behold."

My father declined the offer graciously, as I knew he would. "Sheikh Ruhi, your hospitality is unparalleled. But I am afraid I must return to camp and help my people. We still have many preparations to attend to before we resume our journey."

"Then will you be my guests again for dinner tomorrow?"

Father bowed, "We would be honored. I only hope that we may return the favor someday."

Hallah spoke. "Say'yed Amr, would you permit me to invite your wife and daughters to join me in the morning? As my cousin said, the palace gardens are truly lovely. I would enjoy sharing them with your family." She turned to my mother, "We may make our morning prayers together."

Sawdah could hardly contain her excitement. "Oh Father, could we?"

He smiled, "Of course, my daughter."

Mother asked to be excused from the invitation. "I am needed at the camp," she said gently, "but by all means Noor and Sawdah may attend you in the morning."

"Then it is decided," said Sheikh Ruhi. "Until tomorrow then, Say'yed." He bowed toward my father and smiled at Sawdah.

وَفِيهِنَّ مَلْهًى لِلَّطِيفِ وَمَنْظَرٌ
أَنِيقٌ لِعَيْنِ النَّاظِرِ الْمُتَوَسِّمِ

There are wonders to delight the eyes
And elegance for those who perceive beauty.
-Zuhair

CHAPTER 5
NOOR: HALLAH

Sawdah woke me before sunrise, fully dressed and ready to leave. "Hurry Noor!" she said as she waited for me to dress. She walked so quickly that I struggled to keep up as we hurried toward the palace.

The first rays of sunlight began creeping above the horizon as Hallah walked out to greet us. She led us through the small arched gate to the side of the front courtyard. We followed her around the southern palace wall. When at last we reached the gardens, I was dazzled by the sight before me.

A white stone path, lined with flowers, wound its way through paradise. Palm and fig trees towered over us, and beautiful orchids bloomed under their canopy. The garden fell in terraces down the shallow slope of a hill that seemed to go on forever. Beyond it, sunlight twinkled through the branches of glorious trees.

Sawdah walked before us, gazing at the wondrous sight. "It is so beautiful!" she gushed. "Look, Noor! A peacock!"

Two striking blue males fanned their tails as we walked toward them along the path. I saw a gazelle peeking out from between the branches of a fig tree and pointed it out to Hallah.

"My cousin loves animals," she said. "He keeps a tiger too, a gift from a Bengal lord."

I started at this. I had heard of such beasts and knew them to be terribly dangerous though exceptionally beautiful.

"Don't worry," Hallah said, smiling. "The tiger is well guarded."

The path branched, and Sawdah followed the peacocks as they walked down into the lower gardens. Hallah turned along the second path, which curved toward the rear wall of the palace, inviting me to follow. We reached a surface of fine white stones, and I saw a good-sized well centered on the large terrace. Hallah stopped at an offering table set upon a large flat stone overlooking the lower levels of the garden. "Let us make our prayers," she said.

Hallah poured water into the offering bowl and stood before it to face the rising sun. She held the bowl aloft and called out to the gods, thanking them for the new day. She performed the same water ritual to which I was accustomed, but in her voice, the words took on a special quality I could not explain. Our simple customs seemed magical when I watched her perform them.

When the prayers were done, I heard footsteps behind us. I turned to see Sheikh Ruhi walking from the direction of the palace. This morning, he wore ivory robes that amplified the rich olive tones of his skin. "Good morning," he said, bowing low.

"Good morning, Sheikh Ruhi," I said. "Thank you for honoring us with this treasure of a garden."

He smiled proudly. "I am glad you are enjoying it."

Sawdah ran up another path to where we stood, excited to share some new discovery. "Oh!" she exclaimed, stopping short when she saw our companion.

He bowed again, "Good morning, fair Sawdah." He considered her for a moment, then furrowed his brow and said sternly, "I think you ought not walk in these gardens."

Her face fell at his words. "Why not?"

His eyes twinkled, and his face broke into a smile. "Beside your beauty, my rarest flowers seem like common weeds."

Sawdah's face blossomed at the compliment. She even stood a bit taller. "Thank you." She gazed up at him through her long lashes.

"Have you seen the white peacock?" he asked. She shook her head. "He is a beauty. Very rare. Come. I will introduce you." They walked together along yet another path.

I moved to follow them, but Hallah held my arm. "Let them have time alone. We can see them from here. They will not go far."

I watched them walk down the winding path, stopping now and then to pluck fruit from a tree or admire a blossom.

"Come with me," Hallah said. "I want to show you the healing herbs I keep here." I did not want to take my attention from my sister, but I was curious to learn what Hallah might have to teach me. And I had promised my mother I would bring her something new.

We passed a cragged tree, its branches laden with large yellow gourds. "Colocynth," she said. "Do you know it?"

I shook my head.

"Its fruit is poisonous to us, and very bitter, but its dried flowers can be used as a tonic in very small doses. I will give you some to take to your mother. Only be careful to wash well after touching them."

Hallah showed me an herb garden. I recognized mint growing alone in large stone pots. "Keep it apart, or it will conquer your entire garden," she warned.

I smiled and thought of my small garden at home and how many hours I spent pulling out mint as it threatened to smother its more delicate neighbors. I broke off a leaf and savored its cool scent.

She knelt beside the other plants and showed me each in turn. Some she pulled from the ground, roots and all. "I will wrap these for your mother. She will know what to do with them. I won't be a moment." She stood and walked to the palace, hands full of the small plants.

I returned to the offering place, anxious to catch sight of Sawdah and the Sheikh. I spied them at last, sitting together on a stone bench. He had her hand in his, and I could see their heads bent close together as they spoke. I was not certain my parents would have approved of this intimacy, but I remembered my own romance with my beloved Hassan. I recalled the blush of first love, the joy of stolen moments that ended much too soon. I decided Hallah was right and let them have this time.

Hallah returned to the platform. "They are beautiful," she observed, looking out at Sawdah and Sheikh Ruhi.

"They are," I agreed, "but I'm afraid I need to interrupt them. We must get back to camp."

"I understand." She smiled. "But I'm not sure they will." We laughed and made our way down the path. "You were alone at dinner last night. You are not yet married?"

I smiled. "My husband is meeting us in Mecca. He is taking the desert route with my grandfather's caravan."

"Why did you not join him?" she asked.

"He thought it would be safer for me to stay with my family. My grandfather has only a small party traveling to Mecca. Hassan took two others to help guide them across the desert." I thought longingly of my beloved and wondered where he was now. I said a quiet prayer in my heart that the gods would keep him safe. "And you?" I asked. "Are you married?"

She shook her head. "I almost was, but on the eve of our wedding, I found him with another man. My father discovered his treachery and put him to death." She shrugged. "But that was a long time ago. And now I seem to have lost my taste for marriage."

I had no response for this. I was surprised at how easily she could relate this tale, especially to me, a stranger. She seemed utterly detached from the pain it must have caused her. I marveled at the strength of will required to recover from what must have been a terrible heartbreak.

Sawdah stood quickly when she saw us approach. "It's time to go back," I said. "Thank you, Sheikh Ruhi, for this lovely diversion."

He stood and bowed his head. "It is I who must thank you both for gracing this garden with your presence."

"Come, Sawdah," I said. She nodded. Sheikh Ruhi remained in the garden as we walked away with Hallah.

When we reached the front courtyard, Hallah held out the bundle of herbs she had collected. They were wrapped in a damp cloth to keep their roots alive. "These are for your mother."

I took it and thanked her.

"We will see you tonight for dinner," she added.

Sawdah and I walked back to camp. Her face glowed. I had never seen my sister so happy.

سَتَّتْ عَمَايَاتُ الرِّجَالِ عَنِ الصِّبَا
وَلَيْسَ فُؤَادِي عَنْدَ بِمُنْسَلِ

Let other men forget the passions of their youth.
My heart will never forget my love for you.
-Umr Ul Quais

CHAPTER 6
NOOR: SAWDAH

We walked through the marketplace on our way back into camp. As we passed the stall selling dresses, Sawdah stopped and asked to see the dress I had shown her the day before. It was made of deep blue cotton, elegantly embroidered with delicate gold thread. She held it against her body.

"It will look beautiful," I told her. I pulled out a small purse of coins Father had given me. He wanted me to be free to buy anything I might need during the journey. I wore it on a cord around my neck in order to conceal the coins and keep them safe. "Let me buy it for you."

Sawdah hugged me as the merchant wrapped the dress. Her eyes were shining. She took the package from his hands and held it carefully in her arms as we walked back to our campsite.

Sawdah ran to her tent the moment we arrived. She wanted to try on the dress and no doubt make the small alterations that were her specialty.

I wanted to see Mother and tell her all I had learned, but I could not find her. Walking toward Father's tent, I was surprised to see Sheikh Ruhi's emissary standing outside as though guarding the door.

I inclined my head in greeting, "Good morning, Youssuf." He smiled and nodded but said nothing.

I turned to see Fatima walking toward me. "Good morning, Noor," she said. "Walk with me a little."

We walked to the well, stopping first at the door of the healing tent, so I could place Hallah's package where Mother would find it. "What is happening?" I asked Fatima. "Why is Youssuf here?"

Fatima smiled. "The emissary, you mean? He is here because his master is paying a visit to your father and mother."

"Sheikh Ruhi is coming here?" I asked. "But why?"

She stopped walking and looked at me intently, shaking her head. "Can you not guess?"

I stared at her. "Sawdah?"

She nodded. "It would seem your sister will indeed have her wish." She looked out at the large city and the beautiful palace at its center. "She will be happy here, I think."

"Should we tell her?" I asked, knowing Sawdah was still in her tent and had not seen Youssuf standing guard.

Fatima shook her head. "I'm sure she already knows."

I thought of the blue dress and Sawdah's smile this morning. Joy welled up inside of me at the thought of my sister finding her love here in this beautiful place.

We walked once around the campsite then returned to the main tent. Youssuf and Sheikh Ruhi had already gone. Mother walked outside, smiling when she saw us. "Well?" Fatima said. "Is there news?"

"Yes, Sitt Fatima," Mother said. "There is news, but I think I ought to speak to Sawdah first."

Fatima nodded and embraced my mother. "I am happy for you," she said, "and for her."

"Sawdah was in her tent," I said. "I think she's still there."

Mother smiled at us both and walked on to find my sister. They returned together a few moments later and disappeared inside without a word to either of us. Fatima turned to me, "Let's make something beautiful for your sister."

We walked to the marketplace, and I told Fatima about the blue dress. We bought some gold threads to weave into a circlet to adorn Sawdah's beautiful black hair. By afternoon it was finished, and I brought it to my sister.

"Please wear this tonight," I told her. "It will be lovely with your new dress."

Sawdah beamed when she saw what we had made. She took out the pin that held her hair loosely atop her head, and the ebony locks cascaded down around her shoulders. She shook them out and put on the crown of gold. A golden braid encircled her head with fine strands falling down into her hair. Fatima had knotted the thread into small gold flowers, and these were set along the strands. It was as though stars had fallen from the sky and settled in the black depths of Sawdah's beautiful hair.

"Thank you," she said. She smiled, but I saw tears in her eyes. She took my hand and held it tight. "I'm scared, Noor."

"Of what?"

She shook her head. "I don't know. When I think about this city and the palace and," she paused and looked away, "and him." Her words trailed off. I waited for her to finish her thought.

She looked back at me. "It's everything I ever wanted, but now it just doesn't seem real. And tonight, I'll be with him, and you'll all be leaving, and I won't be going with you." She bit her lip. "My head is spinning."

I hugged her. "You are going to be so happy, Sawdah," I brushed a tear from her cheek. "He obviously adores you."

"I just can't believe it's really happening."

"I know. It's like a dream." She nodded. "I felt the same when Hassan asked Father for my hand. I was more frightened than I had ever been in my life and happier than I could imagine. I was so happy I thought my heart would burst out of my chest and fly away."

She laughed. "That's exactly how I feel."

"I love you, Sawdah," I said. "I'm glad you found your prince."

"Will you sit with me a little longer, Noor?" she asked.

"Of course," I said. "I'll stay as long as you want me to."

We sat together, talking quietly, as she collected the belongings she would take with her. Everything she needed fit easily into the red pouch Sheikh Ruhi had used to wrap his first gifts to us. By the time I left to dress and make the evening offering with Mother, Sawdah was flush with excitement and ready to step onto the new path the gods had presented her.

"How is she?" Mother asked when I arrived at the offering place.

"I think she is ecstatic." We both smiled. "Oh, Mother, I forgot to tell you something. Hallah sent some herbs, and I left them in your tent."

"I found the package this morning. Thank you for bringing them."

We said the evening prayers and walked to where the family waited. Tonight would be a party. Selma and Bassam were joining us, as was Fatima. "Ali is staying to watch over the camp," Bassam told me when I asked after his son. I suspected Ali was staying behind more because of a broken heart than from any real need. The rest of our people would be joining us at the palace after dinner for dancing and music.

We arrived at the palace at dusk. This time my father brought a beautiful young stallion as a present for Sheikh Ruhi. Again, Youssuf opened the doors, and Sheikh Ruhi stood on the threshold to welcome us inside. He stepped outside when he saw the horse and stroked its strong neck. "What a fine animal," he said, "He will be the jewel of my stables. Thank you, Say'yed Amr." Youssuf led the horse away.

Sheikh Ruhi turned back toward the door and stopped when his eyes met Sawdah's. "Good evening," he said softly. She nodded and blushed but held his gaze. He turned to my father. "Please, enter," he said, holding out his hand.

The table in the dining area was much bigger this time. Joining us for dinner were the palace vizier, Ahmed, and several of the more important city merchants and their wives. Tonight's meal was indeed a feast. We shared platters of stuffed peppers, luscious fruits, fish, and roasted lamb.

When the meal ended, we walked into the entry room whose tables were now festooned with flowers of every description. A hush fell over us as Sheikh Ruhi turned to my father, who stood next to him at the front of the room. Lowering his head in an attitude of deep respect, he said, "Say'yed Amr, I would take your daughter into my home as my wife."

My father took Sawdah's hand. "Sheikh Ruhi, you have my blessings, but my daughter is free to choose her own destiny." My mother smiled at these words, knowing as I did the high esteem in which my father held the women of his family.

Sheikh Ruhi turned to Sawdah and smiled, "Would you do me the great honor of becoming my wife?"

She inclined her head then looked back at him. "Yes."

"Then it shall be done," said my father. He moved aside to let Sawdah stand with her betrothed.

By custom, the time of celebration took many days after a formal betrothal. Our imminent departure to Mecca, Sheikh Ruhi's exalted position and my sister's own impetuous nature had conspired to set betrothal and union together in this one night.

Hallah and my mother walked toward the couple to perform the marriage rites. Hallah spoke first. "Sheikh Ruhi Al-Azeem Ibn-Adel Ibn-Ruhi Al-Azeem, do you wish Sawdah Bint Amr Ibn-Ghazi to be your wife this night?"

He nodded.

She turned to Sawdah. "Sawdah Bint Amr Ibn-Ghazi, is this also your wish?"

Sawdah smiled, "Yes." She looked up at her beloved and he took her hand in his. The golden threads sparkled in her hair, and the new blue dress clung to her lovely figure. He also wore blue, and tears filled my eyes, so overwhelmed was I by their beauty and their joy.

Hallah turned to my mother. "Leila Bint Saleem Al-Afhaz, do you also consent to this union?"

My mother bowed her head. As she spoke, her voice trembled. "I do consent."

Hallah continued. "Will you perform the rites with me?" My mother nodded solemnly.

Sheikh Ruhi and Sawdah turned to face one another. These marriage rites were a simple matter. They had expressed their desire to marry. All that remained were the joining and anointing.

A servant brought Hallah a white silk cord. Hallah bound Sawdah's left wrist loosely to Sheikh Ruhi's right. Sawdah touched the cord on her wrist, loosening it a bit. Another woman brought almond oil in a small vial. Mother placed a drop on my sister's forehead, lips and at the base of her throat then did the same to Sheikh Ruhi.

When the rites were completed, my mother lit a small lamp before them. "As it is your desire, you are now joined by the hands of the gods. May they bless this union. May you be pleasing to them." She unwound the cord from their wrists and gave it to Sawdah. The cord had left a pink mark on Sawdah's delicate skin.

Mother gave the lamp to Sheikh Ruhi. "May the light guide your way along your united path and the cord of love bind you to one other."

As the ritual ended, we heard the sounds of cheering and ululating. I turned to see the palace doors had been thrown open. The courtyard was filled with well-wishers. Members of our village and individuals from the city had arrived to celebrate the marriage.

"Some music!" Servants rushed in at their master's summons. The music started, and we moved aside. Sheikh Ruhi clapped the rhythm as Sawdah swayed around him. The party moved outside into the courtyard, so the entire city could join in the celebration.

For hours, we danced and sang and feasted on sweets and fruits brought by Sheikh Ruhi's people as gifts on his wedding day. At last, I saw Father and Mother walk together to a bench on which Sawdah and the Sheikh sat sharing a dish of fruit. They stood when my parents approached.

"The night is old, Sheikh," I heard Father say. "It is time I return to my people. A blessing upon your house."

Sheikh Ruhi bowed his head and embraced my father. "I am honored by your company. You are my family now. If the gods will it, we shall meet again soon."

My father turned to Sawdah. "My daughter, I will miss your laughter." He embraced her. "Goodbye, Sawdah."

"I love you, Baba," she said. He nodded and kissed her face. I saw tears in his eyes as he turned to walk away.

My mother hugged Sawdah and touched a hand to her cheek. "Be happy in this life you have chosen, my daughter." Her voice broke as she spoke. As she released Sawdah, I saw my mother too shed tears.

"Stay and dance, Noor," Mother said when she saw me.

I shook my head. I was ready to go home. I embraced my sister and kissed her forehead. I took both their hands in mine. "May the gods bless you both with long and happy lives," I said.

I knew we would not meet again before our caravan moved on. A week would pass before Sawdah would entertain anyone but her husband. I did not know if we would pass through this city on our way home. There were many roads to and from Mecca. It was often the custom of our people to return by a different way. The journey here from our village was not a simple one, and I felt a pang in my heart knowing there was a good chance I might not see my sister again for many years. I hugged her. "I love you, Sawdah."

Fatima said her goodbyes and walked with me. We saw Bassam and Selma also leaving and waited for them. We walked back to camp in silence. It had been a perfect evening.

Fatima said goodnight and slipped into our tent. I knew she was tired. I told her I would take a walk before retiring. I was too restless for sleep.

The campground was all but deserted. Almost everyone was still in the courtyard of the palace and streets of the city enjoying the festivities. I could hear the music and the voices raised in song. I walked along the wall and found Ali alone grooming his horse.

Ali had been my friend all my life. Unlike Hassan, who craved the excitement of the road, Ali was as content to travel with the caravan as to remain behind in the village. He was a kind and gentle man who composed poetry and loved the peaceful work of tending our animals.

I watched as he gently combed out the horse's beautiful long tail. He separated it into sections and began to braid. He looked up from his work and saw me. "Good evening, Sister Noor," he said. "How was your dinner at the palace?"

I weighed my words carefully. "We had a pleasant time."

"I am glad," he said. He resumed braiding.

"The wedding was lovely." Ali missed a turn in his work but fixed it quickly without comment.

"I hope your sister has found happiness," he said in a low voice.

"As do I." I wanted to talk to him, to draw him out. I worried he would grieve now that Sawdah was gone. I also knew the choice to speak or be silent was his alone.

Ali finished the braid and tied it off with a cord. "I must return to my work. Goodnight, Noor." He spoke without meeting my eyes and turned to walk along the wall.

"Goodnight, Ali." As I watched him walk away, my heart ached for him.

The next morning, after my morning rituals, I sought out the other women of our village to see what I could do to help them prepare for our departure. It would be two weeks yet before we would see Mecca. We would find small settlements along the route but nothing so comfortable and inviting as this city.

I found Selma loading packs and filling jars. She worked as hard as any other, but her face betrayed her fatigue. "Good morning, Daughter," she said when she saw me.

"Good morning, Selma," I replied, helping her move a sack of newly milled flour. We set it down, and I took her hand. "Come, walk with me a bit."

We walked to the shade of a nearby palm. "Sit here. You should not be so long in the sun."

She protested. "Noor, I want to help the other women. There is so much to do. I am only a little tired."

"There are many hands, Selma. The work will be done. You must consider yourself now." I looked at her pale face. "I will find Mother and bring some herbs to help strengthen you."

"I do not wish to trouble her," she said. "She has enough to do."

"You are my family, her family. There is nothing more important."

She smiled. "Thank you, Noor."

"Until then, will you rest awhile in the shade and leave the heavy work to other hands this one time?"

She nodded.

I left her and approached Fatima who was busy salting olives. She agreed to give Selma only the lightest work and promised to keep her eyes upon her and insure she remained in the shade. I left them and went to find my mother.

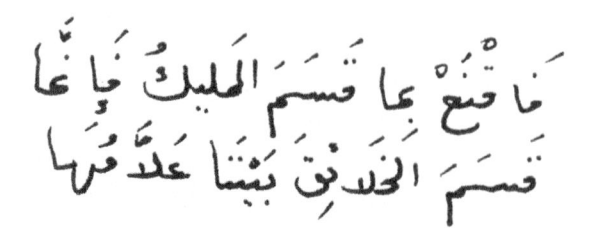

ما تنفع ما قسّم المليك فانّما
قسّم الخلائق بيننا علّام قرّها

Accept that which God in his wisdom
Has divided among us.
-Labid

CHAPTER 7
NOOR: MECCA

J ust before sundown, I took my seat atop the camel. Mother sat facing me as we left my sister's new home behind and made our way across the sands to Mecca. The caravan veered, and we rode along a high ridge of land overlooking the sea. I looked out at the water and the reeds that grew along its shore and wondered at the marvels of creation that water and desert could live alongside one another in such harmony.

When we stopped to rest, I saw my father gazing out at the sea. I walked to his side. Stars reflected upon the water as though the sky had fallen to earth. Father pointed to the shoreline. "Do you see how the desert extends beneath that water? Water gives us life, but never forget that the desert is the soul of this land." He bent to scoop a handful of sand off the rocks below our feet and sifted it back to the earth. "The desert grants us passage but reminds us we will never conquer her."

When we stopped to make camp the next morning, I was surprised to feel my muscles aching again. In the days we had spent in the city of Sheikh Ruhi, I had forgotten how uncomfortable desert travel could be.

At our mealtime, I found I had no appetite. "What is it, Noor?" Mother asked.

"Nothing." I took some cheese and drank a little water. "I'm just tired I suppose."

After the meal, Mother asked me to walk a bit with her. When we were away from the others, she turned to me. "Noor, have you missed your moon cycle?"

I was surprised by the question. My body had worked in rhythm with the moon since I was a young girl. I joined the women in our moon tent every month. For the last few years, I had come to depend on their revelry to help ease my sorrow at not bearing a child with my beloved. Had I missed my visit there this month?

I thought back to our time in the city. I had been with Sawdah almost every day. Her cycles were less consistent than mine. She visited the tent perhaps once a season. With the excitement of meeting Sheikh Ruhi and the thrill of Sawdah's wedding, it had never occurred to me to wonder why I had had no need of the tent myself.

"You have missed it," Mother said, touching a hand to my cheek. "And you have not been eating."

I laughed. "You don't think," I could not finish my sentence. She finished it for me.

"I think you are going to be a mother." She had tears in her eyes as she embraced me. We laughed and cried. After so many years of waiting and hoping, I could hardly believe Hassan and I might finally have a child.

"Rest well today," she said as we resumed our walk hand in hand.

"When we ride out tonight, take with you a bit of mint and ginger. Chew on them throughout the trip. They will help."

"Mother," I said, still overwhelmed by this new information, "I think I would like to wait and tell Hassan first."

She nodded. "I understand. I would do the same in your place." She smiled and squeezed my hand. "I will keep your secret."

"Even from Fatima." We said it together and laughed again.

Later that day, after we made our prayers, Mother gave me a skin of water. "I steeped some ginger and mint for you," she said. "I thought this might be more discrete."

I took it from her and pressed her hand with mine in gratitude. "I had wondered how to explain to Fatima my sudden craving for ginger root."

I sipped the delicious water throughout the days of our journey. It refreshed me and helped ease the discomfort I was beginning to have after meals. I thanked the gods that we would soon be in Mecca. I had helped my mother attend many women through their pregnancies and knew well the trials of the early months. It would be easier to handle the symptoms without a daily camel ride.

Mother prepared herbs for me every day. She told me what foods might help and what to avoid. With her help and the distraction of travel, I was able to keep my secret. I felt a little guilty keeping the news from Hassan's own mother, but I knew Selma would understand my desire to tell her son first.

At long last we arrived at Mecca. I felt a surge of energy as we approached the city. This was the holy land the gods had sanctified. I was excited and anxious to join the other pilgrims in worship and adoration.

Thousands of people in hundreds of caravans had already arrived at the sprawling campsites. I knew more were coming, including the one led by my beloved. We arrived before dawn and soon established camp.

Late that afternoon, Mother found me helping Ali untie some baskets that had been too tightly bound together. My fingers were smaller than his, so I could work the rope more easily. The rope slipped, and the knot fell apart in my hands. I turned the baskets over to Ali and left with my mother to make our evening blessing.

"We have to hurry," she said. "We don't want to be late."

We walked toward a group of perhaps twenty women. These were the servants of Manat who had grouped their tribal icons together on a stone altar. Each had with her a small basin of water. Tomorrow, the icons would return to their home at the Kaaba, from which we would make our prayers for the rest of our stay, but tonight we would say the evening blessing together here at this simple altar at the edge of the desert.

Mother took up a basin from a small pile next to the altar, and I poured water into it from a jug left for this purpose. With the other women, we spoke the ritual prayer, our voices merging until it sounded as though one woman spoke for us all.

When the blessing was complete, we emptied the water into a larger pot. This water we would leave out to help those who might have need of it. Tomorrow, whatever was left would go to the animals that they too might drink of this water blessed by the gods.

I watched my mother greet old friends she had not seen in many years. Her radiant smile shone even brighter when I caught her eye. "Noor!" she called. "Come. I want you to meet everyone." She introduced me to the other priestesses as her acolyte and daughter.

An old woman took me aside and put her hands on my face. Her face was etched with deep lines, but her eyes glittered as starlight. "You are with child," she said. My mother had told me of such women. They saw in their minds what could not be seen with the eyes. I could not deny the truth to one such as her, so I nodded. As she did not know me, I knew my secret would be safe.

She stroked my forehead. Her fingers felt smooth and soft. "There will be great pain. Loss."

I wanted to pull away. I was frightened by her tone and angered by her words. I had not come to Mecca to hear the ravings of a fortuneteller. She seemed to sense my fear and took my hands in hers.

Speaking more gently now, she said, "Your child will be a leader. Speak only the truth to this child, no matter the question."

I smiled, relieved but still anxious to leave her company. "Thank you." I left the old woman and walked to where Mother stood gazing at the rising moon.

My face must have betrayed my discomfort, for her eyes searched my face. "What is it? What's happened?"

"An old woman," I said. "She wanted to tell my fortune."

Mother nodded, "There are those who think we need to know what lies ahead, so we can prepare ourselves."

"What do you think?"

She smiled. "I think it is better if we leave tomorrow in the hands of the gods. If I learn that happiness awaits me, I will be less joyful when it comes. And if I learn that I will meet sorrow, I must grieve twice."

I stood with her in silence and watched the sky fill with twinkling stars. I thought of Hassan. If all had gone as planned, his caravan would arrive in four or five days. I smiled as I imagined the joy he would feel at the news that was awaiting him. Mother was right. Unexpected joy is the sweetest.

Fatima met us on our return to camp. She had been to the marketplace and had her own stories to tell. "There is a crazy man in the city," she said. "He is regaling people with wild stories. He claims to speak to the angels and says he is hearing the words of a powerful god. He condemns our rituals and says we shall all be struck down for our ignorant ways."

"Who is this man?" Mother asked.

"Some shepherd or shopkeeper. Who knows?" Fatima said. "I was told he is a man of little education who claims to be a prophet. If he is a shopkeeper, perhaps business in his shop has been slow, and he hopes to increase sales by making a spectacle of himself."

She shook her head. "The elders are keeping him at bay. I think they see him as a bit of a nuisance now, but if he continues plaguing people with his ravings, they will surely banish him from the city."

"That won't help his business." I smiled.

We laughed. There were always zealots who put forth their own ideas of what others should believe. Mother said, "I have watched these fanatics come and go all my life, and yet the temples and stones of Manat and her sisters remain."

The next morning, Mother and I walked toward the Kaaba, our holiest place. Mother carried the stone of Manat in her arms. I asked to take the burden for her, but she insisted on carrying it herself. "This is my task to complete," she said, and I did not ask again.

The streets were full of people and animals. Some distance from us, I heard shouting and strained to see through the crowd. I climbed onto a low wall and saw a group collected around a man. They were calling out to him, chanting words I could not quite make out. I heard a few words and the name *Mohammed*.

"That must be him," Mother said, craning her neck to see, "the man Fatima spoke of." We watched as a different group of young men surrounded them, jeering and taunting. Some of the men began to fight, but the men nearest the leader stopped them, and the group dispersed.

Mother shook her head. "At least he is not violent. There is some comfort in that."

I stepped off my perch, and we resumed our walk. I stopped as I beheld the Kaaba, deeply moved to be in its presence. I wanted to kneel, to bow, to pray in the sight of this perfect place.

Mother took my hand. "I know, Noor. It is a powerful thing." Our people told stories of the men who had created it at the behest of the gods who ordered this temple to honor the sacred Black Rock that stood as its cornerstone.

As we entered the low, roofless building, I saw hundreds of holy stones set along the inner and outer walls and some statues of figures I did not recognize. I was drawn to a tapestry. "It is poetry," I told my mother. I stopped a moment, reading the beautiful tale of leaders and loss.

Mother shook me from my reverie. "Come, let us do our part for Manat." We walked away from the poems toward a row of idols along the inner Eastern wall.

Mother placed our stone among the others. She spoke a prayer of thanks for the icon of the goddess who had watched over our village these many years. We would leave our stone here while we remained in Mecca. Upon our departure, Mother would choose a different stone to return home with us. This was our tradition, one that had borne our people through the generations. The new stone would stay in our village until we could again return it to this place.

Our faith was our constant, our foundation. I thought of the man in the marketplace and could not fathom why anyone would want to sweep our faith out from under us.

We walked along the wall, and I marveled at the variety of stones I saw. At last, we arrived at the Black Rock. "Token of the gods, Noor." Mother touched its surface. She bent to kiss it then knelt. I did the same. I pressed my lips to the cool sweet-smelling stone. We knelt in silence for perhaps a half hour, meditating upon our holy shrine. At last, Mother stood.

"Wait until the festival begins in earnest, Noor," she told me. "You will see such jubilation as you have never known." She looked around the small building. "Our people will dance here, encircling this holy place and honoring the gods who dwell within its walls." She smiled at me. "I am so grateful to be here." She took my hand, and we walked toward the entrance.

I stopped when I saw an icon of Hadad, god of fertility. I remembered Fatima's prayer the day Hassan and I had parted. I stopped to give thanks that Hadad had heard those prayers and fulfilled the dreams of my heart by granting me the child that grew within me.

I thought eagerly of my reunion with my beloved. I had been separated from Hassan for many weeks now, and my eyes hungered for the sight of his handsome face. My heart trembled at the thought that I would soon hear his voice and feel his touch. As I stood in the Kaaba, I called upon the gods to watch over him and bring him safely to me. I prayed his journey had been uneventful and that we would soon be reunited.

I spent the next few days exploring the wonders of Mecca with Fatima and Mother while Selma rested in her tent. She wanted to regain her strength, so she could participate in the coming festival.

The month of pilgrimage was a time of great celebration every year, but this year, the tenth year, was special. Every ten years, the people of the desert came together as one to honor the gods. People who did not have the means to make the journey every year worked hard to accumulate the resources to come on the tenth year. Within days, they would all arrive, and our celebration would set the city afire.

"The caravan of Al-Afhaz should arrive in the morning," my father said to Mother at dinner one night. He looked at me and smiled.

I slept fitfully that night, so anxious was I to see my beloved. My dreams were strange, and more than once I awoke with a start, not knowing where I was. I was grateful for the dawn.

I completed my rituals with one eye to the horizon, hoping for some glimpse of Hassan astride the black horse he loved.

The sun rose in the sky, and still we had no word of him. I found work to distract me from my vigil. After mid-day, I could distract myself no more. I stood at the edge of the city and strained my eyes for any sign of a rider.

As the afternoon sun filled the western sky, I saw the silhouette of a man on horseback. Two more followed, then the outline of a small group of camels adorned with the green canopies my grandmother had favored. My heart soared at the sight. This had to be my grandfather's caravan. I wanted to run into the desert to meet my beloved, but I knew he was still too far away. I ran to my father's tent to tell him they were coming.

أَلا أَيُّها اللَّيْلُ الطَّويلُ أَلا اجْنَلِ
بِصُبْحٍ وَما الأَصْباحُ مِنْكَ بِأَمْثَلِ

*I beg the long night to make way for the dawn,
Though morning brings no solace.*
-Umr Ul Quais

CHAPTER 8
NOOR: BELOVED

I found my father playing chess in the shade of a large fig tree. Several men had gathered to watch the game's progress and offer advice to his opponent, who appeared to have the upper hand at this point in the game. The man had the advantage of numbers, certainly, but I knew my father's strategies well enough to recognize he was intentionally building the other man's confidence in order to catch him unawares.

The man moved his queen. "Check." The man smiled broadly. "Let's see you get out of this one, Amr."

Father leaned forward, appraising the board. "You put up a good fight, Mahmoud." Father stroked his beard, sighed and nodded, then moved his hand over his king as though preparing to tip it over and concede the game. At the last moment, he touched his knight instead. "Check mate, my friend." He rose from his seat on the ground. The other man stared at the board, speechless.

I caught my father's eye, and he walked toward me. "Congratulations, Baba," I said, kissing his cheek. We walked away from the men who were still examining the game board and discussing Father's strategy. "But why do you have to torment them like that?"

He laughed. "If I win in a few moves, I lose the delight of playing the game."

"Baba, I think I saw a caravan coming in from the desert."

He touched my arm. "Then we should ride out to meet them."

I beamed, and he smiled back. "Let's go find my horse."

His horse was waiting, already saddled. I looked at Father in surprise. "I too was anxious for their arrival," he said. He lifted himself up into his seat then easily lifted me into the saddle behind him. I held on tight as he spoke a command to his horse, and we rode out toward the desert.

The riders were closer now. It was indeed my grandfather's caravan. My heart was pounding in my chest, and I strained to catch a glimpse of Hassan.

In a few minutes, we reached the first riders. Father called out to them, and I saw my grandfather waving back. I had not seen my grandfather in many years. His hair was whiter, but his face seemed not to have aged. He greeted us with a warm smile but reached out a hand, beckoning my father to ride alongside him. I wanted to ask Father to take me to Hassan but could not interrupt their greetings. I turned as much as I could but saw nothing but the camel that loped along behind my grandfather.

"How was your journey?" Father asked.

"We had some trouble," Grandfather replied. I saw sadness in his eyes. "We were attacked in the night."

I gasped. I wanted to cry out, to call for Hassan. Father must have felt my anxiety. He took one hand off the reins and touched my hand. "Was anyone injured?" he asked.

Grandfather nodded slowly. I could bear it no longer. "Where is Hassan?" I cried. "Is he alright? Please, tell me where he is."

"He is riding alongside Braheem," he said. "They are behind the second camel. Amr, take her to him. We can talk later."

Father turned his horse, and we made our way past the lead riders and the first two camels. I saw Braheem on his own horse, leading Shihab. Hassan was astride her, wrapped loosely in a thin blanket. Braheem saw us and spoke some words to Hassan. Hassan looked up and met my eyes. Even as he smiled, there was sorrow in his beautiful eyes.

Father moved his horse around and rode at Hassan's left. "You'll be alright, Son," he said. "We'll take care of you."

Hassan nodded but said nothing. "I love you," he whispered to me. His voice was weak, and fear filled my heart.

We passed through the walls of Mecca. While Grandfather led his caravan to his campsite, we rode with Hassan and Braheem toward our own camp. Mother saw us coming. "What has happened?" she asked.

"Hassan's been injured," Father told her, getting off his horse and helping me down. Mother rushed into her tent. Braheem held the horses while Father attended Hassan. "Can you walk?" he asked softly. Hassan shook his head. Ali ran up to us. Without a word, he helped my father lift Hassan off his horse and carry him to blankets Mother was already spreading out on the soft ground.

I stood by, helpless, while Mother moved the coverings aside to examine his wounds. She sent Ali for water and told my father to summon the other healers. "Come, Noor," she said. "Sit with him."

I knelt on the ground and stroked Hassan's hair. His eyes were closed now, and his jaw was set. He was in pain. I kissed his forehead. It was cold and wet with perspiration. His eyes opened. "Noor," he whispered. With difficulty, he moved his hand up to stroke my cheek. I felt tears fill my eyes. "Shh," he said, "It's alright." I kissed his face and a tear dropped onto his cheek. I wiped it away.

He closed his eyes again, and I looked at my mother. She was wringing out a cloth, and I could see the water ran red with blood.

Father had returned, followed by several women I recognized as priestesses and healers.

"It's bad," Mother whispered when one of the women came to her side. "I don't know if I can help him."

I heard Selma's voice and found her kneeling beside me. Hassan opened his eyes and reached for her. "Mother," he said. She took his hand, pressing her lips against it. She kissed his forehead then put his hand in mine. She was crying now. She pressed her hands to his face and kissed him again. She swallowed hard and struggled to stand. Fatima came to her side and held her.

"Let's try to make him comfortable," I heard Mother say.

Bassam and Ali knelt beside Hassan across from me. Hassan's eyes were closed again, and his father kissed them gently. "I love you, my son," he said, his voice cracking. "You have always made me proud." He turned away, tears running down his face.

Ali touched his brother's hair and kissed the top of his head. "Ride with the gods, brother," he said softly. "You will be a king among them." Tears fell from his eyes, splashing onto the cloth that covered Hassan's chest. Ali sat back, putting his arms around his father. They stood together and went to Selma.

I saw all these things as if in a dream. I was confused and frightened.

"Noor," Hassan whispered. His eyes were still closed.

"I'm here," I said, bending toward him.

"Be happy, my love." His breathing was more difficult now. "Smile when you think of me. I will always be with you."

I swallowed back my tears. "I will find you," I said. "I will search among the stars, and I will find you again."

He opened his eyes and looked at me. "I will wait for you."

I pressed my cheek to his. "I love you," I whispered.

I felt his breath against my face, then nothing. I sat up and looked at his beautiful face. His eyes were closed. I stroked his hair.

I heard my mother speaking. "He's gone."

I felt strong arms around me. My father knelt at my side. I heard

Selma wailing. I looked around frantically. "No," I said. "No. He's not gone."

Father held me tight. "You have to let him go, Noor."

"It's not true," I said, balling my fists against his chest. "He can't be gone. He can't be." Father kissed my head. I pushed him away and looked up at my mother. "You have to help him. You have to do something."

She sat with us. "I'm so sorry, Noor. There was nothing I could do. His injuries were too great."

"No!" I cried. "Please. He has to live. I have to tell him." I fell upon Hassan's still body, weeping. "I didn't tell him," I said in a hoarse voice. "He doesn't know." I felt my mother stroking my hair. I sat up and looked at her. "I didn't tell him."

Mother kissed my head. "He knows, Noor," she said gently. "He knows everything now." I fell into her arms and wept for my beloved. I heard my own heartbeat pounding in my ears and wondered how my heart could still beat now that he was gone.

Father helped me to my feet. I buried my face in his chest. "I'm sorry, Baba," I said. "I'm sorry I yelled at you."

His voice broke as he spoke. "I'm sorry I can't bring him back to you." He held me tight.

I felt a gentle hand on my shoulder. Fatima was at my side. "Let me take you to our tent."

I protested. I wanted to stay with Hassan's body.

"No, Noor," she said. "He is gone now. Let the others do the work that must be done."

"Go Noor," Father said.

"Just give me a moment." I knelt at Hassan's side and put my hands on his face. I stroked his hair and ran my fingers along his dark brows. I wanted to remember every feature, to etch his face into my heart, so it would be there always. I touched his lips, his strong jaw. I put my cheek against his and held him. "Goodbye, my love," I whispered in his ear. I lifted his limp hand and placed it upon my abdomen. "We have a child, my beloved." I could bear no more. The tears flowed faster now, and I felt my body fall.

I opened my eyes and felt strong arms helping me to my feet. Ali stood there. His eyes were red, and his face was wet. My throat closed, and I could not speak. He held me, and we cried together. "He was the best of us all," Ali said. "He loved you, Noor. You were his queen."

When I felt I could trust my legs to hold me upright, he left me with Fatima. I looked around and saw Selma crumpled in her husband's arms. Ali went to his mother. I could not bear her sorrow atop mine, so I turned to Fatima and nodded. She held my arm and led me to our tent.

Fatima sat with me all the rest of that day. When I wanted to talk, she talked. When I needed to cry, she held me in her arms. When I was overwhelmed by sorrow, she said prayers with me, begging the gods to give me the courage to go on.

That night, we gave Hassan to the heavens. I stood with my mother while the men lowered his body into the ground. Fatima stayed at camp with Selma, who could not bear to watch the earth consume her son's body. My grandfather looked on silently. In the light of the fires that burned around us, I saw his face wracked with grief. As the flames illuminated the desert sky, Ali sang a poem of lamentation.

We sat together afterwards in my father's tent. Grandfather spoke quietly to Bassam and my father, but I could still hear their words. "I blame myself, Amr," I heard him say. "It was foolish of me to make that journey."

He shook his head. "I trusted the peace of Al-Hurum. I trusted no one would breach the promise of peace." Father nodded slowly, tears in his eyes. My grandfather said, "I was a fool."

Father shook his head. "I should have taken the desert route with you. We could have met at Al-Jawl and crossed together."

Bassam, sitting at my father's right, spoke now, "Let us not blame ourselves for the crimes of infidels." He sighed.

My grandfather reached across my father to touch Bassam's hand. "Your son was a great and honorable man," he said softly. "His name will be spoken by the gods for evermore." Bassam looked down at the ground. I saw his shoulders shake.

I did not want to hear the story. My beloved, my light was gone. I did not need to know more. Still, I listened. I held my mother's hand with my brother's arm around my shoulders and honored the memory of my beloved as my grandfather recounted the tale.

"If they had come for the camels, we would have given them. We were outnumbered, and most of my men are too old to fight. They surrounded one of the camels and took four of our women, including Samira." His voice broke. Samira was my cousin. She was only twelve years old, and this was her first trip to Mecca.

"Hassan gave chase, leading the other men. We had five young men to battle twenty. Hassan did not leave one of those criminals standing. When he brought Samira to me, she was frightened but unharmed."

He looked down and sighed. "He had been injured and yet kept on fighting." He looked at Bassam. "Hassan was the bravest man I have ever known. My people and their children will remember his name always." His voice broke, and Father put a hand on my grandfather's shoulder while the older man silently wept.

قِفَا نَبْكِ مِنْ ذِكْرَى حَبِيبٍ وَمَنْزِلِ
بِسِقْطِ اللِّوَى بَيْنَ الدَّخُولِ فَحَوْمَلِ

Pause here while we weep at the memory
Of the one we loved and the place he lived.
-Umr Ul Quais

CHAPTER 9
NOOR: HOME

I did not want to enter my tent that night. I stayed outside, looking out at the mound of earth that covered Hassan's body, my body wracked with sobs, my eyes burning from tears that would not stop falling. Mother brought me a drink that calmed me. She led me to the tent where Fatima was waiting. I could not speak. Mother sat me on a bed, and the drink helped me sleep. I dreamed of Hassan sweeping me onto his horse and riding fast with me across the desert, the wind whipping at our faces. I dreamt we made love under a canopy of stars. I did not want the dream to end. The morning sun brought with it renewed sorrow when I woke and remembered I would never again feel his arms around me or hear his voice whispering in my ear.

I saw Fatima sitting at my feet. She had fallen asleep keeping vigil. She stirred then settled back against the tent post and slept on. I did not want to wake her. I wanted to find my mother.

I cried when I saw her waiting for me outside the tent. She held me and stroked my hair then dried my tears. "Let us go talk to the gods," she said softly. "I think something of the familiar will help today."

I nodded and walked with her to the altar where the other women waited. They gathered around me to offer their condolences. I knew I should feel grateful for their kindness but did not want to hear the words of encouragement they offered. I could not stand to hear them assuring me I would be alright, that I would smile again, that life would go on. I was angry when they said those things. These women did not understand. They did not know that were it not for the life growing within me, I would have thrown myself into that grave last night rather than face a lifetime without my beloved. I bit my tongue and muttered empty words of thanks.

I was grateful when my mother began the morning prayers. The familiar words soothed my heart. When she offered a special prayer in honor of Hassan, everyone stood in silence, to honor his memory. I saw his face in my mind, heard his voice in my heart and wept.

I returned to camp the moment the prayers were completed. I did not want to risk another onslaught of well-wishers. In my tent, I found Fatima awake and dressed. I told her what I had felt at the altar, the resentment I carried against those women and their honeyed words.

She nodded. "I felt that too when I lost my own husband. I think none of us can truly comprehend another's loss. We speak those words to console ourselves, to ease our own fears. We mean well, but the words do not console those who mourn."

"What consoled you?" I asked.

She considered that a moment. "My daughter. She was so young. I had to care for her. I could not allow myself to fall into despair. I had to rise every morning to feed her, bathe her, clothe her, love her. Caring for her gave me the courage to go on. You will find the thing that keeps you going, and it will see you through."

"I should be comforting Selma." I realized she must be suffering as I was. "I am selfish to be dwelling on my own pain."

"Selma is not alone," she said, "She has Bassam and Ali. They share the same grief she does. Do not concern yourself with her." She put her arm around me. "Give yourself leave to grieve, Noor. The tears that flow from your eyes nourish the ground from which you will someday reap smiles."

She stroked my hair and looked into my eyes. "Now let us go find some food for you. For you both."

I looked up at her, surprised. "Your mother told me yesterday. She was worried about you and the baby." She took my hand. "The gods carry us through, Noor. They never give us more than we can bear. Even in your hour of sorrow, they have brought you joy." Tears were running down her face now. "You will be a wonderful mother, Noor. That child is blessed."

I fell into her arms, grateful that mother had shared the secret with Fatima. I had wanted her to know but could not have spoken the words myself. I did not know how to be happy and sad at the same time.

We left the tent and joined Mother in the morning meal. The food tasted like ash in my mouth, but Mother persuaded me to eat something. Ali came to us. I stood to embrace him, both of us grieving for the man we had loved so well. "How is Selma?" I asked.

He shook his head. "She is devastated, as are we all." He looked at Mother. "The broth you sent did help. She is sleeping now. Baba too." His voice broke as he spoke. "He was at her side all night. I hope he gets some rest today."

"What about you?" Mother asked him. "Did you sleep?"

"I'm alright." He avoided the question. "I have work to do, and I am grateful for it."

He kissed my cheek and took his leave of us.

"He is a good man," Fatima said.

When we finished our meal, Fatima walked with me through the city. The sights and sounds kept my attention focused away from the grief. The festival was scheduled to begin the next day. I did not know how I would bear it. I could not imagine participating in any sort of celebration.

"Tomorrow, we will walk toward Minah," Fatima said, as though reading my thoughts. "It is well enough away from the city for us to avoid the first day's revelry." She gripped my hand. "The other days will be calmer, more bearable."

When we returned to camp, I stopped at Selma's tent. She was sitting with my mother, her hands in her lap. Her face was lined, and her long black hair, always peppered with strands of grey, seemed to have whitened overnight. It fell over her shoulders, disheveled and ignored. She looked up when I entered and cried out to me. She held me close and wept for her lost son.

When she was calmer, I took up a comb and ran it through her hair. I often braided it for her. As I took up the strands in my hands, I felt her body relax. Mother smiled. I wove Selma's hair into a smooth braid that ran the length of her back. I found a cord and used it to tie the end tight before wrapping the braid up against Selma's head the way she liked it. I fastened it with the slender wooden sticks that Ali had whittled for her.

"Thank you." She took my hand. "Noor, you are a daughter to me. I know my son adored you. You made him so happy. I thank the gods for you." She cried again.

"Selma," I said, gently, "There is something you should know."

She looked up at me through her tears.

My throat tightened as a wave of sorrow overtook me. I looked at my mother. She smiled and nodded as though to encourage me. I took a deep breath and said, "The gods have given Hassan a child."

"What?" She looked at my mother then back at me. "What do you mean?"

I touched her face. "Selma, I am pregnant." My eyes filled with tears.

She turned to my mother again. "Is it true?"

Mother nodded. "In the summer she will bear their child."

Selma cried out. "Praise the gods!" She gripped my hands. "Praise the gods."

For the next week, Fatima and I kept together, avoiding the crowds as best we could. Selma wanted to stay in her tent, but we convinced her to join us on some of our outings. The walks and rides helped us both, and made the days pass more quickly.

Soon it was time for our journey home. My father and grandfather had decided our caravans would make the journey north together, then part at the oasis of Al-Jawl, where we would take the western route, while grandfather's caravan would travel east. The protection of Al-Hurum still stood, but even criminals who did not respect our laws would not dare attack so large a party as we would now be.

I helped prepare for the journey and found I did not want to leave the place where my beloved had died. I wanted to be close to where he had taken his final breath, to touch the earth upon which his body had lain. But I knew I had to journey home. I did my part, feeding goats, filling baskets, scrubbing clothes, but my heart was not in the work. It traveled with my beloved Hassan, along a glistening river, toward the realm of the gods and that land which no living man may enter.

We left Mecca at dusk, traveling home by a different route. We did not pass through Sheikh Ruhi's lands and did not visit Sawdah in her new home. My father sent a rider to tell her what had happened. The messenger returned to us some days later, bearing lavish gifts for me and Selma along with a letter from my sister expressing her deep sorrow at our loss. We could not bear to look on the gifts and asked my mother to give them away. We wanted only Hassan's return, and that was a thing neither man nor god could bestow.

The journey across the desert was a difficult one and many days longer than our journey along the coast had been. I was sick every day despite the ginger and mint Mother prepared for me. I hated the rolling camel ride. After three days during which I could not keep down food of any kind, Mother spoke to Father about my condition. He offered to let me ride Shihab so long as I wore male clothing to protect me from any outlaw who might see me as an easy target.

Grateful for the respite, I dressed myself in some of Hassan's clothes and wrapped my face to shield it from the wind, then took up the reins of Hassan's beautiful horse. Wrapped in his things, riding his horse, I felt he was with me. I loved the freedom of horseback. I rode in the middle of the caravan with whichever of the men was taking a turn there. Each night the riders rotated spots, alternating between leading, following or keeping pace with the caravan.

I looked forward to the times when I rode with my father. If it was not too windy, he talked as we rode, sharing stories of the desert and reciting poems he had learned in Mecca. I cherished these hours. Father was the wisest man I have ever known. He had an answer for every question and never faltered when once he had set upon a course of action.

We reached Al-Jawl after three weeks. When we had replenished our supply of water and sufficiently rested the horses and camels, we said our goodbyes to my grandfather and took up the westward route home.

When at last we arrived at our village, Rullah ran to meet us. Tears ran down her face when she heard our news. "Oh, Noor, I'm so sorry." I fell into her arms, helpless and home.

The journey had been a blessed distraction. Now home, I could no longer hide from my sorrow. I tried as best I could to return to a normal life. I helped unload the camels and put away supplies.

Fatima gave me extra tasks to keep my thoughts busy. She knew I did not dare sit idle. It was then that the sorrow overtook me. It was then that I heard his voice in all the places we had laughed together. I felt his arms around me as I passed the trees under which we had walked. When evening fell and everyone retreated to their homes for the night, I dared not enter the home that had been ours.

Fatima sat with me then, looking at the stars, talking if I wished to talk. She seemed to know precisely what to say and when to be silent. I could not have asked for a more perfect companion in my grief. She took me into her home and let me sleep there, sitting up with me until at last sleep overcame me.

As the days passed, the pain became easier to bear. I stayed with Fatima at night and did my work in the day. One night, when we had been home a month, Fatima took my hand and led me home. "Sleep in your own bed tonight, Noor," she said. "It is time."

She sat with me, talking and telling stories as you would to a child until at last I fell asleep. I dreamed of Hassan. When I opened my eyes, it was still night, and Fatima was asleep. I covered her with a blanket, careful not to wake her. I stood and walked outside. The sky was full of stars. Sorrow overtook me as I gazed upon them.

"I miss you," I spoke aloud in the dark. "If only you were here, you could hold me, and I would have the strength to carry on."

I felt strong arms encircle me, and I turned to see who was there. I was alone. A breeze blew against my face, and I heard a voice say, "I am here." The arms held tighter then suddenly they were gone. I looked at the stars. They had sent my beloved to visit me one last time.

I stood wrapped in the memory of that embrace until dawn when Fatima walked out of the house to find me.

"He came to me in the night," I told her. "I felt his arms and heard his voice."

She nodded. "He will be with you all the days of your life." Tears streamed down my face, and she took me in her arms. "The joy will come again," she whispered.

PART TWO

وَلَقَدْ نَزَلْتِ فَلا تَظُنِّي غَيْرَهُ
مِنِّي بِمَنْزِلَةِ المُحِبِّ المُكَرَّمِ

Never question that you dwell in my heart,
Beloved, and most highly esteemed.
-Antarah

CHAPTER 10
SAWDAH: SHEIKH RUHI

I remember the day I learned what was possible. I was a little girl, watching a caravan enter our village, each of its camels laden with treasures. The caravan's leaders dined with us that night, bringing with them their wives and daughters. I was entranced by these beautiful women, by their hair, their faces, and their clothes. They wore the most beautiful garments I had ever seen. Rich with color, the fine cloth moved like liquid over their beautiful bodies. I had never seen dresses like this in my village. I had never seen silk before, nor dresses cut as these had been.

I watched these women and others like them who passed through our village. I learned to make dresses like the ones they wore. I embroidered beautiful designs on cloths I could trade for silk. I copied their hairstyles and learned to apply kohl and henna to my face as they did.

The leaders of these caravans were wealthy merchants, traveling from the East, bearing riches and silks for the kings of Damascus and beyond. I often heard them tell Father about the schedules they had to keep lest they incur the wrath of some powerful sheikh. These merchants were wealthy and powerful men but still the inferiors of the kings and sheikhs they served. I swore even then that I would one day marry a man who could drive such men as these to do his bidding.

On the road to Mecca, I met and married such a man.

I knew I had won him when we walked together in his garden. After he spoke with my father, asking for my hand, Father gave the choice to me. My father was a wise man. He let me be responsible for my own life. Whatever sorrow or joy might come, he wanted me to know they would come from choices I had made.

I was swept away by the lushness of my surroundings and pledged my life to this man, this stranger, before my family. I knew I might never see them again, but any grief I had at that parting was consumed by the thrill of what I had achieved.

I watched my father bow to my husband, wishing him good fortune. Father embraced me and kissed my face. He seemed smaller to me, somehow. I believed I had surpassed him now that I had married a man I thought was more than his equal. I said goodbye to them all, saddened as I watched them go back to their humble existence. A moment later, my heart leapt as I imagined the opulent life that awaited me as I began my life as the wife of a great and glorious sheikh.

Soon after my family returned to their camp, my husband put his arms around me and whispered in my ear. "Let us go inside. They won't even notice we've gone." I looked out at the crowd of revelers. They would dance and sing until dawn, all the time drinking to the health of their leader and his bride. I giggled and nodded. He took my hand and led me back inside the palace.

Intoxicated by my luxurious surroundings and by the man who

possessed it all, I fell into my husband's arms as we crossed the threshold. He kissed my mouth and moved his hands along my body. I heard a cough and felt him pull away. I turned to see a small, ugly man standing in the doorway opposite us, my husband's vizier, Ahmed. He had been vizier to Ruhi's father and now fulfilled the same role for the son. He had a craggy, pockmarked face, and I could not bear to look at him. I found myself wishing I could eliminate this horrid little man from our beautiful surroundings.

Ahmed had not followed the celebration outside, preferring to remain in the palace. "Many pardons." He bowed to his master. "A small matter requires your attention."

My husband kissed my hands and whispered to me. "Shall I kill him quickly now or drag out his death over many days?" I laughed with him. "I won't be a moment," he said aloud.

I waited while he crossed the room to join Ahmed. They spoke quietly together for a few minutes.

"As you wish," Ahmed said, bowing again. He nodded toward me then turned and left the room.

"What was it?" I asked Ruhi as he returned to my side.

He shook his head. "Some of our guests got out of hand and started a fight in the streets. They damaged some statue or other. I told Ahmed that so long as no one was killed, he should douse the drunkards with cold water and see that they get home without doing any more mischief." He stroked my cheek. "I am in a forgiving mood tonight."

He swept me up into his arms. I held onto his neck, laughing. "I have waited for this moment since I first beheld you in the marketplace." He kissed me. My body melted into him as I felt his mouth moving on mine. He kissed my neck, and I shivered with anticipation. I wanted it never to end. He whispered in my ear as he carried me out of the room, and my senses tingled with the excitement of what was to come.

He walked behind a large tapestry that concealed a hidden door. Through it was a corridor that led at last to his quarters. He laid me on a bed so soft I felt I might never stand again. The silk of his blankets and pillows caressed my skin. He knelt at the side of the bed and touched my face. He moved his thumb over my lips, and I kissed it.

He took my hand, kissing each finger in turn. Slowly, gently, he brought his lips to my wrist, my arm, my shoulder, my neck. I felt his hot breath and wrapped my arms around his shoulders, lifting my body up to meet his. I wanted him closer. I wanted to feel his body over mine. Our mouths met, and I felt his hand slide along the top edge of my dress to the slender cord that held it closed at my back. He pulled, and I felt the dress slip over my shoulders. I had never been touched like this before, had never been with a man in this way. I had dreamed it, and I had imagined it, but no fantasy could have prepared me for the thrill I felt at the touch of his hands on my naked body.

"You are so beautiful," he whispered. I gasped as he ran his fingers over my breasts.

His hands slid down over my belly, and I shuddered as he moved his hand ever so slowly between my legs, encouraging them to part. He smiled and kissed me again. He slipped off his own clothes, and I ran my hands through the dark hairs that covered his powerful chest. I felt the muscles of his arms as he held himself up over me. He looked in my eyes, and I felt him enter me slowly, gently. I opened my legs wider, and he moved deeper. I felt a pain and let out a soft cry. "Please, don't stop," I said, when I felt him pulling out. The pain was gone in an instant, and in its place a pleasure I could hardly bear.

He smiled. We were both breathing heavily now. He pressed deeper, and I felt a jolt as though lightning were shooting from my belly into my throat. I could feel him inside me now, pressing up deep inside my abdomen. My body was on fire. I put my hands on his arms and pulled him into me. I buried my head in his neck, breathing in his scent and muffling my cries as our bodies joined in a rhythm we could no longer control.

There was a soft knock on the door after sunrise. I opened my eyes and met my husband's gaze. "The servants have brought our breakfast."

He leapt out of bed and recovered his loincloth. Pushing aside the fabric that separated his sleeping chamber from the entry room, he walked through.

I sat up and looked around, noticing another doorway on the far side of the room. My husband returned with the tray of food the servant had left for us. I sat up and covered myself with a blanket as he brought the food to our bed. He broke open a fig and fed one half to me then put the other half in his own mouth. He fed me cheese and bread, each time first touching the food lightly to my lips. We shared a large cup of some hot spicy beverage. At last, he put the tray on the floor and pulled my body in to meet his.

Afterwards, I noticed blood on the sheets and some on his body. I was frightened, but he only laughed and touched my chin.

"It is the mark of a virgin," he said. "I will be right back." He walked out through the second door. When he returned, he had with him a damp cloth. He used it to clean the blood from my legs.

His touch thrilled me, and we laughed as we fell into each other's arms again. Later, I lay wrapped in his arms as he slept. When he rolled over, deeply asleep, I slipped out of the bed. I was curious to see what lay beyond the other door. I found another room, much smaller than the bedchamber, with a basin and jug of clean water on a table and an empty bathing tub in the corner. A further door led outside. When I walked through it, I saw a fire pit over which servants probably heated his bath water. Around a low wall, I found a private latrine.

I had never seen such rooms as these. Servants to attend to his every need, baths prepared for him, food brought to him. This was my life now. These were my rooms now. They would be my servants too.

I imagined the life I would lead in this beautiful place with this beautiful, powerful man. I knew I would have every luxury. Never again would I have to burn spices and apply oils to rid my room and myself of the odor of camels and goats or endure the wretched smell of shared latrines. Servants would now cook and clean for me. I had overcome my humble beginnings and accomplished my life's goal. I reveled in my new freedom, flushed with victory and thrilled with the passion I felt for this man and the power he bore.

I spent six months in paradise. My husband and I explored every passion, indulging our senses in a whirlwind of delights. Every night he brought me some rare fruit, delicate fabric, or priceless jewel. Every morning we walked in his garden, where he chose the most beautiful flowers to adorn my hair. We made love under cover of the same trees where we had shared our first private moments.

I hardly left our rooms in those first months. Other than the gardens, I knew very little of the rest of the palace, let alone the city in which it stood. I spoke to no one save Hallah and the servants. Even these were brief conversations or a few words of thanks after a meal. There would be time to explore everything. Now, I only wanted to explore my husband. I came alive at his touch, and he at mine. I felt I existed only to belong to him.

One evening, he looked at me and frowned. "Are you ill?" he asked. "You look pale."

"I have not been feeling well for some days, but it is nothing. It will pass. I did not want to trouble you."

He shook his head, lifted me from the bed, blankets and all and carried me to his cousin's apartments at the other end of the palace. He pounded on the door, and Hallah answered quickly. She saw us and opened the door wide to let us in. "What has happened?" she asked.

"Sawdah is sick," he said. "Please make her well."

I had to smile at his concern for me. He was so worried. "It's nothing, Hallah, really," I said. "I just haven't felt much like eating lately. I'm sure it will pass."

He set me down on a chair, and Hallah came to my side. She felt my face then took my hands in hers. "Are you with child?"

My eyes grew wide, "I don't know. How would I know?"

She shook her head. "Have you experienced your moon cycles?"

I thought a while. I had been too busy, too entranced with my new life to notice. I shook my head.

"Well, there you have it." She turned to her cousin. "She's not sick at all." She smiled at me. "I have some herbs that will help you eat. Come to me in the morning, and I'll have them ready for you."

I nodded and glanced at my husband. He seemed frozen to the spot. Hallah laughed. "It is typical, Sawdah. He is a man. Thank the gods they do not bear the children themselves. They would stand stock still waiting for the gods to rescue them from their predicament."

This seemed to rouse him from his reverie, and his eyes met mine. He laughed out loud and swept me into his arms again. He spun me around the room then suddenly stopped and frowned.

"What's wrong?" Hallah asked.

"I don't want to hurt the baby," he said.

She laughed. "You won't hurt her. Trust me, the baby is not hanging by a cotton thread. Just do what you like. The baby will be fine."

He grinned like a boy and, still carrying me, ran out of the room, not stopping until we were back at our bed. He laid me down gently and sat at my side. I had never seen him so happy. He kissed and held me, and we made love until we fell asleep in each other's arms.

تُضِيءُ الظَّلامَ بِالعِشَاءِ كَأَنَّها
مَنارَةُ مُمْسَى رَاهِبٍ مُتَبَتِّلِ

*She illumines the dark of evening
As the lamp carried by the faithful one at prayers*
-Umr Ul Quais

CHAPTER 11
NOOR: AMIRA

Seven times the moon waxed and waned from the day I last held my beloved Hassan. Seven months without him. Seven eternities. I dreamt of him every night and woke each morning to another empty day.

I drank the herbs Mother gave me and ate the food Fatima prepared. I helped Selma pick fruit in the orchard. Neither of us spoke, afraid to set loose the sorrow in both our hearts. Time passed, and my child grew within me. When I felt I could not bear to go on another day without my love, I thought of our child and remembered I must carry on.

As the full moon shone in the evening sky, I sat in my house with Mother and Selma weaving small clothes and blankets for the baby. Ali had made a cradle, and Selma was decorating it with ribbons and the small flowers Fatima had woven.

When I felt the first pain, they looked up at me as though they had felt it too. I smiled.

"Come Noor, let us walk awhile," Mother said, standing. "It will help the baby come more quickly."

Selma took my hand in hers. "The gods are with you, my daughter." I smiled at her and kissed her face.

Mother helped me to my feet, and we walked together through the streets of our little village. I saw everything as if with new eyes. Tomorrow I would be a mother. I would join the legions of women who have brought forth life unto the world. I felt afraid and gripped my mother's hand more tightly.

"It will be alright, Noor," she said. "You will see."

We walked by Rullah and Ghazi, playing with their baby, whom they had named Jaleel to honor Rullah's father. They smiled when they saw us. I watched the baby crawling on the sandy ground. He put his hands on his father's knee and pulled himself up to stand on wobbly legs. At that moment, I felt another pain, much stronger than the last. I bent forward but my mother held me upright.

"Breathe, Noor," she said gently. "It will pass."

Rullah realized what was happening. "I will come to you when the baby is asleep," she said.

The pain did pass, and we walked on. We stopped at the well, and Mother drew out some water. She ladled it into a cup.

"Sip slowly," she said, pressing the cup to my lips. I felt the cool liquid glide down my throat. It felt wonderful. I wanted to drink more. Mother took the cup away, and I knew well enough to trust her judgment.

The pains continued. As they came, Mother reminded me to breathe, to relax. "The gods have created your body to do this thing," she said. "Just let your body do what it was born to do."

We walked along another small road and stopped for a rest at the village wall. I squatted with my back against it. Rullah had taught me this position as it had helped ease her labors. Another pain came, and I let my body fall into it.

"Good," Mother said, as the pain passed, and she helped me once again to my feet. "Remember, the pains will flow like a wave, becoming gradually stronger, then ebbing again. They will not linger long."

The pains were coming more quickly now. We walked around to the birthing tent Ghazi and Ali had erected for me away from the noise of the village. Fatima stood in the doorway waiting for us.

"Not long now," Mother said, touching my abdomen. "This baby is ready to see the world."

Mother ushered me into the tent which was large enough to fit us all with room to spare. Fatima had a basin of water ready. She dipped in a cloth, wrung out the water, and used it to wipe my face. "Have your waters broken?"

"Not yet."

The floor was bare but for a low bed along one side. Fatima spread cloths on the floor near the opposite wall. I leaned against the tent post while Mother lit a lamp and loosened the flap that covered the doorway. She returned to me and let down a rope that had been tied to the tent's frame.

"Take this, Noor," she said, putting the rope in my hand. "When you squat down, the rope will help you stay upright."

I nodded and did my best to breathe through the pain. In my head, I repeated my mother's words, that this was my body's birthright. I had nothing to fear. These pains were bringing my child into the world.

With the next pain, I felt a sudden flow of water down my legs. I held the rope tight and squatted down. The pressure built inside my womb. Fatima stood at my side, wiping the sweat that fell from my brow. When the pain passed, Mother felt for the baby's head.

"Push into the pains now, Noor," she told me.

I felt the next wave come. I held onto the rope and bore down as hard as I could.

"Breathe, child," Fatima whispered in my ear.

"I am breathing!" I gasped then laughed when I realized I had been holding my breath without knowing it.

I pushed again and again. My arms shook, and my legs ached. The rope cut into my hands. "I can't do it," I gasped. "I'm not strong enough." Fatima moved behind me and put her arms under mine.

Mother put her hand on my face and looked into my eyes. "You are stronger than you know. You will do this. You must do this," she said. "You must do this for your baby. Bring Hassan's baby into the world."

I felt a rush like flame coursing through my body, and a new strength flowed through me. I pushed again with the next pain and cried out as the baby's head emerged. I thought I might split in two. Then suddenly the pain was over.

Mother eased the baby out, and I gasped with relief.

"A girl, Noor," she said with a cry in her voice. "You have a baby girl." She cleaned the baby's mouth with a sweep of her finger. The baby cried, and I fell back into Fatima's arms, sobbing.

Fatima helped me to sit, and Mother put the baby in my arms. I opened the top of my birthing shift and helped the baby find her way to my breast. She latched on instinctively and began to suckle. I looked down at her. She was so tiny. I stroked her little hand. Her foot was smaller than my thumb. Impossibly small. I looked up at my mother. She smiled.

"She's fine, Noor," she said as though reading my mind. "She is perfect."

Fatima laid a blanket over us as my mother waited for the cord to stop pulsing. She tied it with a small strip of cloth. "Do you want to cut it, Noor?" she asked gently.

I took the knife in my hand, but it shook, and I knew I could not wield it. Mother put her hand on mine and together we cut the cord that had bound my child to me.

After some minutes, I pushed again, and my body expelled the organ that had nourished my child. Mother wrapped it in a cloth and gave it to Fatima. She would bury it in the desert for me.

I closed my eyes and leaned back against the post. I opened them again when I felt Rullah's touch. I had not heard her come in. "She is beautiful, Noor," she said, kissing the top of my head. "She is blessed to be yours."

Mother took the baby and swaddled her in a blanket while Rullah helped me take off my soiled clothes and gave me a dry shift to wear. She and Fatima helped me onto the bed. Mother laid the baby at my side. She was already asleep. I heard my mother's voice fading into the distance. Soon I too was asleep.

I woke to the sound of the baby crying. Mother was still there. My breasts were aching.

"Your milk has come," Mother said.

She helped me position the baby at my breast and showed me how to support her head as she nursed. My breasts had doubled in size, and I had to laugh at the sight of them dwarfing this little baby.

"You must nurse her often in these early days," Mother said. "The milk you give her now will be with her all the days of her life." She stroked the baby's soft head. "The more frequently she feeds, the more milk your body will make for her."

Fatima returned to the tent. "Let me have a turn at the watch, Leila," she said. "Go rest a while. Selma will come at dawn."

For the whole of the next day, Fatima, Mother, Selma and Rullah, sat with me, each in turn. They swaddled and changed the baby and brought me food and drink. At noon, Fatima put another pillow behind my back and fed me a sandwich of cucumber, mint, and strained yogurt.

"I feel like a queen, Auntie," I said to Fatima.

"So you should, Noor," she said. "So should every mother."

My family stood with me as I presented my daughter to the gods on her seventh day. I named her Amira for my father's mother. My father sacrificed a sheep in thanks for her birth. Selma gifted her with a beautiful blanket woven in secret in anticipation of this birth. Such was her skill that Selma had worked our names into designs in the cloth.

Hassan, Noor, Amira, woven together with golden threads on a field of ivory.

Ali wrote a poem in her honor. It told the tale of her father's noble sacrifice and reminded us all that Hassan would live again through his beautiful daughter.

The entire village celebrated her naming that night. We danced and sang and feasted. Each family presented Amira with gifts. I was overwhelmed by the generosity of our people. I knew my child would want for nothing. And yet, whatever treasures she might receive, I would forsake them all could she have but known her father.

As I watched her sleeping in my lap, with all our people reveling in her name around her, I whispered a silent promise. "You will know him, my beloved one. Your father was a great man. We will remember him together."

وَمَا ذَرَفَتْ عَيْنَاكِ إِلَّا لِتَقْدَحِي
بِسَهْمَيْكِ فِي أَعْشَارِ قَلْبٍ مُقَتَّلِ

Your eyes only cry to strike arrows
At my shattered heart.
-Umr Ul Quais

CHAPTER 12
SAWDAH: HALLAH

Hallah's herbs helped me to eat, and my abdomen began to swell. My husband loved the new curves developing in my body. With every day that passed, he seemed to love me even more. He sent emissaries to bring me treasures. He wanted everything perfect for me and for our child. I was thrilled at his attentions.

"How is the mother of my son today?" Ruhi asked as he swept me into his arms and swung me around the room. I laughed and kissed him. He set me on the bed and handed me a soft package. His eyes were wide as a child's as he waited for me to open it.

I undid the cord, and the package fell open to reveal bedding fit for the tiniest of beds. "They're so small," I said, holding the blanket in my hands. "And so soft."

He took my hand. "Come with me." I followed him. "Close your eyes," he said. I obeyed, and he led me to the entryway. "Open them now."

I looked down and saw a cradle, delicately crafted and beautifully carved. I knew my husband must have searched to the ends of his lands for the craftsman who could create such a treasure. "It's wonderful!" I said, falling to my knees to caress its gentle curves. I looked up at Ruhi who was grinning now.

He carried the cradle into the room and helped me fit it with the impossibly soft bedding. When it was finished, he sat back and smiled. "Perfect," he said. He touched my abdomen. "Now we wait for him to arrive, so he can sleep in it."

"And what if she is a girl?" I asked, smiling.

He frowned, "Then I shall build iron gates around the wall of the palace and set armed guards at every entrance."

I laughed. "Don't forget you will also need the tiger to guard the door to her room."

"Come here," he said, pulling me into him. He kissed me, and I felt my body melt. The baby kicked. "I felt that!" he said, grinning again.

That night, while Ruhi slept, I looked at the new cradle, bathed in moonlight at the foot of our bed. I could see the swell of my abdomen, could feel the baby's every movement, but somehow it was this small bed that made the baby a reality for me.

I had never considered having children. I would hear the other girls in the village talk about babies and watch them play at dolls. I was always too busy imagining what my rooms would look like if I lived in a palace, how I would arrange the gardens, how best to sew a dress that would catch the eye of a king. I never considered that being the wife of a king involved bearing that king an heir.

I missed my mother. I missed Noor. They seemed so much better suited to motherhood than I would ever be. Maybe there was some magic, some trick they could have taught me to make me want to be a mother. I did not like babies. I had never had patience for the crying, their constant need. I wanted to be free to enjoy my husband without sharing his attention.

I looked at Ruhi's sleeping face. He was so happy at the thought of our child. He desperately wanted to be a father. He told me he wanted ten children, enough to fill the rooms of this palace. "If we don't have enough rooms, we'll build more," he had said.

I knew my feelings were selfish and felt guilty for them. I tried to put my fears and doubts aside. I reminded myself that we had many servants. I knew they would attend to our child's every need.

As for my husband, I knew I could always entice him into our bed. That time, at least, we would have together. I snuggled against his warm body and finally fell asleep.

I visited Hallah the next morning. We met regularly now, so she could give me the helpful herbs and check the size of my growing womb.

"How are you feeling, Sawdah?" She asked after counting the baby's kicks. "Did you sleep any better last night?"

I nodded. "It was late when I fell asleep, but I slept."

"Be sure to nap today," she said. I was tired all the time now and took to my bed more and more during the day.

"How about your food? Are you eating well?" she asked.

"Everything you told me," I said. "I just don't want any of it."

"Eat it anyway," she said. "The baby needs nourishment, especially now." She placed a gentle hand on my abdomen. "How is the pain? Any better?"

"It comes and goes."

She nodded. "It's part of growing a baby," she said. "Your body is expanding to make room for him."

I did not like the sound of that. I did not want to have a mother's body. I prayed mine would return to normal once this baby came.

Hallah seemed to read my thoughts. "Don't worry, Sawdah," she said. "You are young. After the baby comes, your body will return to you."

I smiled. "Do you promise?"

"I do. Now go eat your breakfast."

That night I dreamt I was alone in the desert. I stumbled over rocks and fell in the sand. A man walked toward me. It was Ruhi. I held out my hand to him, begging him to save me. He pulled out a knife. I cried out as a stabbing pain overwhelmed me.

Ruhi sat up and put his hand on my shoulder. "What is it?" he asked.

"I don't know," I said, "I think it was a dream." Another pain pierced my body, and I cried out again. "It's too soon for the baby to be coming," I cried. I grabbed his hand. "It hurts so much. What's happening to me?"

Ruhi wasted no time. Leaping from the bed, he took me in his arms and carried me to Hallah. He pushed his way into her rooms without waiting for her to open the door. She ran out from her bedchamber, a blanket hastily wrapped around her body. She looked at us, and I saw fear in her eyes.

Hallah threw on a dress and lit a lamp as Ruhi brought me into the small room she used for treating the ill.

"Here," she said. "Put her here on the bed."

As my husband laid me down on the blankets, I felt cold, wet fabric clinging to my legs. Ruhi looked down at his hands. "What is this?" he asked Hallah.

She took his hand in hers and spoke quietly. "It is blood."

My heart sank. "Send someone to bring Misha," Hallah said, naming another healer. Ruhi looked at me. He did not want to leave.

"Go now," she said. Her voice was calm but firm. He ran from the room.

Hallah sighed as she poured water into a bowl. She came to me and gently lifted the soiled sheet off my body. I sat up and groaned, clutching my abdomen. I grabbed her arm. "Tell me what's happening," I pleaded.

She set her face. "The baby is coming."

"But it's too soon," I said. "It's not due for weeks."

She nodded. "I know." Her voice broke. "Only the gods know why these things come to pass."

I realized what she was saying. "Can't you do anything?"

She shook her head. "No one can." She got up and mixed some herbs with water. "Drink this," she said softly.

Misha ran into the room. "Sheikh Ruhi brought me from my home himself," she said to Hallah. "What is happening?" Misha saw the blood and stopped. "Praise the gods," she said quietly. She knelt with Hallah. "How long?"

I did not hear the answer. I did not even feel my head fall into the pillow.

I opened my eyes and saw daylight in the room. I heard voices. Then I felt pain. "Push, Sawdah," Hallah said in a deliberate, rigid tone. I obeyed. I felt my body expel something. I could not remember where I was or what was happening. I was crying and did not know why. I only knew pain.

"It is done," Hallah said. Misha wiped my brow with a cloth, and I suddenly remembered.

"The baby!" I cried. "Where's the baby?"

Hallah stood and came around the bed carrying a small bundle wrapped in a blanket. "He is with the gods, Sawdah."

I looked at the blanket in her arms and realized I would never have the chance to be overwhelmed by my baby's needs or annoyed by his cries. I cried for him. I cried because he never would.

"Do you want to see him?" she asked me. I shook my head. She gave the bundle to Misha and sat at my side. "You bled a great deal, Sawdah," Hallah said. "You are still bleeding. I have to help you now." She gave me a cup. "There are herbs in here that will ease some of the pain." I drank the liquid and felt warmth flow through my body.

I don't know what Hallah did to me. For hours, she worked to stop the bleeding in my womb. I wanted to sleep. I wanted to die. She would not allow it. She called my name, and Misha splashed cool water on my face to keep me with them. I felt Hallah's hands inside my body and screamed at the pain. Misha held my arms so I would not disrupt what Hallah was doing.

"Hush, Sawdah," Hallah said, "I'm going to save you." She took fresh cloths from a basket at her side and used them to pack my womb. I bit my lip to keep from screaming again.

"The bleeding is less severe now," she said softly as she washed the blood off her hands. "You will stay with me until you heal."

Hallah and Misha cleaned me and covered me with a fresh blanket. "What happened, Hallah?" I asked. "What happened to my baby?"

She sighed and took my hand. "There is an organ the mother's body produces that sustains the baby until his birth. It tore, and your body expelled it and the baby. The baby was too young to survive."

I saw tears in her eyes. "I'm sorry, Sawdah, but there is more that you have to know."

I waited. My baby was dead. What more could she have to say?

"When the organ ruptured, it injured your womb. I think you will survive, but I am certain you will never again bear a child." Tears ran down her face as she spoke.

I nodded slowly. "Does Ruhi know?"

She shook her head. "Not yet. He is waiting outside. I have told him nothing. I wanted to be sure you would live before I spoke to him."

"Please," I begged her, "please tell him everything. I can't bear to be the one to let him know."

She nodded and went out into the next room. I saw my husband in the doorway. I wanted to cry out to him but did not have the strength. I saw Hallah show him the small bundle and speak to him softly. I watched his face fall, and he crumpled onto the floor, weeping.

Hallah kept me in her room for ten days and nights. Servants came and went, helping her to care for me. They brought me food and drink I did not care to touch. My husband never entered the room. He did not visit me in all that time. I asked Hallah where he was.

"He is busy, Sawdah," she said. She would not look in my eyes.

"Please, Hallah," I begged. "Please tell me the truth."

"Sawdah," she sighed. "He speaks to no one. He says nothing. He rides for hours in the desert or sits alone in the garden. I have come to him each day, to tell him how you are."

"Have you told him to come to me? Does he know how much I need him?"

She took my hand. "Sawdah, he is grieving. I think he grieves for the baby and for you."

"For me? But I'm here. I'm alright now. You've said I'm getting stronger every day."

"You are," she said. "But you will never be the mother of his child. He set all his hopes on the children you would have together. That hope is gone, and he grieves for what he has lost."

"But we can go on together. We still have each other."

She nodded and touched my hand. "It will take time."

When at last she was certain the bleeding had stopped completely, Hallah helped me walk to the rooms my husband and I had shared. He was not there. I fell asleep alone in our bed.

When I woke, I walked out of the room and found Ahmed in the corridor. He nodded. "Greetings, *Say'yedah*." The coldness in his eyes contradicted the politeness of his words. I asked after his master. Ahmed pressed his hands together and paused a moment in thought. "I believe he is in the garden." As I walked away, he called after me. "Many condolences on your most unfortunate loss." I did not turn back. I knew his concern was insincere.

I found Ruhi standing at the foot of our tree, beside a small mound covered with flowers. My abdomen ached, but I ran to hold him. He did not return my embrace. He would not look at me.

He turned to go, and I grabbed his hand, falling to my knees. "Please, my love, look at me. Please don't leave me now."

He looked at me, and I saw his eyes. They were vacant, empty. His jaw was set. "I have to go."

I dropped his hand and watched him walk away.

إنَّ الزَّمانَ وَما يَفْنى لَهُ عَجَبٌ
أَبْقى لَنا ذَنَباً وَاسْتُوْمِلَ الرَّأْسُ

Amazing how time cuts off the grain
Leaving only the chaff behind for us.
-Al-Khansa

CHAPTER 13
NOOR: LEILA

Though a night did not pass that I did not yearn for the touch of my beloved Hassan, the passing years dulled the pain I felt in my heart. Amira was my joy, my hope, and I devoted myself to her care. She thrived under the watchful eyes of a loving family and an adoring village.

When Amira first learned to talk, she would walk to my mother's house demanding of her grandmother, "Sittu, carry me!" My mother did that gladly. She tied a long wide cloth around her body, so she could carry Amira on her back as she walked through the village. Amira called out a cheerful hello to everyone she passed. She often returned home with arms full of fruits and sweets our neighbors had given her.

Rullah and Ghazi had two children now, both boys. Their second, Samir, was born within a year of Amira, and the three children played together every day. When the boys pretended to be robbers, my daughter stole the treasures from under their noses. As they learned to climb palm trees, she scampered up the tree ahead of them both. They came home bruised and bloodied from each day's new misadventure. All three bore their injuries as marks of glory.

"You're not raising a daughter. You're raising a *jinn*," Fatima teased me as we sent Amira back outside with another warning to stay off the rooftops no matter how badly she and the boys insisted they needed a higher vantage point to effectively protect the village from incoming marauders.

As much as she loved games of adventure with the boys, Amira adored sitting at her grandmother's feet learning the names of herbs, the history of the gods and goddesses, and the words of sacred prayers. As she had from the day of her birth, she joined us each morning and evening for the ritual prayers. Of course, she ran off immediately afterwards to find her devoted cousins and wreak some new havoc.

Caravans regularly passed through our village, stopping to trade wares or have bags of grain milled into flour. They brought us the world in their songs, poems, and stories. Sometimes they brought news from my sister. Her messages were brief, glowing reports of the luxurious life she led in her gilded palace.

"Mohammed has fled to Yathrib," I heard a Bedouin leader tell my father late one night as I sat with Amira's head in my lap. She had fallen asleep watching their musicians and dancers.

"At least Mecca is rid of him," Father said. He shook his head. "And his ridiculous prophecies."

The man nodded. "We have enough problems as it is. Tribal wars are already decimating our people. We don't need another zealot calling our gods into question."

"I hear he has developed quite a following."

"Yes, unfortunately there are all too many young men and women eager to follow whatever new fanaticism exploits their natural desire to rebel."

"I just hope they do not take up arms," Father said. "If they keep to themselves like the Jews, all the better. Let them have their notion of their god but leave us be."

The older man sighed. "I fear these men will not be satisfied until their faith conquers the world. They are worse than the Christians in the West. Mark my words, Amr, there will be fighting. There will be death on both sides."

"I hope you are wrong, my friend," Father said. "But our traditions have survived such threats before. They will prevail beyond the words of an unschooled shepherd as well."

I looked down at Amira's innocent face and beseeched the gods to spare us the agonies of war. I knew men like my father would die for what they believed. If this Mohammed challenged our ways, I feared for the deaths that would surely come.

I lifted Amira gently to my shoulder and stood. "Good night, Baba," I said to my father. He stood and kissed the back of Amira's head, then kissed my cheek. I looked at his face. I wanted to say what was in my heart, that fighting one another in the name of the gods, or of any god, seemed the pinnacle of foolishness. But I had to take my daughter to bed, and I knew Father would only smile and insist that no war would come.

The next morning, Rullah and her boys collected Amira so they could spend the day playing with the children of our Bedouin visitors. I rolled up our beds and finished my morning tasks then joined my mother in the healing tent.

I smiled as I walked up to the small house. It had been nearly five years since Father had replaced the old tent with a new building and yet we still referred to it as the healing tent.

I opened the door and inhaled the scent of spices as familiar to me as my mother's eyes. Whenever I entered this room, the scents and sights of Mother's collections lightened my heart and brought a smile to my face.

I touched the stone that hung on a leather braid over the edge of a shelf. Smooth and cool under my fingers, the deep blue stone was the symbol of my mother's skill as a healer. Even after so many years watching her heal the sick and comfort the despairing, I was still mesmerized by her words and her movements. She had trained me in the healing arts, but I could not hope to match her abilities. She seemed to have an intuition, a second sight that helped her look in someone's eyes and know immediately what ailed them and how best to heal them.

I brought down the mortar and pestle off a shelf. We would be making medicine today from some flowers the Bedouin healer had given us.

"Good morning, Noor," Mother said as she walked through the door. "Here are the flowers." She handed me the small package.

I took it from her hand and opened it, sliding the small blue petals into the mortar. I tossed the petals gently then lifted them out of the bowl. Mother poured the seeds and chaff onto a parchment. We would plant the seeds later in the garden.

I returned the petals to the bowl and ground them into a thick paste that Mother sealed in a flask with olive oil. She marked the flask to remind her of its contents.

"Now the roses, Noor," Mother said. We went out to her garden where she had left a much larger package. She unwrapped it, and I could see the contents were damp. We dug holes in the moist dirt and carefully planted the mass of roots and small branches that, if the gods permitted it, would someday bear beautiful roses.

Mother smiled as she looked over the garden. "The gods have provided us with so many wonderful remedies," she said. "Come, Noor. I have a surprise."

She lit a small fire under a large pot. "Bring me a brick. There are some over there." I walked to the wall she had indicated and found three clay bricks, the sort we used to build houses. "The biggest one, please," she said. I brought it to her.

She set a large pot on the ground beside her and had me stand the brick up in the middle of the pot.

"What are we doing?" I asked.

"You'll see." She pulled out another large package and emptied its contents into the pot.

"Rose water!" I clapped my hands and mother smiled.

"Exactly." The rose petals filled the pot, coming just below the top edge of the brick. "Bring some water." She handed me another large pot.

I walked to the well and drew cool water into the stone basin. I carried it back to her, careful not to spill a drop, and poured the water into the pot so it just covered the petals.

Mother stood and tried to lift the pot onto the fire. "I need your help," she said. I lifted the pot with her, and we set it down carefully. She placed a small bowl on top of the brick and covered the pot.

"Noor, I am trusting you with this task. When the water boils, steam will collect in the lid where it will cool and fall into the bowl. As it collects, you must remove the water quickly into this." She showed me another flask. "Don't leave the water in the bowl too long, or it will be ruined."

"Don't worry, Mother. I'll take care of it."

She smiled. "I know you will." She kissed my cheek. "You have become quite an excellent healer, Noor. I am proud of you."

Mother left to tend to the garden and remove the few weeds she had noticed while we were planting the roses. I attended to the rose petals. When I heard the water boiling, I waited a few minutes then quickly lifted the lid. Water dripped from it back into the boiling mass while I used a spoon to collect what had already fallen into the small bowl. I worked as quickly as I could but was careful not to lose any of the precious liquid. I tended the fire too, keeping it low, so as not to boil the water too quickly. The work took an hour. I passed the time watching Mother and reflecting on all she had taught me.

My mother had learned her art from some Eastern wise men who had traveled to her father's city when she was but a child. She learned at her mother's side and soon was helping to heal the sick of their city. People came from other villages, seeking her mother's help, only to find that a little girl named Leila was the one the healer trusted to better diagnose their maladies. Over the years, other women had learned from my mother and took her knowledge with them to their own villages. When she left her city to marry my father, many people begged my mother to stay, to bring her husband to their city, so they would not lose her.

"I go with him to his lands," she had told them. "My mother and sisters are here. They will serve you as well as I have."

"I knew the gods had given me a gift," she had said to me when I was a little girl, "but I knew that if I began to believe I was special, that my power came from myself and not the gods, I would be forsaking all they had given me. I did not want to be the famous healer anymore. I did not want their accolades to go to my head."

She became the priestess and healer of our village. When I was old enough to begin my training, she taught the healing art to me. One day the knowledge would pass to Amira.

My mother held her faith above all other things. This too she had learned at her mother's side. She showed me the beauty of sacred rituals and reminded me to thank the gods in all things. Thus we carried on together the traditions of our grandmothers, honoring the gods they had adored.

Mother came to my side as I carefully spooned the last of the rosewater into the small flask. "You have done well, daughter," she said with a smile. I took the pot off the fire and doused the flames with some water.

Mother inspected the pot. "Let us mash what is left and give some to each household in the village. Those petals will still give a lovely fragrance."

One morning, when Amira was just four, I sent her to play with her cousins and went to look for my mother to begin the day's work. I found her sitting on the ground, her head drooping. The pouches of herbs and healing stones she was bundling lay before her. She had fallen asleep at her work.

As I watched her sleep, I took notice of her lined face and suddenly felt afraid. She seemed so pale, so drawn. How could I not have noticed this before? I felt I was seeing my mother for the first time.

I knelt at her side and gently stroked her hair. When had it turned so white?

She lifted her head and blinked awake. "Ah, Noor. Forgive me. I am tired today."

"Mother, go and rest. I can do your work."

She smiled faintly as she took my hands in hers. "No. There is work we must do together. Come, sit by me. I have much to tell you."

I did not protest. I sat on the rug beside her and took up the work of bundling herbs. She stopped me with a touch. "Not now, my daughter. There is a thing which we must first discuss."

I looked up into her beautiful face and saw how thin she had become. "What is it, Mother?"

She took my hands again. "I am dying, Noor. I have done all that I know how. I must accept the truth, and so must you."

I knew she had been battling an illness for some weeks, but we had not spoken much about it. I did not know it was as serious as this. "Mother, can nothing be done?"

A fit of coughing took her, and I watched her slender body shake. When it passed, she spoke again. "No, my child. Your father even brought a healer from Damascus. She said there is nothing to be done. I did not want to tell you, but you must know if you are to take my place when I am gone."

She coughed. "My time is coming. It is the will of the gods. It is what must be. And you must be ready to take my place with our people."

I shook my head. "No, Mother, please. I'm not ready for that. I can't."

She smiled and kissed my cheek. "The gods will help you, my daughter. You will see. This is your destiny."

Tears filled my eyes. The gods had taken Hassan and now would take my beloved mother. It could not be. I could not bear it.

She held my hand as she went on, "Your father will need your support, child. Like you, he does not want to believe it is so, but he has seen my body wither. He has seen what you have not. These past few nights have been very hard. I am finding it hard to breathe sometimes."

She took some water and sipped it slowly. "Your father may not want to believe, but he knows in his heart that my time is short. Noor, you must know that too. I think I will not be here to witness the birth of Ghazi's next child."

I turned away, not wanting her to see my tears. She touched my cheek.

"The gods have given you the same gift of intuition they gave me. Use it well, Noor. It is a precious gift, but it comes with a hard price. Your heart will not always see what you would have it see, but it will always speak the truth. Trust in that, child, and let it guide you when I am gone."

"Mother, shall I send for Sawdah?"

She shook her head. "Do not burden her with this. She has her own life to lead now, and her city is too great a distance away. There is nothing she could do for me in any case."

"But she would want to see you," I protested.

"No," she said firmly. "By the time she could come, it would be too late. And if she did not arrive in time, she would carry that guilt forever. Only send word to her when I have gone and tell her that I loved her very much."

She coughed again, "Noor, you will be midwife to Rullah. She has birthed two before. This birth will be easy for her, but she will still need you."

I knew she wanted to give me a task to hold onto. She wanted me to have the great strength that comes from great responsibility, but in that moment, I found no solace in my vocation. I trembled and could not stop the tears. My mother held me in her arms, stroking my hair and rocking me gently.

أَعَزَّكِ مِنِّي أَنْ هَبَّكِ مَا يَلِي
وَأَنَّكِ مَهْمَا تَأْمُرِي الْقَلْبَ يَفْعَلُ

Are you satisfied? My love for you is killing me.
Ask of it what you will. My heart will obey.
-Umr Ul Quais

CHAPTER 14
SAWDAH: NADIA

The months passed, and still my husband did not speak to me. Hallah was my only link to him, and she did not know how to help. "He is suffering too," she said.

It was Hallah who told me my husband was setting out on a long journey. "He will not return for half a year," she said. "Perhaps when he returns, he will be yours again."

I stayed within the palace walls for six months waiting for his return, waiting for any word of my husband. The treasures of the palace, which had once brought me so much joy, now brought only renewed sorrow. My only solace was the garden. I walked its winding path for hours every day. I buried my hands and my sorrow deep in the soft earth, planting delicate flowers and eliminating the weeds that threatened to overpower them. When I passed the small grave, I fell to my knees and wept.

I ate meals alone. I spoke with no one but Hallah, and to her only when she called me to her rooms to check my healing body. She heard no news of her cousin. As I grew stronger, our visits grew more infrequent. I did not want her company. I did not want any company. I wanted only my husband.

At long last, he returned. My heart felt it would burst from joy when I saw him riding toward the palace on his beautiful white horse. I ran to him as a servant led the horse away.

He looked down at me and asked. "How are you feeling?"

"Happy now you are here," I said, reaching out my arms, but he clasped his hands behind his back, and I dared not touch him.

He looked away over my shoulder. "Hallah told me you can no longer bear children. Is that still true?"

I nodded. "I'm sorry, my love."

He looked at my face now, avoiding my eyes. "You understand, of course, that I must have an heir." It was not a question. "I must take another wife." He paused and looked away again. "You may remain with me if you wish."

I did not know what to say. Of course it was his right to marry again. "Do you want me to leave?" I asked.

He shook his head but still would not meet my eyes. "No."

His voice was flat and empty. I wanted him to weep. I wanted to see him shatter. I wanted to see him as devastated as I was. I could not bear to see him so resolute, so stern. I wanted to scream. I wanted to run away. But where would I go? Back to my father's village? Return to the stench of camels and sheep when I could spend my days surrounded by flowers and my nights nestled in perfumed sheets? I could not make that choice. I sold my soul for silk that day as I bowed my head and said, "Of course. I understand. I will be honored to stay."

He walked into the palace, and I followed a few steps behind. In my heart, I knew I was no longer his equal. I had failed him.

Ahmed approached and bowed to his master. I felt a chill as his eyes met mine. I always felt uneasy in the horrible man's presence. As I left the room, I heard Sheikh Ruhi speaking in a low voice. "Send word to Say'yed Azeez. His family is visiting the city for the festivals. I should like to meet his daughter, Nadia. Arrange a dinner tonight."

I did not attend that dinner. Alone in my room, I heard music and imagined Nadia dancing for my husband as I had once danced for him. I covered my head with pillows and wept.

My husband took Nadia as his wife the next month. They left the city together and did not return for nearly a season. Hallah told me it was her cousin's wish that I keep the rooms I had shared with him. He would continue to live in the rooms he had been using and would give Nadia her own apartments. The palace was large enough to accommodate us all.

On the evening of their return, I heard a knock on my outer door. "Enter," I said.

A beautiful young woman stood in my doorway. Her hair was covered with a scarf whose ends fell gently over her shoulders. She bowed before me and held out a package with both hands. "Say'yedah," she said, addressing me in the formal way. "I am Nadia, daughter of Azeez. I thank you for giving me leave to live in your home and offer this small token of my esteem."

I took the package from her hands. She looked up at me. "I cannot hope for your friendship," she said gently. "I only ask that you not hate me."

She turned to leave but stopped and looked at me. Her eyes were shining, and a tear slid down her cheek. "I cannot imagine your grief. Praise *Allah* you will find peace in this life."

These kind words overwhelmed my lonely heart, and I felt my eyes fill with tears. I nodded, unable to speak, gripping her gift in my clenched hands. I turned away. I did not want her to see me cry.

I heard her softly shut the door then felt an arm around my shoulders. Wracked with sobs, I wept as she held me. She let me cry without words of consolation, without once offering to dry my tears. She waited until the tears subsided, and only then did she gently dry my face with the edge of her scarf. She led me to a low bench where we sat together.

"Breathe," she counseled when I tried to speak through the spasms of the remaining tears. "Just breathe."

I took a few deep breaths and looked at her face. She was younger than me but not by much. Her eyes were a deep hazel, almost green. They were kind, gentle eyes.

"What must you think of me?" I said, wiping my face with a soft cloth she found on a side table.

She put her hands on mine. "I think you are a beautiful young woman who has been handed a terrible burden of grief that you have had to bear alone."

I smiled at her. "You are very kind. I'm sorry you had to see this display."

"Never apologize for your feelings," she said. "I know what you have suffered. I want to help you if I can."

"Thank you," I said, "but I don't think you can help."

"You may be right," she said. "But I believe there is One who can. There is One who can ease your pain."

"Who?" I asked, unable to hide the scorn in my voice.

"Not now." She smiled. "The hour is late. Let us talk another day." She let go of my hands, and we stood. "Would you join me tomorrow for the mid-day meal? We could eat in the gardens if you like."

"Yes," I said, standing. "I would like that very much." We walked together to the door, and I opened it. "Thank you."

She kissed my cheek. "I will see you tomorrow."

I walked into the garden the next day and found her kneeling on the plateau where Noor had once stood with Hallah. Nadia bowed her head low to the ground, reciting words I could not make out. She stood, then stooped to retrieve a small rug on which she had been kneeling. She folded it carefully, ensuring the edges met just so before rolling it.

"Sawdah!" she called out when she noticed me there. She walked towards me but stopped suddenly, lowering her eyes. "I'm sorry for my presumption, Say'yedah," she said. "May I call you by your given name?"

"Of course," I said. I pointed to the rug in her hands. "What is that?"

She held it out to me, so I could examine the workmanship. I felt the material with my fingertips. It was soft and very well made. I could see that it had been woven with care. "It is my prayer rug," she said. "I made it to always have a clean surface on which to pray."

"It is lovely. You are very talented."

"Praise *Allah*. I pray only to be of service to Him. Come," She beckoned me to walk by her side. "Let us walk in the garden a while."

"My mother was the Priestess for our village," I said as we walked, "but I don't recall her ever performing any prayers like the ones I saw you doing."

She nodded. "My grandmother was Priestess for ours, but that was a long time ago." She stopped and looked at me. "I don't practice the ways of my grandmother or my mother. I follow the laws set down by *Allah*, given us through the Prophet Mohammed, praised be his name."

"Mohammed?" I asked, "Who is that?"

"He is a great man, Sawdah," she said, her eyes shining. "*Allah* speaks to him that he may speak to us all." She smiled as though reliving a fond memory. "I had the fortune to meet some of his closest followers in Medina."

"Medina?" I asked. I had never heard of that city.

She smiled. "You might know the city as Yathrib. The believers have changed the name. It is to be known now as the city of The Prophet. So we call it Medina."

She clasped the prayer rug in front of her as she spoke. "Oh, Sawdah, the Prophet speaks of the living words of *Allah*. Even though I have only heard of him, I feel the power of *Allah* flowing through his words."

"Al-Lah," I said, trying to remember some of what my mother had taught us of the gods. "He is the father of Al-Lat and Manat, right?" Spirituality had always been Noor's domain, and I had been happy to leave her to it.

"No," Nadia said. "Al-Lat and the others, even what you call Al-Lah, these are false gods. There is only one true God, *Allah*, and His Prophet is Mohammed."

"What about the rest of the gods?" I asked, "There are hundreds of them. I heard they surround the Kaaba in Mecca."

"All false idols," she said, "born of ignorance."

We had been walking again as we spoke and had now arrived at the table where servants had set out our meal. Nadia set her rug on a bench before taking her seat. I found myself lost in thought. For some time, we ate without speaking.

"You said last night that there was one who could help me," I said. "Did you mean this *Allah*?"

"I did." She smiled. "*Allah* is merciful and just. *Allah* will guide you and help you in your need. I know it."

I examined her face for deception and saw none. These words were her truth. "Nadia," I said, "I never really followed the gods of my mother. I'm not certain I can believe in any of this."

"I understand." She touched my arm. "I only ask that you give me leave to talk to you of what I believe."

I considered this a moment. I had not had a friend, a true friend, in a very long time. Nadia seemed honest and kind. She wanted to help me. It would do me no harm to listen to her. "I would like it very much if you would share your beliefs with me," I said at last.

She smiled and took my hand. "Then I would be honored to talk with you of *Allah*."

We finished our meal and left the garden together. "I have something I would like to show you," she said. "Come with me."

We walked through the palace to her quarters and entered her sitting room. She first set the prayer rug on a small shelf then stood at a table which held a large basin and a full pitcher of water. She poured water over her hands and washed them carefully. She dried them with a cloth that she folded neatly before setting it back on the table.

From a shelf below the one on which she had placed her prayer rug, she lifted the top page of a sheaf of parchment. She held it out, so I could read what was written upon it. The handwriting was lovely. I read the first line: *In the name of Allah, the merciful, the compassionate*, it began.

"These are the words of *Allah*," she said, her voice catching as she spoke in a reverent tone. "They were spoken to the Prophet Mohammed and given to all who live by His words."

"Where did you get these?" I asked, noting the beautifully precise calligraphy.

"I wrote them," she said. "I took down the words as I heard them and copied them again on these pages." She gently set the parchment back on top of the others. "I listened to those who had witnessed his revelations. I wanted to devour their words. I wanted to learn all I could."

I marveled at her patience and her skill.

"There is more, Sawdah," she said. "The Prophet Mohammed continues to speak the word of *Allah* in Medina."

"When did your family leave Medina?" I asked.

She bowed her head. "They are there now." Her face reddened, and she did not look up. "We only came to this city at Sheikh Ruhi's invitation."

I realized then that they had returned to the city with him on his way home from his travels. He had known, even as he had spoken to me in the courtyard, that he would take this woman as his wife.

I looked at her kind and beautiful face. "I understand, Nadia," I said. "I don't blame you."

She nodded her head but did not look at me. "I knew he had a wife, but people said you were a monster, that you had shunned him and shut him out of your rooms, cursing his name. People told me you refused to bear his children. I just accepted that and never asked Sheikh Ruhi any questions about you."

She looked at me now with tears in her eyes. "While we were away, when we had been wed but two weeks, one of the servants came to me in secret and told me how you had lost your baby. She was one who had cared for you as you healed. She felt you had been abandoned in your grief, and she wanted me to know the truth so I might be kind to you. She asked me to release her from her service, and I let her remain in Egypt as she desired."

"Thank you for believing her," I said.

She dried her tears. "Thank you for allowing me to be your friend."

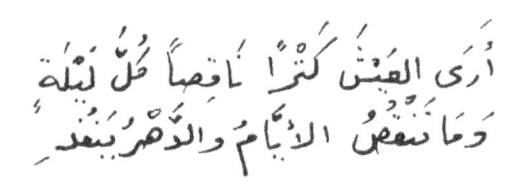

أَرَى الْعَيْشَ كَنْزاً نَاقِصاً كُلَّ لَيْلَةٍ
وَمَا تَنْقُصُ الْأَيَّامُ وَالدَّهْرُ يَنْفَدُ

The treasure of life dwindles as the nights pass.
The days go on counting, while time draws to an end.
-Tarafah

CHAPTER 15
NOOR: PRIESTESS STONE

In the next weeks, Mother and I did not again speak aloud of her illness, yet I saw the truth of it reflected in her weakening body each time we met. She wanted to teach me everything she knew, so I could take her knowledge with me as I journeyed forward without her. As the days went on, she tired more easily, and I took on most of her duties, so she could rest. I cared for the sick and attended to Rullah in her pregnancy. I brought the news of the village to my mother's bedside and asked for her counsel.

"Thank you, Noor," she said one evening when I sought advice about what herbs might best help Rullah in her labors.

"For what?" I asked.

She smiled. "For making me feel useful." She took my hand. "I know you no longer need to consult me. You have the tools and wisdom you need to carry on in my place."

I shook my head and tried to protest. She only kissed my forehead. "I love you, Noor," she said. "Thank you."

As her illness worsened, she could no longer join me even for our daily prayers. I brought her the prayer waters every morning if she was awake. I brought them again each evening and sat at her side until Father came in for the night. When she could, she spoke of sacred things. When her voice failed her, I told her stories about Amira.

One morning, I came to her door and called softly, "Mother?"

"I'm awake," she said. I walked inside and set the basin of water on a table. She smiled up at me from her bed, and I sat in my usual place at her side.

I helped her sit up in bed and covered her with another blanket. "I have exciting news, Mother," I said with a smile. "Rullah's baby was born at dawn."

She gripped my hand.

"I'm so happy for them," she said. "Tell me about the birth."

"It was an easy one," I said. "Rullah knew just what to do. She told me when she wanted help and when to stand aside."

Mother smiled. "She is strong. She trusts her body. Just remind her to rest."

She put her hand on my face and spoke quietly. "Noor, I fear my end is near."

"They want to present the baby to you if you feel able. Rullah is well. Rullah says," the words stuck in my throat, and I swallowed back tears. I could no longer pretend not to have heard her. "Shall I get Father?"

She hesitated, as if the words were difficult to form. "Not yet. First, there is a thing I need to tell you. Before I go." She looked hard into my eyes. "Noor, you must remember. Whatever happens, whatever changes, remember who you are. Remember your gifts. You are my daughter, a daughter of healers and keeper of the sacred heritage of our ancestors. Remember that, Noor. Promise me, you will always remember."

"Yes, Mother. Of course, I promise. I will not forget what you have taught me."

She smiled, then let go of my hands. She reached across to the table at her side and lifted the Priestess Stone from the cloth on which it had been lying. She had kept it with her during her illness. She now lifted it carefully and held it out to me.

I knew what she was doing. She had prepared me for this moment, but it was a moment I had dreaded. I lay my hand upon the stone as she spoke again, this time in the strong, clear voice of ritual. I had not heard her speak so powerfully these many months. She summoned every bit of strength left in her body as she spoke the words.

"Noor, this is the Priestess Stone. The women of my family have carried it for countless generations. I pass it now to my daughter as my mother passed it to me. Honor the women who have held it before you. Honor the people you serve. You are Priestess now, Daughter. Wear that title with honor."

I held the stone and spoke the ritual words. "May I honor our mothers as they honor me today." I kissed her hand. "May the gods direct my hands and my heart that I may be of service to my people." I raised the braided cord over my head. "And when my time is done, may my daughters follow in the footsteps of the ages." I put it on and felt the leather pull against the back of my neck. I looked down at the dark jewel, now mine to hold, and felt the weight of its legacy upon me.

My mother sighed and nodded. "It is done, Noor. May the gods bless you and keep you safe." She touched my face softly, and I covered her hand with mine. "I love you, my daughter. Remember that I shall always be with you." She coughed and held a cloth to her mouth. She crumpled it in her hand, but I could see the blood upon it. "Please," she said, struggling to speak. "Please get your father."

I squeezed her hand and ran out into the courtyard where I had seen him talking with Bassam. I found him alone in the garden examining some flowers. "Baba!" I called. He looked up and met my eyes.

Without a word, he walked quickly into the house in which my mother lay. He closed the door behind him as he entered.

My father sat with her all that day and into the night. She did not ask for any other visitors. She had made her peace and said her goodbyes. She wanted only her beloved by her side.

Amira and I stayed with Fatima that night. Fatima and I could not sleep and did not wish to speak. We watched Amira sleeping peacefully in Fatima's bed. Before dawn, I walked outside and saw my father emerging from their house.

His face was drawn and pale. As I walked toward him, our eyes met. His face moved as if he were trying to speak, yet no words came. He turned away from me and walked out to the desert, his shoulders shaking.

I entered their house and knelt at my mother's side. Her eyes were closed, and her arms folded across her body. A single white flower lay upon her chest. I kissed her cheek and said goodbye.

I walked back to Fatima's house. I did not know what I would say to my daughter. She knew her grandmother was ill. I had prepared her as best I could but feared she was still too young to truly understand.

Fatima met me outside her door. She saw my face, and her eyes filled with tears. I put my arms around her. "She was so young," Fatima said, shaking her head, "too young."

She pulled away and looked at me. She wiped the tears that were running down my face.

"What do I tell Amira?" I asked.

"Tell her the truth," Fatima said. "You must always tell her the truth." She put her hand on my cheek. "Ask the gods for help. They will give you the words to say."

I nodded and walked inside. Amira was sitting up in the bed playing with a doll Ali had made for her. She looked up at me. "Good morning, Mama."

"Amira." I sat next to her on the bed. "Something has happened."

She looked up at me with big, inquisitive eyes. A part of me hated the gods for taking first her father and now her beloved grandmother. I wanted to spare her this news, spare her the grim realities of life. But I could not pretend her beloved grandmother was coming back. I had to speak the truth.

I took her little hand in mine. "Sittu's body stopped working. She went to live with the gods. She's not with us anymore."

"Not working?" she asked. Then after a moment, "Like Baba?"

I swallowed back tears. "Yes, just like Baba. They're both with the gods now, watching out for us together."

"Okay, Mama," she said.

"Would you like to see her body and say goodbye?"

She nodded. "Yes, I will say goodbye."

I held her hand, and we walked to my mother's house, where she still lay peacefully upon her bed. Fatima was there now, kneeling at my mother's side. She stood when we walked in. Amira walked to her grandmother's body and touched her face. "Sittu is not working," she said to me.

She turned back to her grandmother's body. "Love you, Sittu," she said, giving her a kiss on the cheek. Amira looked at me again. "Sittu will be with Baba now?"

"Yes," I said, tears filling my eyes. "Sittu is with Baba."

"Okay Mama," she said. She touched her grandmother's soft hand. "Sittu can't carry Amira now?"

"No."

"Okay." She thought for a moment then looked at me again. "Amira is sad now."

"I know," I said, kneeling at her side. "Mama is sad too."

I held her little body, and we wept softly together. After a moment, I dried her tears and asked, "Amira, can Mama carry you now?"

"Yes, Mama. Goodbye, Sittu." Amira waved at her grandmother's body then held up her hands to me. I lifted her into my arms, and we followed Fatima to her house. We sat together, weaving the cloth that would wrap my mother's body when we laid her in the ground. Selma joined us in our task. Even Amira helped. I gave her small, colored pieces of cloth that she worked into the shroud like the many colorful flowers in my mother's garden. I knew my mother would have liked that.

From time to time, Amira would stop what she was doing, turn to me and say, "Sittu is not working," as though to remind herself. "Amira said goodbye to Sittu. Sittu is with Baba now." I nodded each time, grateful to the gods for helping her make some sense of it all.

My father returned to the village before the sun set that night. All who were able walked with my family into the desert to a lone palm tree under which Mother had asked to be buried in the custom of her ancestors. Even Rullah joined us, carrying her newborn baby girl in her arms. Her sons and Amira stood silently near Fatima.

Jibran and Ghazi carried Mother's body on a flat board to the deep grave they had dug with my father in the hot sands. Her body was wrapped now in the shroud we had prepared for her. Father touched the part that covered her face, and I heard him whisper, "Goodbye, my beloved one."

Ali brought ropes that he used to help my brothers gently lower her body into the deep grave. The women of our village carried white flowers, which they scattered over her body. Each one whispered words of farewell to the woman who had birthed their children, healed their bodies, and dried their tears. When they were done, Father turned to me, his voice cracking with emotion.

"Noor," he began. He could not finish the question. I knew what needed to be done. I touched my hand to his shoulder and nodded.

I took a handful of sand and cast it into her grave. After a silent prayer for strength, I spoke. "As our bodies begin, so do they end. May the spirit of this woman rise above this desert grave. May those who loved her shed their grief by remembering the life she spent so well. Let them weep now, so their hearts will be free to go forward tomorrow. May we honor her in passing as we honored her in life."

I nodded to my father. He sifted a handful of sand gently into the grave. He took a breath and spoke in a hoarse whisper. "Beloved, I honor you, and I love you. Go in peace." His hands trembled as he turned to Ghazi.

Ghazi lifted sand into the grave and spoke. "Mother, I honor you, and I love you. Go in peace."

Ghazi turned to Jibran, and he repeated the ritual as his brother had, placing sand into the grave. "Mother, I honor you, and I love you. Go in peace." Then it came to me.

I cast sand again into her grave and spoke. "Mother, I honor you, and I love you." A sob escaped my lips, and I could speak no more, bowing my head with grief.

A glint of light caught my eyes, and I looked down at the Priestess Stone hanging from my neck. I thought of my mother, of her eyes, of her courage. I thought of all she had taught me, and all she had borne for our people. I remembered my promise. I breathed deeply and felt my body straighten and strengthen.

"Thank you, Mama," I whispered.

With renewed strength, I finished the ritual in a strong, clear voice. "We, your family and all who love you, honor your passing. May your spirit find safe harbor in the loving arms of those who have gone before. Let us speak your name often that you may always be among us."

Along with their friends, Sameer and Braheem, my brothers and Ali filled her grave as I spoke the final lines. "From the desert we are born, and so must we return. May the gods bless our beloved Leila who has walked so well among us. We give her up now to their keeping."

We stood together, weeping over her grave, holding one another for strength as the sun slowly set.

Seven days later, Rullah and Ghazi presented their baby to the gods and their family. They named her Leila.

$$\text{مَا مَتَّ دُمُوعُ العَيْنِ مِنِّي صَبَابَةً}$$
$$\text{عَلَى النَّحْرِ حَتَّى بَلَّ دَمْعِي مَحْمَلِي}$$

The tears of my love poured from my eyes, flowing down my neck,
Drowning even the sheath of my sword.
-Umr Ul Quais

CHAPTER 16
SAWDAH: ALLAH

As the days passed, my friendship with Nadia grew. We sat for hours together in the afternoons, braiding one another's hair as we discussed the word of *Allah*. She recited passages of the Prophet's revelations from memory and explained their meanings to me. She was a true friend, one who asked nothing in return. Those days we spent together were golden moments for me. My nights were a different matter, and I still weep when I recollect them.

Sheikh Ruhi spent his evenings in Nadia's company. I had asked her to take my place at his table, so I would be spared the agony of being in his company. I took my evening meal alone in my rooms and spent my evenings working at needlework while I memorized the passages Nadia had left for me to learn.

One night, as I was putting away my work and preparing for bed, there was a knock at my door. A servant entered. "Say'yedah, Sheikh Ruhi commands your presence in his chambers." I was surprised, as I had not set eyes on my husband in some weeks, but I only nodded, set aside my work and followed the man to where his master awaited me.

I found him alone in his room, drinking from a goblet. He smiled when he saw me enter. "My love," he said, slowly, "come to me. How I have missed you."

My heart leapt at his words. I had longed for this moment! I ran to his side and embraced him. He smiled again. "Do you hear the music? Dance for me, my gazelle." There was indeed the rhythm of a drum playing outside. Hallah was entertaining friends in the garden. "Dance, my beloved," he said again. His words were slurred now. He seemed tired, languid. He sat, watching me.

I danced for him. My body came alive, and I remembered again what it was to feel the thrill of passion course through my veins as I moved to the sound of that drum.

"Whore!" He was on his feet now, screaming at me. I had never heard him raise his voice in anger before. "Whore!" He shouted it at me again and threw his goblet. It shattered crystal and crimson across the hard floor. I fell to the ground and covered my face with my hands.

"What is it?" I asked. "What have I done wrong?"

"What have you done?" he asked. He moved toward me. "What have you done?" He shouted the words, towering over me, then stumbled back onto the bed. "Go," he whispered. "Just go."

I stumbled to my feet and ran from the room. I did not stop until I reached my own. I barred the door behind me and flung myself onto my bed. He had been so kind, so loving. What had I done to incur his wrath? I had not danced in almost a year. Perhaps I had danced poorly. Yes, that was it. I needed practice. And I had not taken enough time with my appearance. He must have been displeased, thinking I did not respect him. These thoughts spun through my mind with endless questions. I pleaded with the gods. No, not the gods. I begged *Allah* to help me know how to please my husband. He did love me. I was sure of it. If I could but learn what had displeased him, then certainly he would take me in his arms again, and we would be happy.

I said nothing to Nadia when we met the next day. "What is it, Sawdah?" she asked. "You seem so pale. Has something happened?"

"No. I am just a bit tired," I lied. "Perhaps I ate something that disagreed with me yesterday. I did not sleep well last night."

Her face was distressed. "Please go to Hallah and let her help you."

I nodded. "If you will excuse me, I think I will go now. Maybe I just need to rest."

"Shall I come with you?"

"No. Thank you, Nadia. It is a lovely day. You stay and enjoy the garden."

I did not go to Hallah. I returned to my room and sat on my bed, wondering if he would summon me again tonight. I let down my hair and brushed it. He liked when I wore it down around my shoulders. I took out a dress I had worn when we were newly married. He had said that he liked the way it looked on me. I set it on the bed, happy with my preparations. He would call for me. I was certain of it. This time I would be ready. I lay on my bed imagining a proper reunion with my beloved husband and drifted to sleep.

He did not call for me that night, nor the next. Every night I dressed for him. I applied kohl to my eyes and perfume to my wrists. I practiced my dancing in the solitude of my room. Still he did not call for me. Almost a week passed before once again the servant came to the door. I hardly believed it when I heard the knock.

"Sheikh Ruhi commands your presence," he said.

I rose from the bed and checked my appearance in a glass. Confident that I would now be pleasing to my husband, I followed the servant down the corridor. He left me at the door of my husband's chambers. I opened it and entered.

He was sitting on cushions, again holding a goblet in his hand. "Come, drink with me, my love." I came to his side. He held the cup to my lips, and I drank. It was sweet with a heady perfume. It was not wine. There was something different about this drink. He tipped the glass again to my lips. My head swam as though I had drunk too much, though I had but two sips.

"They call it opium," he said, drawing out his words slowly. "I brought it from Egypt. Isn't it wonderful?" I looked at his eyes. He seemed very far away. He gave me another drink, and the heat filled my body. I fell into his arms.

He drew me into him, his body pressed against mine. I melted. He moved his hands over my body. "So beautiful," he whispered. He took another drink and tipped the glass again to my lips. The smooth liquid burned in my throat. I was dizzy now, and the room was spinning. "This drink makes you forget," he said. "It takes everything away." My dress vanished, and he was inside of me, loving me.

I woke to find myself alone in his bed. It was day now, and sunlight filled the room. My head throbbed. "Ruhi?" I called, searching for him. He was not in his rooms. I dressed and walked quickly to my own. I washed and changed my clothes, then went to Hallah's door and knocked.

"I have a bit of a headache," I told her when she let me inside. "I wondered if there was something you could give me."

She looked into my eyes. "What did you drink last night?"

I blushed. "I had something with," I paused, uncertain if I should share my secret with her. "Ruhi gave me something to drink."

"Ah," she said, "was it the opium?"

I nodded. "What is it?"

"It is made from a flower. I have used it in small doses to remedy certain illnesses. In large quantities, however, it," she paused. "How shall I say this? It softens the mind."

She cut some dried herbs and gave them to me. "Boil these and drink their waters. They will help your head."

I thanked her.

"Be careful, Sawdah," she said. "My cousin is not in his right mind when he is taking this drug. Nor are you."

"I don't like the way it felt. I don't remember some of what happened."

She nodded. "The drug will do that. It will make you forget."

I smiled grimly, remembering what my husband had said.

She walked me to the door. "Be careful."

"I will," I promised.

The herbs did help, and that afternoon I joined Nadia in the garden. I had not seen her all that week. "You look so much better now," she said. "Your face is full of color. I'm glad you're feeling well."

I smiled and took her arm as we walked along the sunlit path.

That night, I waited for my husband's summons. It did not come. Days passed, and still I waited. When at last the servant knocked, I was ready. At the door to my husband's room, I stopped to arrange my hair. The door opened and a servant girl walked out, giggling. She saw me and bowed. "Good evening, Say'yedah," she said. Her hair was disheveled and her dress askew. She moved her hands quickly to smooth her hair and straighten the dress, then walked past me and hurried down the corridor as I walked into the room.

Ruhi was lounging on his bed. I saw a goblet on the table at his side. It was empty. His robes were open to the waist. "Come." He waved a limp hand toward me. I went to his side. "Dance for me."

"But there is no music."

"You've danced without music before." His eyes were closed now. He seemed to be falling asleep. "You danced for me." His eyes snapped open suddenly. "Get out!" He shouted at me and pointed to the door.

I ran to his side. "No, my love. Let me stay with you."

He pushed me away, and I fell to the floor. "Get out!"

"But why?" I was crying now. "Why must I go?"

He collapsed back in the bed. "She was so beautiful," he whispered. "We had the world." His head fell forward.

I stood looking at him. He was asleep. I covered him with a blanket and kissed his face. It was the drug, I thought. He had had too much. He did not know what he was doing.

Some weeks passed before he again summoned me to his chambers. I found him bent over a table, befuddled by his drugs. I tried to lift his hand, to take the goblet away from him, afraid he would be overcome.

"Don't touch that!" He struck my face. I was stunned. "You did this to me," he said. "You drove me to this madness." He struck me again, and I fell to the floor. He pushed himself away from the table and stood over me. His face was red and menacing, and his eyes shone with rage. I was terrified.

"I loved you!" he said in a cold, hoarse voice.

"I loved you," he whispered again. He fell to the ground, weeping, his body shaking. I went to his side and held him.

"I can't do it. I can't go on. I want to die." His voice was thin as though the words were being slowly dragged from his mouth. I felt his body go limp, and he was asleep. I did not want to let go. I stayed on the floor, holding him. I prayed for this powerful man whose heart could soar higher than ordinary mortals and whose pain could drive even a god to his knees. When I woke up, I found myself alone in my own bed. I did not remember how I came to be there. I did not have strength even to rise.

Nadia came looking for me. We had planned to pick grape leaves together. When I did not answer her knock, she came in and saw me still lying in my bed.

"Sawdah, what's wrong?" She rushed to my side. When she saw my face, she gasped. "What has happened to you?"

I touched a hand to my cheek and winced from the pain. "I fell from the bed in my sleep," I said. I would not tell her the truth. I could not betray my husband, even as the drugs drove him to the edge of madness.

"Let me take you to Hallah," she said. "I'm certain she has a poultice you can use."

"No!" I shouted and pulled away from her. "I'm sorry, Nadia," I said in a calmer voice. "Please, understand, I do not want to go to Hallah."

"Then let me go to her for you."

I did not stop her as she got up and left the room. She returned several minutes later with some leaves. She applied them to my face with a gentle touch. "Tell me what happened, Sawdah. Please. Let me help you."

I shook my head. "It's not important." I looked at her imploring face. "Please don't ask me again."

She helped me to my feet and bathed my face with a cool wet cloth. She took me to the bed and helped me into it. She put the leaves back onto my cheek. "Keep these here and try to rest. I will come to you again in the afternoon."

I closed my eyes and slept. When I awoke, I sat awhile in silence, hearing my husband's words repeating endlessly inside my head. He hated me. He wanted to die. I cursed my body's treachery. I cursed myself. I wanted to save him. I knew what I must do. I bathed and dressed and hurried out of the palace. I did not wish to speak to Nadia again. I ran to the stables and found them deserted. I saddled Karim, the horse that had been my dowry. I rode him hard and fast out into the city streets. When I reached the city walls, I pulled back his reins and stopped. I looked out onto the road that led to Damascus, the road that would take me to my father's village, the same road which had brought me here. What would happen if I just kept riding? I could be with my family in a few weeks' time. I could leave this place forever.

Then I remembered the smell of the camels, the black stains around my fingernails from peeling pomegranates all day. I remembered the simple brick huts, the old clothes.

I thought of the soft bed and beautiful dresses I had in the palace. I thought of the gardens, the peacocks, the gazelles, the scent of jasmine. How could I leave this place? Even now, after all that had happened, I could not go. If I returned to my father's home, broken and barren, I would be condemned to a mundane and empty life. I dared not return to the world I had known before.

But how could I return to the palace? How could I return, knowing my very presence was like a dagger in my husband's heart? Staying might destroy him. Leaving would surely destroy me.

I turned Karim and rode slowly back to the palace. It was dusk when I returned to my rooms. Nadia had been there. She had brought me food and drink. I set the tray aside and got on my knees at the side of my bed. I turned to face Mecca, as Nadia said she did.

"*Allah*, if You are truly with us, I ask for Your help. I do not know if

I believe in You, but I do not know what else to do. My life is forfeit. Please, help me know what I should do."

With that prayer, I gave my life to the service of *Allah*. I woke the next morning at dawn and fell to my knees. I did not know the words Nadia used for her prayers, so I only said, "*Allah*, please be with me this day. Help me know what to do."

I examined my face in the glass, then applied powder to hide the bruise. I braided my hair carefully and dressed for the day. I walked outside and found Nadia in the garden, picking figs.

"They looked so beautiful yesterday. I had to have some for my breakfast." She held out a basket full of the plump, black fruit. "Come and eat with me."

We sat on a bench and ate figs together. "I want to know more about *Allah*," I told her. "Please, teach me how to pray."

$$\text{وَنَحْنُ الحَاكِمُونَ إِذَا أُطِعْنَا}$$
$$\text{وَنَحْنُ العَازِمُونَ إِذَا عُصِينَا}$$

We are the rulers, if obeyed
And we take action against those who challenge us.
-Amr Ibn Kulthum

CHAPTER 17
NOOR: ABDULLAH

My father had always insisted on educating his people. Every man and woman of our village could read and write as well as calculate sums. These skills stood us in good stead in the markets when it came time to barter and sell. Even children could be relied upon to make a good trade and bargain with their elders without fear of deception.

Rullah, a natural teacher, taught all the children of the village. From her, they learned Arabic, poetry, mathematics, and astronomy. Amira and her cousins took their lessons together.

Amira was fascinated by mathematics and opened her own shop, selling dates and almonds door to door off the back of a small cart she and the boys had built together. Amira was the darling of the village. In the mornings, she walked the route she had often taken with her grandmother, trading her wares for kisses and sweets.

In the evenings, Ali spent time with her teaching her about horses. When she was old enough to learn to ride, he gave her Shihab, Hassan's horse.

"This horse loved your father," he told her.

She stood on a stool at his side, feeding the horse treats as Ali braided his long, black tail. She sat in front of him as he taught her to hold the reins and let the horse feel where she wanted him to go. She was soon riding Shihab alone while Ali rode his own horse at her side.

Each night before retiring to bed, Amira sought out her Jiddu for a game of backgammon. If he was traveling, she went to her Uncle Ghazi. They taught her to play the way my father had taught me and my brothers. They played to her level and let her win some of the time. They made the games harder little by little, strengthening her abilities until she was adept enough to beat them on her own. When she showed an interest in chess, they taught her that game too.

Auntie Fatima taught Amira to dance, and her Jiddu Bassam taught her to play beautiful music on the *oud*. Amira sat at her Sittu Selma's side and learned to weave designs in cloth. I watched my daughter grow and play, astonished by how quickly she learned, proud of her strength and character, but always with an ache in my heart that her father was not here to share my delight. Amira was beloved by our family, indeed, by all who knew her. She brought us joy. She was my treasure.

My father continued traveling to Mecca at least once a year, usually during the months of Al-Hurum, the months when warfare was forbidden, and pilgrims could safely travel in peace. Since the terrible day that took from us my beloved Hassan, my father had traveled only along the desert route, meeting a party from my grandfather's village at Al-Jawl, which had become a prosperous center of trade. He avoided the coastal route. Out of deference to custom, he would not impose on the hospitality of Sheikh Ruhi without invitation, and no invitation ever came. In all these years, I had not accompanied him on any of these journeys. I had no wish to return again to Mecca.

In the year after my mother's death, my father traveled more frequently. Leaving Ghazi in charge of the village, he set out with Bassam and Jibran for Damascus, Mecca and even once went East beyond Baghdad. He was restless now and seemed not to want to remain at home. He always returned with presents and stories. Amira would sit with him for hours as he regaled her with tales of his latest adventures over endless games of backgammon and chess.

One of these journeys took him to Yathrib, a city some days' travel from Mecca. From that trip, my father returned a changed man and changed forever the destiny of our people.

"Daughter, sit with me," he called out as he rode back into the village. "I have much to tell you." He lifted me onto his horse, and we rode to the stables together.

"How was your trip, Baba? Was it a prosperous one?"

"Daughter, could I but share with you one part of it, you would know that it was a most blessed adventure." He dismounted, then helped me off. I brought him combs and cloths as he unsaddled his horse.

He spoke as he worked. "We met some men on the road to Mecca. They told us they were traveling to Yathrib to see the Prophet Mohammed, messenger of *Allah*."

He shook his head. "In my heart, I scorned their ideas, but I let them talk. I had heard of this man. I told you about him. Do you remember?" I nodded, remembering the group in the marketplace Mother and I had passed on the road to the Kaaba.

"In the years since he took up residence in Yathrib, Mohammed has gained a large following. I wanted to see for myself what would possess thousands of our people to deny their faith and take up the cause of this shepherd." He poured water into a trough, and his horse bent his head to drink.

Father looked at me. "Noor, I confess I followed them to Yathrib intending to seek out this Mohammed and kill him. I wanted to end the life of this heretic and prevent the bloodshed that I knew would come when his believers set out to conquer the world." He combed the horse's sleek body and said nothing for several minutes while I waited in silence.

"Along the way, our companions told us fantastic tales of this Mohammed. They said he was the chosen of God, of the One God, *Allah*, and that *Allah* was speaking through him to us all. They recited passages of beautiful poetry Mohammed claimed were the words of *Allah*, spoken by the angels themselves." He shook his head and laughed. "Do you know, this Mohammed has had almost no education and yet he recites endless lines of poetry whose beauty and perfection rival the masters themselves!"

My father stopped working. "I arrived in Yathrib prepared to kill. I spoke to no one of my plan. Not even Bassam knew my true motive for coming to this city. We walked to the center of the town where Mohammed was speaking to a crowd of hundreds who had gathered around him. I watched them prostrate themselves on the ground, heard them cry out in adoration of this man and the God for whom he spoke. I listened to the words of Mohammed as he spoke to the crowd that afternoon."

Father took my hands in his. There were tears in his eyes now. "Noor, this was no ordinary man. Indeed, he is the Prophet of *Allah*."

I thought I must have misunderstood. "You can't mean that you believe him?"

He nodded. "Yes. He is the Prophet of the One True God, *Allah*." These words drove a stake into my heart. Had my father gone mad? I started to speak, but he went on, still gripping my hands.

"He spoke of many things, Daughter, things I did not always understand completely. What I do understand is that there is one God, *Allah*, and Mohammed is His Prophet. This I believe with my whole heart. It is as if I have been blind my whole life, but now I can see."

I wanted to scream, to slap my father's face and wake him from this terrible nightmare. His words were a profanation of all that our people believed, all that my mother had held dear. Still he went on. "Oh, Noor, if you could have heard him, seen him, you would know the truth of which he speaks."

"But Father," I said, finally finding my voice, "we have always spoken of the god Al-Lah. He is a king among our gods. We worship him and his daughters already."

He smiled. "Noor, *Allah* is not a god of stone to be passed from hand to hand. He is The God. The only one. There are no others before Him nor ever shall be. The stones we have worshipped and deified are empty idols, the products of our ignorance."

I shook my head, confused. "But Baba, what about our rituals, our shrines? These gods have protected us and borne us through difficult times. You would have us forsake them now because of the words of one man?"

Father began braiding his horse's long brown tail. "I know, Noor. I know it is difficult for you to comprehend. I was surprised myself at how my heart changed that day in Yathrib."

He finished the braid and tied it off at the end. "That is why it is critical for you to learn what I have learned, see what I have seen. Since your mother's death, you have been responsible for guiding our people in the worship of our gods. If our people are to see the truth, it must come from you."

"Baba, I don't understand how any of this can possibly be true. This man is claiming to speak the words of a new god, reviling the gods we have adored for countless generations," I shook my head. "How can I teach our people to believe something I do not?"

"Noor, you will believe. You will see with your own eyes." Father put away his tools and walked outside to wash his hands in a basin. "There is a man, Abdullah, who has traveled with us from Yathrib. He has spent some years there, learning the word of *Allah* from the Prophet Mohammed himself. Abdullah has come to teach us. When you hear him, you will know the truth. He will speak to us tonight after the evening meal. I wish you to be there."

My face felt hot. I was angry but dared not show it. "Of course, Father," I said, inclining my head. "Of course I will be there."

At that moment, Amira ran across the courtyard and flung herself into my father's arms. "Jiddu!" she cried. "I missed you!"

He swung her around, and her peals of laughter rained upon us. He set her down gently and considered her for a moment.

"Amira!" he said, his face set with mock sternness. "Have you been growing while I have been away?"

She giggled and stood as tall as she could. "Auntie Fatima says I am tall enough now to get water from the well all by myself."

He patted her head. "Soon you will be even taller than me."

"Will you play chess with me tonight, Jiddu?" she asked, grabbing his wrist. She laughed as he lifted his arm and swung her.

He smiled and set her down gently. "Not tonight, Amira. But bring the board to me tomorrow. I want to see if you have been practicing."

She grinned and ran off to play with her cousins.

"She is beautiful, Noor," he said, watching her run away. "You are truly blessed." I nodded and he kissed my cheek. "Come to the gathering place tonight, and let us both learn of *Allah*."

"Yes, Baba," I said. I walked away from him, reeling. I went to the eastern wall of the village, to the temple of Manat and stood alone. Hot tears fell from my eyes.

I could not fight my father's will. If he intended to bring this sacrilege upon our people, I was powerless to stop him. I begged the gods to forgive us all and prayed for the courage to walk with them along the path my father had chosen for us.

That evening, as was my custom, I took my dinner with Fatima and Amira. After Amira had fallen asleep, I walked to the healing tent. I took the Priestess Stone off its hook and set it around my neck, letting it fall under the fabric of my dress. I felt the cool weight of the stone against my skin. "Mother," I whispered, "give me strength."

I walked to my father's meeting place where I found him sitting with my brothers, Bassam, and another man about my father's age.

My father stood and held a hand out to me. "Abdullah, allow me to present my daughter, Noor. She is our High Priestess and Healer and one of my most trusted counselors."

Abdullah put the tips of his fingers together and bowed to me. I despised him instantly.

"Please, let us all sit and speak of the great Prophet of *Allah*." My father turned to Abdullah. "In the city of Yathrib, where I saw the Prophet," he began, but was interrupted by a soft cough from Abdullah.

"Permit me, Say'yed," the man said, "it is the will of *Allah* that we now address that place as Medina, the city of the Prophet."

"Very well then," said my father, "In Medina, I was told that the stone idols we keep in the village and carry to Mecca are," Abdullah did not let him finish the sentence.

"Blasphemies!" Abdullah cried. "False icons! They are nothing more than stones. Only the ignorant could believe them anything else."

I felt my father's hand on mine and looked at him. His eyes asked for my indulgence. I wanted to leave the room. There was nothing of god in this man, nothing he could possibly teach me of faith. Still, I had a responsibility to my father and to my people. More importantly, my father wanted me there. Out of love and respect for him, I stayed.

"Well, Abdullah," Father said, when the man had ended his tirade. "Please speak to us of Mohammed and Al-Islam."

Abdullah bowed his head. "As you wish, Say'yed. I am honored to spread the word of *Allah*. *Allahu Akbar!*" He cried out the words, raising his hands to the heavens. "In the name of *Allah*, the most merciful, the most compassionate." He bowed his head and smiled. "There is one God, *Allah*, and Mohammed is His Prophet."

Abdullah spoke well into the night. He talked about Mohammed and the miraculous prophecies and revelations that had come to him in visions. He spoke of *Allah*, the one true God. He spoke of Al-Islam, the one true faith.

When Abdullah showed signs of fatigue, Father stood. "Thank you, my friend, for coming to us. I want to offer you a place in our village. Please, stay as long as you can and continue teaching us what you know. You have been with the Prophet for many years. We are blessed to have you among us."

Abdullah rose and bowed to my father. "Of course, Say'yed, I would be honored to speak what I know of *Allah*, though it is but little."

"Bassam," Father said, "would you escort our guest to the house we have prepared for him?" Bassam bowed his head and stood. Father turned to Abdullah. "I trust you will find everything you need there. Please do not hesitate to ask if any comfort is lacking."

Abdullah nodded and left with Bassam. When they were gone, Father sat with me and my brothers. He turned to me first. "I can see you had a difficult start with Abdullah. But do you see now the power of *Allah* and the beauty of the Prophet's words?"

I considered this before speaking. "Baba, I truly do not know what to make of all this. I can only say that Abdullah believes this Mohammed has truly been visited by angels. I don't know enough about his faith to judge its veracity."

He turned to my brother, "And you, Jibran? What do you make of Al-Islam?"

Jibran's eyes were bright. "I am curious to know more. I felt a chill in my body when Abdullah spoke of *Allah*." He looked at me. "Noor, I mean no disrespect, but I have never felt drawn to the gods of our people. Now, suddenly, I feel a pull in my very being, a longing to learn all I can of *Allah*."

"So you shall learn," Father said. "Ghazi? What do you have to say?"

"Thank you, Baba, for bringing this man to us. I believe we have much to learn from him." My brother Ghazi was ever the diplomat.

Father smiled. "We will discuss this more tomorrow." Jibran and Ghazi stood and exited the room. Father turned to me. "Good night, my beloved daughter." He helped me to my feet and kissed my forehead.

"Father," I asked, "what do you think Mother would say to all this?"

He wore a sober expression. "I don't know, Noor." He smiled. "I do believe she would have been proud of you tonight. I know you did not take well to Abdullah. I thank you for staying. Try to give him a chance to alter your impressions of him and of this faith. I hope that as you get to know him, you will see him for the truly pious and passionate man I have come to know."

"Good night, Baba."

"Good night, Noor."

As I walked to my tent, I thought of what had passed this night. Questions stirred inside of me. I thought especially of what Abdullah had said about our stone idols, our gods, and the ignorance of those who worshipped them. I had spent my whole life learning the ways of Manat. I had walked at my mother's side from childhood, repeating the sacred words, learning the sacred rituals. My mother was a strong, wise woman. This agent of a self-proclaimed prophet dared to characterize all she had believed in as the ravings of ignorance. I hated him. I hated everything about him and the god he purported to serve.

If only my mother were here. She would have spoken the sweetest words, and they would have cloven that man in two. If only my beloved were here. He would have helped to shore up the walls of my spirit as they crumbled down around me.

بُوَرِّثَنِي التَّذَكُّرَ حِينَ أُمْسِي
أَصْبِحُ وَقَدْ بُلِيتُ بِفَرْطِ نُكْسِ

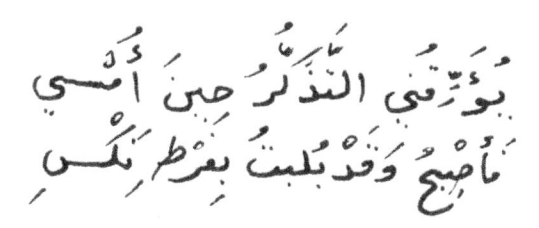

Memories keep me awake at night,
And I rise in the morning exhausted by the never-ending tragedy.
-Al Khansa

CHAPTER 18
SAWDAH: AL-ISLAM

Nadia taught me to pray. She showed me how I must wash my hands and feet to make myself worthy of *Allah*. She gave me a clean rug to use for my prayers and taught me how to stand and kneel and bow before Him. We prayed together at dawn and dusk, at mid-day, mid-afternoon and again at late evening. She spoke the words for us both until I learned them too.

Nadia suggested I cover my hair with a scarf as she did, especially when in the company of men. "*Allah* asks for our modesty," she explained. "In my family, we are taught married women should wear a scarf over our hair and modest clothing over our figures to save our beauty for the eyes of our husbands alone. For my part, I choose to cover my hair as a symbol of my fidelity to *Allah*." It seemed a small enough gesture to honor a great and glorious God. We sat together, embroidering the edges of the sheer silk, discussing and praising the wisdom of *Allah*.

Sometimes a caravan would pass through bearing news from Nadia's family in Medina. They sent her the latest words of the Prophet, so she might know what he had taught his people in her absence and follow the decree of *Allah* more faithfully. Her mother took down the words as she learned them, passing them on to her daughter by messenger. We pored over those words day after day, learning and repeating them together. We read one day that the Prophet spoke of a promise of everlasting life.

"Think of it, Sawdah," Nadia said, "a Paradise with no concern and no remorse. Why, it would be like walking in our garden always."

To feel no remorse. To walk in the gardens of *Allah*'s mercy forevermore and shed the grief and regret that had become my living shroud would be a Paradise indeed. I longed for such a day. When Sheikh Ruhi next summoned me, I vowed to imagine myself cloaked in *Allah*'s love and benevolence.

Nadia and I were alone in our worship. Sheikh Ruhi had not embraced Al-Islam, nor had his people. This was a source of pain to Nadia who worried her husband would be easy prey for the demon, Shaitan. "I know he drinks too much," she said one morning as we walked together in the garden. She turned to me. "I know he has struck you."

I said nothing. It was rare that we spoke of him at all, and I had never told her what passed between us.

Nadia went on. "*Allah* prohibits the use of intoxicants. He wants us to be clearheaded and pure. If only Ruhi could see the beauty of Al-Islam. If only he could embrace the word of *Allah*." She stopped. "I'm sorry, Sawdah. We should talk about something else."

"It's alright, Nadia. He is your husband too. I know you want what is best for him."

She smiled. "Thank you for saying so." She paused and turned to look at me. Her face was pale. "Sawdah, I am carrying his child."

Although I had suspected this, her words still cut. I did my best to conceal my feelings, but still she blushed and turned away.

I took her hand. "Nadia, you are my friend. I am happy for your happiness." She embraced me, and I held her, celebrating with her even as her joy reminded me of my sorrow.

Nadia was a kind girl. I could not hate her. She was not at fault for my lot in life. As her pregnancy progressed, I retreated farther back into the shadows of palace life, allowing her to take my place in its hierarchy. When her son was born, her place as first wife would be sealed forever. I knew Ruhi would lavish every comfort upon her and the baby. I hoped too that this baby might heal some of the pain Ruhi still carried in his heart.

When the baby was one week old, Nadia brought him to me for the first time. I knew Sheikh Ruhi would want to be with her in this special time, and I had not wanted to impose myself on their newfound joy. I had not visited her apartments since receiving news of his birth. She held the baby out to me, and I took him in my arms.

"He's so beautiful." I stroked his round, pink head. "And so small."

She smiled at me. "He will be called Adel. His naming ceremony is tonight. I suspected you would not want to come, and I wanted to be sure you could meet him today."

"Thank you," I said, returning the baby. "May he be blessed beyond other men."

She smiled. "This ceremony tonight will involve the gods of ignorance. I have asked *Allah* to forgive my child his father's pagan ways." She looked down at the baby in her arms. "I want my son raised with the faith of Al-Islam. I pray every day for *Allah* to turn his father's heart."

I put my hand on her shoulder. "You can give your son your faith," I said. "Teach him as you have taught me, and he will come to love *Allah* as I do."

She smiled, blinking back tears. I kissed her cheek. "Go and celebrate in the name of your son," I told her. "Tomorrow, we'll take him for a walk in the garden and start teaching him all about Al-Islam."

When she left, I was surprised to find myself truly happy for her. I loved her. I asked *Allah* to protect her and her child.

We did meet in the garden the next day. We made our ablutions and prayers while Adel slept in a cradle alongside us. Over the months that followed, I watched Adel grow and marveled at the world as I tried to see it through his eyes. I loved that child as I loved his mother.

We giggled together the day he said "lahoobar," knowing it was his way of saying *Allahu Akbar*, the words he heard us speak so many times each day. Nadia and I held his hands as he learned to walk and made him his own little prayer rug to sit on when he began mimicking our actions.

One afternoon, as we sat together in the garden watching Adel nap under the shade of a fig tree, I looked at his beautiful little face and thought of my own child. Had he lived, he would have been five years old today. Tears welled in my eyes. Nadia saw them and touched my hand.

"What is it, Sawdah?" she asked, gently.

I looked at the ground. "It's my fault I lost my baby." I had never spoken these words aloud though they had tormented my heart. The tears fell faster now.

"What do you mean?" Nadia asked.

I turned to her. "I think *Allah* must have known I did not really want a baby. I was not ready. I was too frightened. I kept worrying I would lose my figure. I was jealous of the time it would take to feed him and bathe him and clothe him. I was afraid I would not have time to play with my husband." I shook my head. "I was selfish and ungrateful, and *Allah* punished me. I killed our baby with my horrid thoughts."

Nadia held my arms. "Is that really what you think, Sawdah?" I nodded. "No," she said, "you did not kill your baby. No." She touched my face. "Every mother worries. We all wonder what childbirth will do to our bodies, how motherhood will alter our lives. We all fear we will be unfit parents. You are not the first woman to have had these thoughts. They are normal."

She sighed. "We are not spirits, Sawdah. You are a woman with real feelings and fears and doubts and failings. *Allah* forgives us our humanness. *Allah* would never punish you for that."

I wiped the tears from my face. "You don't understand. You are so kind and generous. You could never know the evil thoughts I had."

"But I do know them, Sawdah," she said. "When I learned I was with child, I was filled with joy and fear in equal measure. There were days I wished I had never conceived a child. It pains me to say this as I look at my beautiful boy, but I want you to know that I have felt what you felt."

She looked away. "Sawdah, I know my husband does not love me as he once loved you." She shook her head and placed a hand over my lips to stop my protestations. "I feared that once I brought his child into the world, he would cease to seek me out at all except when he was ready for another son." She laughed bitterly. "And I was right."

She looked back at her baby. "But I love my son. I would give my life for him. You would have done the same if you had been given the choice." Her eyes met mine. "Please, Sawdah, don't bear the burden of that guilt. It will destroy you. You must seek *Allah*'s compassion. He will save you from this demon you are carrying in your heart."

I nodded. I heard her words and appreciated her candor. But the doubt remained. When I saw my husband in his drugged state, heard his shouts, felt the blow to my heart when he blamed me for his sorrows and wished himself dead, a part of me knew it was my penance for the secret guilt I harbored in my soul.

He continued to summon me to his room in his drunken stupors. Sometimes he only yelled, after first speaking to me with the opium's sweet, honeyed voice. Sometimes he wept in my arms, only to stop suddenly and cast me out of the room. Sometimes, the drug worked its evil most deeply. It was then that he laid his hands upon me in anger.

He hated me, yet I stayed with him. I was trapped and did not dare set myself free. Only the promises of *Allah* and a joyful hereafter gave me any solace from my shame. Some nights I vowed that I would leave at the dawn, but when I awoke to silken sheets and perfumed water and the memory of what awaited me outside the palace walls, I was loathe to abandon this luxurious prison. And that shame haunted me most of all.

When Adel was two years old, Sheikh Ruhi took up the study of Al-Islam with Nadia, who was then pregnant with their second child. Al-Islam appeared to pacify his rages and, under Nadia's stern eye, quelled his use of the drugs as well. His sole vice then remained his harem, the female slaves he kept for his selfish pleasure. Nadia abided their presence because they satisfied his desires and freed her to raise her sons and run her household as she wished.

As he stopped drinking his opium wine, he also stopped summoning me to his rooms. I missed him terribly, though I was grateful the ordeal seemed finally at its end. I thanked *Allah* for finding His way into my husband's heart. I prayed He would heal Ruhi's wounds and give him peace. He and Nadia began to travel, taking their children to see her home in Medina or voyaging back to Egypt to see the ancient sights there.

I was alone now. In truth, I had been alone for a very long time. I had my faith and my comfortable rooms. I resigned myself to a life apart and vowed to devote my life to learning the will of *Allah*. I was content in my solitude and found comfort in the life I had chosen. I no longer considered escaping, but oh how I wish I had.

وَمَهْما تَكُنْ عِنْدَ امْرِئٍ مِنْ خَليقَةٍ
وَإِنْ خَالَها تَخْفَى عَلَى النَّاسِ تُعْلَمِ

The true quality of a man shall be known
Even though he thinks he has concealed it.
-Zuhair

CHAPTER 19
NOOR: AL-ISLAM

My father gave Abdullah a small house to use as his own while he stayed in our village. It had belonged to Bassam's aunt until her death and had sat vacant in the months since. Father intended Abdullah to live among us as we learned to embrace the faith of Al-Islam.

The morning after Abdullah's arrival, I said the morning blessing at the temple of Manat as I had done since I was a child at my mother's feet. As the sun dawned, I heard a man's voice cry out, "*Allahu Akbar!*" I walked toward the village center and saw Abdullah standing atop a mound of stone calling out those words.

I watched him a moment, uncertain of what was to come. I saw others, my family, my friends, standing in doorways or walking toward the sound of his cry. I stopped at the well and stood in silence, listening to his words.

"*Allah* is Great! There is no god before *Allah*! Mohammed is the Prophet of *Allah*!"

Fatima came to my side. "Who is this man, Noor?" she whispered as he continued chanting.

"He claims to be a messenger of the Prophet Mohammed bringing a new faith to our people."

"Mohammed?" she asked. "You mean that lunatic we saw in Mecca?"

I nodded. "Mohammed says we are to worship only *Allah* now and follow the ways of Al-Islam."

She shook her head. "What of our other gods? What of the goddesses?"

I shook my head. "Mohammed says these are false idols, relics of our ignorance."

She laughed softly. "No one will accept this. We have worshipped our gods for so long. None of our people will listen to this teller of tales."

"My father believes him."

Fatima searched my face. "You can't mean that."

I nodded. "He has invited this man, Abdullah, to stay and teach our people the ways of Al-Islam."

She looked up at Abdullah who had come down from his perch and was on his knees now upon a small carpet he had placed on the ground. He was speaking what sounded like a prayer. Fatima took my hand. "What will you do, Noor?"

"I will wait."

When Abdullah had finished his prayers, he spoke to the people who had now gathered around him. "I bring you a message from the Prophet of *Allah*. *Allah* is great. There is no god but *Allah*."

"We worship Manat as well as her father Al-Lah!" a woman cried out.

Abdullah sighed. "What you call gods are but worthless bits of stone. You have dwelt in ignorance all your lives."

I watched the faces of those around him. Some looked angry, others merely surprised. A few seemed curious.

"You must pray to *Allah*," Abdullah continued, "and ask Him to forgive your ignorance. Prostrate yourself before *Allah*. I will teach you to pray in His name."

I did not want to hear any more. I went to my house where Amira was just waking. "Good morning, Mama." Her eyes sparkled. "I'm going to play backgammon with Jiddu today!"

I stroked her dark hair and kissed her cheek. "Come. Let's eat something."

We ate our meal together, then walked to Rullah's house where Amira's cousins were already playing in the yard. She ran to join them, and Rullah invited me inside.

"What's going on?" she asked. "Who is that man?"

"Ghazi did not tell you?" I asked.

She shook her head. "He came in late last night after I was already asleep. He left early this morning, saying he had to attend to your father. We had no time to talk of anything."

I told her about Abdullah and what he had said the night before. She absorbed it all then asked, "Is it your father's wish that we embrace the faith of Al-Islam?"

I nodded.

She smiled. "Then that is what will be."

I did not feel like arguing with her. Rullah had always been a kind and gentle soul. She would never speak ill of anyone nor rebel against the wishes of her people. She walked her path, following where it led her, accepting the road before her.

"Yes," I said. "It is what will be." I kissed her cheek and left her house. Amira waved at me from the top of a tree as I walked toward the house of healing.

Fatima came to me later that day. I sat on the floor setting mint out to dry.

"Noor, may I sit with you a moment?"

"Of course, Auntie." I made a space for her at my side.

She sat, arranging her robes carefully around her. "Noor, I am afraid."

I looked up. "What is it, Fatima?"

"This man, this messenger. He is mesmerizing the people. He ridicules the very foundations of our faith, yet the people are listening to him. Have you heard his latest decree? He says women ought to cover their hair and faces to be modest before their god."

I nodded.

"Are we to just sit back and allow this scourge to lay waste everything we have believed?" She shook her head, clearly frustrated. "Noor, I am no Priestess, but our gods, our goddesses, the rituals we perform, these are the cornerstones of our civilization. I cannot just turn my back on the faith of my ancestors."

"I know," I said. "I sit here thinking of my mother, of all she entrusted to me." I touched the Priestess Stone. "I feel helpless before this onslaught. I cannot stand against my father. I cannot stand against the will of my people." I swallowed back the tears that threatened to flow, and I could say no more.

"Come, Noor," Fatima said, unable to bear my pain on top of hers. "Let us have some gossip." I smiled, relieved at the change of topic. "Let's see. Whom shall we slander today?" We laughed together.

We talked about betrothals we knew were planned and a few liaisons we knew were not. Fatima talked about the men who were staying in our campgrounds. One was too old, one too fat. There was one, however, who had caught her fancy, and we giggled as she plotted schemes with which to entrap him into her bed for a night. "Only let me be rid of him the next morning," she teased.

Fatima had an easy way about her that drew men to her. She had declined many offers of marriage over the years, preferring instead the freedom to come and go as she pleased. I had asked her once why she did not marry. "I can bear solitude," she had said. "I am not afraid to be alone. But to find myself living day upon day with a man and still feeling alone, that is a loneliness I do not wish to risk."

I put the tray of mint on a shelf. Fatima watched me.

"Have you ever considered marrying again, Noor?"

I shook my head. "No, Fatima. I am content with my work and my daughter." The pain of Hassan's death still burned in my heart. I could not imagine loving another.

Fatima sighed. "So many men, so many hearts to break." Fatima pulled a length of cloth off a nearby table and held it across her face. She blinked at me over top of it. Fatima's eyes were renowned for their great beauty. They sparkled black as the night sky. "Do you think men would want me less if they could only see my eyes?"

"No, Auntie Fatima. They would want you more."

We laughed together. It felt good to laugh with her. Those moments helped me to feel less alone and less afraid.

The days of Abdullah's stay passed painfully, made bearable only by Fatima's company and her courage. We attended his speeches together and watched in amazement as our people began to forget all that had been, embracing fully this new and unfamiliar faith.

Abdullah stayed in our village for many months, teaching and praying and spreading the word of Al-Islam. Among the speeches he gave, there was one in particular that moved many of my people to faith. It was Abdullah's explanation of death, and *Allah*'s promises for the afterlife. As Abdullah spoke these words, I thought of my mother and watched the faith that had been her life's work crumble and fall.

"*Allahu Akbar!*" he cried, "God is great!" Abdullah stood upon the mound of stones that had been the temple of Manat. When he had been in our village a month, he had taken down the sacred stone and cast it aside. He had claimed our holiest space in the name of *Allah* and called our people to worship and learn with him there. Every day, the village gathered around him as he spoke the words of *Allah*.

"My friends, I must tell you now what *Allah* has promised us after death." His eyes scanned the crowd and the people fell silent, pressing closer to better hear his words.

"*Allah* has told us that our lives will not end when we die. No!" He shouted. "We are not animals! We are men! It is at our deaths that our lives will truly begin!"

He looked out at the crowd, fire in his eyes. "If we break the commandments of Allah, we will spend eternity in the hell fires of *J'hannam*. But if we obey Him," his voice grew louder now, "If we obey Him, He promises us glory and riches and pleasure!" A quiet murmur swept through the crowd.

Abdullah continued. "If we obey the commands of Allah, if we follow His laws all our lives, we will find ourselves in a palace of gold. There will be an end of thirst and hunger, for food and drink shall flow like the water of the seas. We will dine on sweetmeats and drink the finest wine. Our sacrifices will be richly rewarded!" This moved the crowd. He had taught them that among the laws of Al-Islam was a moral prohibition against the drinking of spirits.

And still there was more. "Every desire shall be granted us. Houris and virgins shall wait upon our every need and exist only for our pleasure." This roused the men of the village, as one would expect.

"My friends, declare your faith in *Allah*, follow the laws He has lain down for us, and all this shall be yours!"

I shook my head. Virgins, wine, feasts, what man could resist such a temptation? As he spoke, I scanned the crowd. Like the men, the women of the village nodded and beamed at Abdullah's words. They heard what they wanted to hear. Like sheep thronging to the slaughter, they fell to the sweet temptations of Al-Islam.

My brother Jibran took to Al-Islam as a thirsty man takes to water. I watched the fever of it burn in him and change him. Where once he had been withdrawn, self-conscious and shy, he now became before my eyes a man, strong and confident, passionate, and fierce. I could have been proud of him then, but his eyes had grown cold and distant. He spent most of his days in the company of Abdullah and had taken on many of the man's predilections, including his condescending attitudes and tones. I did not know my brother anymore.

Ghazi took the changes in his stride, letting the wave of Al-Islam carry him on its course. He followed the faith, not from any passion of the spirit, but more because it was proper to do so. And mostly because it was his father's will.

Rullah, always modest and unassuming, was among the first of our women to begin covering her hair in public. She did this as she did all things, with poise and dignity. On her lovely face, the scarf seemed a crown. I watched her as she set it gracefully upon her head. She wore it with love, a love I did not comprehend. Other of the women followed her lead, covering their hair as a devotion.

I could not match their faith, so I imitated their actions. I watched Rullah walk like a goddess, head erect, shoulders back, carrying her faith like a torch in the dark. I tried to walk as she did, no longer daring to betray my unbelieving heart now that so many of my people had embraced Al-Islam.

As Abdullah's visit drew to an end, even Fatima, my friend, my hope, fell to Al-Islam, lost in this terrible war for the human soul. I knew the change had come over her even before she did. I watched her face as she listened to Abdullah's speeches, her eyes gleaming with unshed tears as he spoke of *Allah*'s benevolence and love and the promise of glory in the next life. In her lovely face, lined with age, I saw fear in her beautiful eyes. It was the fear of growing old, the fear of death. Our eyes met, and my throat tightened with a stifled cry when I saw her smile the benevolent smile of Al-Islam.

One by one, the people of my village fell prostrate before their new God. I watched them bow. I watched them break. I watched them fall. I stood with them in labor, knelt with them in prayer, but I was not among them. More than at any other time in my life, I was completely and utterly alone.

I dared not reveal my doubts, my disbelief. I was, if nothing else, my father's daughter. I knew my place in the village. I knew the women looked to me for guidance and healing. They trusted me. I could not divide my family. I would not.

I drew a scarf over my head and face as a shield, protecting me from eyes that might see the truth and hate me for it. I wore my costume and played the role Al-Islam demanded of me.

I listened to the prayers as I spoke their words, listened and learned the words of *Allah* as Abdullah recited them. The words raised in me no flame of passionate faith, only questions that haunted my dreams and surrounded my heart with walls of stone.

دَقوما بِها مَشيي علَىَّ مَطيَّهِم
بَعَدَ كون لا تَهلَك أسَىً وتَجَمَّل

My friends stop in their journey and stand over me, saying,
"Don't destroy yourself with grief. Be patient."
-Umr Ul Quais

CHAPTER 20
SAWDAH: AHMED

When I had been wed nearly eight years, a servant came to me as I sat sewing in the garden. "Sheikh Ruhi Al-Azeem commands your presence in his audience chamber."

I was surprised. Never in all the years I had lived in this palace had he demanded my presence in his public rooms. I followed the man back into the palace and walked behind him to the large room that was used to impress and overwhelm foreign visitors and tradesmen.

I entered the chamber and found my husband sitting on an elevated platform surrounded by luxurious cushions. He was examining a set of carved chess pieces as a young craftsman stood below him. "I hope the work is pleasing to you," the man said.

Sheikh Ruhi picked up the black queen and turned it over in his hands. "The work is excellent," he said. "Youssuf, see that this man is well compensated." He smiled at the artist. "Bring me more of your work."

The man stood and bowed deeply. "You honor me, Sheikh Al-Azeem." He was dismissed with a wave, and the man walked to where Youssuf waited with a pouch of gold coins.

A servant approached his master with some documents. While they worked, I looked at my husband. I had not seen him in nearly half a year. He and Nadia had only now returned from a long voyage. His face was lined but still handsome. His hair was thick, but I could see strands of white now overtaking the black.

Sheikh Ruhi finished his business and looked at me. "Sawdah," he said, "come." I heard a buzz of whispered conversation from the other men in the room.

I approached and bowed my head. "What is your bidding, my husband?"

His look was cold, but as his eyes met mine, they softened. "Youssuf," he called. The man appeared at his side. Sheikh Ruhi spoke with him a moment then Youssuf returned to his place with the other men.

"Come," my husband said to me. "Let us walk." He helped me up onto the platform and let me out through the hidden door behind it. He nodded to the guard keeping watch in the corridor and walked outside with me into the garden. We stood together, looking out at the paradise we had shared so very long ago.

"Sawdah," he said, his voice hoarse, "Sawdah, I cannot continue this charade." He looked up at the sky and sighed. "I have not been a husband to you. *Allah* asks us to forgive, but I cannot find forgiveness for what has passed between us. I cannot forgive *Allah*, I cannot forgive myself and I cannot forgive," here he paused and ran a hand through his hair, "you." The word was small but filled his throat so he could hardly speak it.

"My husband, I understand," I told him. "I bear you no ill will."

He turned to me now. "You do not understand. When I see you, when I hear your voice, I am tormented by the shame of what I have done and by grief for what has become of us." He took my hand. "A wife is to be revered, adored and honored," he said. "I have done none of those things. Now I find I cannot even love you. I can no longer be your husband."

I protested again. "I am satisfied in my life," I said. And indeed I was, for as painful as his words were, I found my heart had strengthened some over these lonely years.

"I am not," he said. "I am tormented by guilt and shame. The pain of it afflicts me now even as I do my work. I must be able to be a leader to my people. I must be able to be a father to my children. I cannot allow this to go on any longer." He let go of my hand. "When we return to the audience chamber, I will speak the words that will free you from me. I return you to your father with your dowry and a fortune that will keep you. I am sorry there is not more that I can do."

I looked at his face and knew it was over. I could not protest. I could make no argument. I would not remain in this place to cause the man I had loved any greater pain.

We walked back inside. At the threshold, he cleared his throat. "If you would perhaps send news to Nadia sometimes, I know she would want to hear that you are well." He took a long breath and walked inside his palace, master of himself once more.

In the audience chamber, before all who waited there, my heart broke as I heard Sheikh Ruhi's voice utter the words that would sever my life from his. "I grant your desire to leave this place and be free of my company. I divorce you. I divorce you. I divorce you." And so the deed was done.

Sheikh Ruhi brought Youssuf to his side once more. One of his most trusted servants, this man was relied upon to carry out his most important tasks. "Youssuf," he said, "this lady desires to return to her family. I trust her to your care. See that she receives every comfort as you guide her to her home."

"As you wish, my master," Youssuf bowed deeply, then turned to me. "If you will follow me, my lady."

Before we left the room, I looked once more upon the man who had been my husband. Our eyes met and he nodded once. I bowed toward him. "Fare well, Sheikh Ruhi Al-Azeem." I turned and followed Youssuf as he led me out toward my chambers.

Nadia was waiting for me when I arrived. The look on her face told me she knew everything. She had been my friend, but she was a woman too. My departure freed her husband. I knew that in her heart, down beyond the depths of our friendship, she would not grieve my absence. I could not blame her. I would have felt the same in her place. Would that I had been in her place.

She gave me a package wrapped in strong fabric. "The words of the Prophet," she said. "May they guide your way always." I held the pages to my heart, and she hugged me.

"I'm sorry it has to be this way, Sawdah. I'm sorry." Tears fell from her eyes, and she turned, running down the corridor away from me.

I stared after her until a soft cough broke the silence. Youssuf stood in the doorway, waiting for me to enter my rooms.

"Pack whatever you need," he said. "The rest has already been prepared and awaits you outside."

I walked past him into my rooms. "There is a caravan leaving at dusk," he said. "It is my master's wish that we join it. If you would meet me before sundown outside the northern doors, I will escort you." He turned and left the room, closing the door behind him.

I looked around the room that had been my home. I touched the beautiful things that had brought me joy. I wanted none of them now. I wanted no silks, no lovely dresses, no trinkets. I wanted my husband, the man I had married. That, I could never have.

I met Youssuf at the door after I made my prayers before dusk. I had with me only Nadia's package and a small bag of simple garments I would need for the journey home. I could not bear to bring anything else. Youssuf was dressed for travel and wore a cloth around his head. It covered all his face. In the dim light, I could not even see his eyes.

He gave me a long black scarf. "The desert winds blow strong tonight. This will protect you." His voice was muffled by the cloth he wore. "Wrap it well around your face." I did so while he readied the horse.

Karim's back was laden with packages. I knew these were Sheikh Ruhi's gifts to me, the treasure he hoped would comfort me. Youssuf took my bag of clothing and helped me onto the horse. I still clutched Nadia's gift. It gave me comfort, and I could not part with it. He took the reins to guide Karim toward the encampments and our caravan. As we neared the campgrounds, Youssuf turned and led the horse into the heart of the city.

"Where are we going?" I asked.

"With your permission," he said, "I want only to say goodbye to my sister before we leave. It won't take a moment."

I said nothing. On my account, Youssuf would be away from the city for months. I could not deny him his goodbyes.

We stopped outside a small house. Youssuf led Karim back behind the stable and tethered him there. He held out a hand to help me down. I would have preferred to wait with Karim, but I did not want to offend his family by remaining outside. Youssuf opened the door and motioned for me to enter.

I walked through the doorway ahead of him and looked around. Youssuf's sister had not yet lit her lamps, and I could see only dimly in the fading sunset. I wondered why no one came to greet us. I heard the door close behind me and turned. Youssuf stood against it. He removed the cloth from his face, and I gasped. It was not Youssuf's face I beheld, but the ugly, cruel face of the vizier. Ahmed sneered at me, and I took steps backward, stumbling over something as I did.

I looked down and cried out. Youssuf's body lay upon the carpet. His neck had been slit. He was dead. I stared up at Ahmed. He was wielding a long, thin knife. "Be silent," he ordered. "Or suffer his fate."

I dared not speak. I dared not move. I stared at the knife in his hand, the stain of Youssuf's blood still upon it. I still held Nadia's package to my chest. I had not wanted to leave it outside. I clung to it now, beseeching *Allah* to save me.

"You will help me move his body outside," he said.

"I cannot," I whispered, horrified at even the thought.

"You must," he said, "or you will die." He moved to the end of the carpet. "Come on girl, pull."

I stood frozen to the spot. Ahmed struck me, the palm of his hand stinging my face. Tears welled up in my eyes. I could not stop them. "You will obey me," he said roughly, "or suffer for your insolence." He dragged me to his side and snatched the package from my hands, throwing it into a corner of the room. He forced me to help him wrap Youssuf's body in the carpet then drag it outside. I could hardly breathe for weeping.

Behind the stable, I saw a hole already dug in the ground. When Youssuf's body lay inside it, Ahmed pushed a shovel at me. Again wielding the knife, he made me fill the hole. My arms, already aching from the effort of moving the body, now burned. And still Ahmed forced me to carry on. If I cried out, even from the pain in my arms, he flashed the knife in my face, and I had to carry on in silence.

At last, the hole was full. Ahmed seized the shovel from my hands and leveled the ground. "Get inside," he ordered.

"What about my things?" I asked, looking at Karim still tethered outside the stable.

Ahmed laughed. "I will take care of your pretty things." He spoke harshly into my ear and forced me back inside the house where he struck me again, driving me to my knees. "Where is your haughty pride now?" he asked. "I watched you plot against me, whispering to my master, telling him to send me from the palace."

"No," I said, "I did none of those things."

"Silence!" he shouted. "I could do nothing, say nothing against you so long as you were under the protection of that house, but there is no one to protect you now. I have suffered your scorn for eight years," he said. "I will show you scorn now such as you have never known." He pulled a leather strap off a table and held it between his hands.

"You will live here at my pleasure, and you will serve me. You will obey me."

"No," I whispered, "I will not stay here."

He laughed. "Where will you go? What value do you have now beyond your pretty face? Rejected by your husband, barren, worthless. You have nowhere to go."

"I will go to my father's house," I said.

"Hah!" Ahmed laughed, a cruel, scornful laugh. "You think he will take you in and bring shame upon his family? You think he will risk losing the fame he gained when he sold his daughter to the most powerful sheikh in the land?"

"He didn't sell me," I whimpered.

"What is marriage but a sale of goods? And in your case, damaged ones at that."

I prayed, desperately begging *Allah's* mercy.

"You will not leave this house except with me. You may have a horse, but you have nowhere to ride it. You may have a pretty face, but no one will see it."

He pointed at the cloth that still covered my face. "You will wear this at all times, in and out of the house. You will keep your body covered completely and speak to no one. If you do not obey, you will die."

I nodded slowly. I could not believe this was happening. Was I dreaming? Oh, that this nightmare would end!

"In the morning, I will leave for the palace. I expect my house to be clean when I return." He laughed. "Now I will see to your pretty things." He walked through the door, barring it behind him.

When he was gone, I fell to my knees. I prayed for salvation, asked *Allah* for mercy. What sin had I committed that for which I was being punished? I thought of the baby I had forsaken, the home I had reviled, the luxuries I had coveted. Greed. Pride. Selfishness. These were my sins. I did not deserve to seek *Allah's* protection.

I looked up with a start to find Ahmed standing over me. "Get up!" he snarled. I stood, trembling. What evil did he have planned for me now? "I cannot trust you in my house when I am sleeping," he said. "You will sleep in the stable until you earn a place on my floor." He took up the lamp and led me into the stable where Karim now stood eating his feed. The stench of animals filled my nostrils. Ahmed threw some blankets on the ground.

"Sleep there," he said. "Tomorrow you will clean the house."

He locked the door, leaving me in the dark. I heard the soft whinny of the horse and curled up on the blankets. With tears streaming down my face, I asked *Allah* to forgive my sins. I fell asleep still weeping.

I woke the next morning when Ahmed opened the stable door. He forced me back into the house and left me there, locking the doors behind him. I was stiff and sore from the labors of the day before and paralyzed by the horror of my situation, but I feared his wrath if I did not clean his house as he had commanded.

When he was gone, I found a broom and used it to sweep the floor of the two rooms that made up Ahmed's house. I picked up soiled clothes and piled them near the door. I could not wash them for I had no water. I shook the mattress and straightened the covers then rolled up the bed. I found Nadia's package, against the wall where Ahmed had discarded it. I sat on the floor and opened the bundle. My eyes filled with tears as I beheld its contents, pages of Nadia's clear, neat writing, a copy of the Prophet's words. These precious pages were all I had now, and I feared their destruction. I found an empty basket in the stable and hid them inside under some rags.

When darkness fell, I made my evening prayers then sat on the floor, waiting. I heard the lock moving and stood as Ahmed entered the room. He had a lamp in his hand, which he set on a table. He examined the two rooms. "Your work is pleasing to me," he said, mimicking his master. "You may eat." He handed me a crust of bread and a handful of dates. I had not eaten in nearly two days. I was hungry, so I ate, sitting on the floor, as he stood over me.

I woke when Ahmed opened the stable door the next morning. "Before I leave for the day," he said, "you will launder my clothes." He took me to a walled courtyard where a large pot sat above a low fire. I retrieved the pile of clothes and put them in the water. I stirred and added the soaps and scents I found nearby. When they were done, I pulled the clothes from the pot, wrung them, and hung them to dry on a line. Ahmed ate his breakfast watching me work.

When I was done, he led me back in the stable and gave me a half-eaten bit of bread and cheese. "That is all you get," he said. "There will be no roast lamb for you in this house." He brought the pot of water I had used for his clothes. "Use this to clean the stable."

He saddled Karim and led him out, locking the door behind him. The stable had no windows, but sunlight streamed through small cracks in the roof and walls and in the space below the door. I set to my work, cleaning the horse's trough and the walls and floors of the stable, stopping always to pray at the appointed times.

I slept in the stable for a month before Ahmed gave me leave to move my blankets to the floor of his house. At night, he barred the doors from the inside. I did not dare try to escape as he was a light sleeper, and I knew he kept his knife with him even as he slept. My one comfort was that he did not force me to share his bed.

Afraid to disobey his orders and too ashamed to attempt escape, I resigned myself to my fate, finding solace only in my faith. I followed whatever command Ahmed gave me. If I failed or objected, he whipped me with the strap. I kept my face veiled and my voice low.

Ahmed left each morning to attend to his work, leaving me with strict instructions for what I was to do that day. He gave me only the bag of clothes I had packed when I left the palace. He laughed when I asked what had become of the treasures Sheikh Ruhi had sent with me.

"They brought a good price in the market," he said. "I think I will let you have a bit of fish with your bread now."

He locked the door behind him when he left for the day. I was a prisoner, though where I would have gone had I been able to escape, I cannot say. I stayed because I had nowhere else to go. I endured his treatment because I knew no way to stop it. Indeed, as the months passed and his dominion over me grew, he ceased even to lock the door, knowing that I would not try to leave. He relished his power over me.

I cleaned his house and stable. I washed his clothes. I waited on him at meals. I endured his beatings and survived in this life that was no life.

In the horror of this prison, my faith was a garden of hope. In the silence of the day, I spoke only to my God. In this place where I lost my dignity and my pride, I repeated the words Nadia had taught me over and over again in my heart. I read the pages she had given me. The words strengthened me and connected me to *Allah*. My faith grew, and it sustained me.

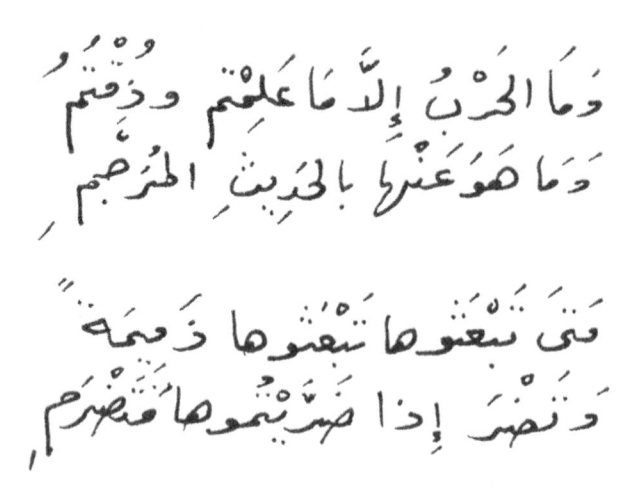

وَمَا الْحَرْبُ إِلَّا مَا عَلِمْتُمْ وَذُقْتُمُ
وَمَا هُوَ عَنْهَا بِالْحَدِيثِ الْمُرَجَّمِ

مَتَى تَبْعَثُوهَا تَبْعَثُوهَا ذَمِيمَةً
وَتَضْرَ إِذَا ضَرَّيْتُمُوهَا فَتَضْرَمِ

What is war? You have known it and tasted it. It is not a tale to be told. Once you light the flame, it becomes an inferno.
-Zuhair

CHAPTER 21
NOOR: AMR

As the years passed, the people of my village forgot the gods of our ancestors and gave themselves entirely to the worship of Allah. I beseeched the gods I knew to help me along this path I did not understand. I asked for their favor, grace, and wisdom. I asked for courage and strength, that I might better do their will and serve my people. I knew no other recourse. Prayer became my one solace, my one friend. I could not bring myself to abandon the gods of my mother, gods I had worshipped so long. And yet I had no choice but to make a show of my allegiance to the God of my father.

My father continued to be mesmerized by the Prophet's teachings and sought new ways to incorporate the ways of Al-Islam into the lives of our people. He took down the tent that had served as his meeting place and began construction of a place of worship.

He continued his travels, going to Medina sometimes three times in a year. Empowered by his growing legion of followers, Mohammed was no longer content to preach the word of *Allah* from Medina alone. He was now building an army. The forces of Mohammed sought to spread the word of *Allah* throughout our lands.

The growing voice of Al-Islam did not sit well with the tribes who had remained true to our traditional beliefs. They saw this new faith as a scourge and sought to obliterate those who preached its word. They hoped to destroy the work of the Prophet. First, they had forced him to flee Mecca and seek refuge in Medina. Now, they had openly declared war on all who followed him.

The Prophet answered them in kind. He called on his people to wage war against the unbelievers. Everywhere, men were dying, killed by the blades of those who claimed to be acting in the name of a god. Whether killed in the name of one god or many gods, the blood of those men ran just as red across the desert sands.

One evening, when Amira was about seven years old, we sat together on the floor of the house of healing, pulling the petals off rosebuds from the bushes that now blossomed from the small plants I had planted with my mother. I was teaching Amira how we would make rose water from them. We were interrupted by loud voices, and both looked up when my door flew open. Jibran rushed inside, breathless.

"We need help. Hurry."

Amira stood to follow me, but I stopped her. I did not know what awaited us. Looking at my brother's face, I felt afraid. "Amira, stay here and wait for me."

I ran out of the house and followed my brother to the village center. I saw my father lying prone on a crimson rug outside the door of the new place of worship. Bassam was leaning over him, his hands on my father's chest. I knelt at Father's side. The ground was wet around him. With horror, I realized there was no rug. He lay on a bed of sand stained red with his blood.

His face was pale and grey. His breath came rapidly, and he clenched his hands tightly at his sides. I saw the blood soaking his robes, the stain growing, spreading outward, moving away from his body and taking his life with it as it flowed.

Bassam was pressing his hands on the wound, trying desperately to stop the bleeding. I looked up at Bassam, both of us powerless. I put my hands next to his and felt my father's strong heart pounding beneath my hands, each beat pushing his life farther and farther away from me.

Father opened his eyes, looking up at us, eyes drifting, spirit fleeing. He reached one weak hand to my face and spoke so quietly I could barely hear. I bent closer. His breath caressed my face as he struggled to speak. "Your brother, Noor," he whispered, his words coming slowly and with great difficulty. "Do not let him go. Stop him. He must not go. Please stop him." My father's words drifted away, and his hand fell.

Bassam and I watched, helpless, as my father's life slipped through our hands. Father's head fell to one side. Bassam's tears fell onto his hands, still pressed to Father's chest.

I looked up and met Jibran's eyes. He looked at our father's body then reached for his sword. I cried out to him as he ran off, but he would not stop.

Ghazi came to us, stopping short when he saw our father on the ground. He looked at me, and I shook my head. "No," he whispered. "What happened?" He looked at Bassam. "Who did this?"

Bassam closed his eyes. "They were two traders who arrived with the caravan last night. Your father invited them to join us for a meal today, so they could show him their wares. When they arrived at mid-day and saw the mosque, they argued with him, saying that Al-Islam was a mockery of faith and an insult to the gods."

Bassam choked back a sob. "They returned with their horses at sunset and stabbed him in his heart. I was walking here to meet him for prayers when I saw it happen. I ran to him and tried to help him." He moaned.

"You did all anyone could have done," I told him. We were surrounded by people now. Men and women who had been gathering to pray stood in the road weeping at the sight of their fallen leader.

"Jibran knows who they were," Bassam said to Ghazi. "He was with us today when they threatened to wipe the name of *Allah* off the face of the earth."

"Where are these men now?" Ghazi asked.

"They fled south," Bassam said.

"I think Jibran went to find them," I told Ghazi. "He was running toward the stables."

"Stay here," Ghazi said. He called to some of the men. "Bring the horses!" Ali and Braheem joined Ghazi, and the three men ran in the direction of the caravan camp.

Ghazi returned a half hour later. I was sitting with Amira, whom I had fetched from the house of healing. I held her as she wept for her grandfather. Bassam had moved Father's body, but the dark stain of his blood still lay upon the ground. Rullah came to my side and took Amira, so I could talk with my brother.

People still milled about in the courtyard, anxious to hear news from any who would give it. They came toward Ghazi, but Bassam stopped them. "Not now," he said. "Give him peace."

"Jibran is dead, Noor," Ghazi said when we were alone. "We found his body at the village gate."

I was sad but not surprised. I shook my head. "What are we to do?"

"I don't know," he said. "There was another man dead on the ground next to him. Jibran's knife was still plunged in his back. The second man must have fled into the desert. Sameer led a team of riders to find him. I told them to return before sundown whether they find him or not."

Ghazi shook tears away. "I spoke to the leader of the caravan. He said he met the two men in Mecca. They asked him for safe passage through these lands, so they could trade in safety. He did not know what they intended to do. I believe him." He looked at the stain of Father's blood and sighed.

An old man, the caravan leader, came to our side at that moment and knelt at Ghazi's feet. "Please forgive me for bringing death to your door."

Ghazi helped the man to stand. "Do not blame yourself."

"But I do," he said. Tears ran down his face. "Permit me to make some amends. Let me do something. I offer any of my flock, any of my goods. I could never hope to make right what I have done wrong."

"These were fanatics," Ghazi told him. "You could not have known their true intentions."

The old man nodded. He looked at me. "Say'yedah," he said, "I grieve for your loss. I know my continued presence here will only bring you pain. My caravan will leave in the morning."

I shook my head. "Don't go. You are still welcome in this village. You offered harbor to those in need as our ancestors have done from time immemorial. You did not know how those criminals would repay your kindness."

"If only I had known what they planned to do," he said, his voice breaking. "They would have died by my hand before they set foot on your father's land."

"I know that," I said. "And I forgive you for that which you did not know."

He bowed his head and walked back toward his encampment. When he had gone, I turned back to look at Ghazi. His face was pale. "You are our leader now." I spoke quietly so none but Ghazi could hear. "Our people will draw their strength from you."

He turned to Ali and Braheem who had returned while we had been talking. "We will bury them before sundown."

Ali nodded. "We carried Jibran's body into your father's house."

"We will bury the other man as well," Ghazi said.

Braheem looked shocked. "That jackal deserves to be left in the desert to rot and be feasted on by carrion birds."

Ghazi shook his head. "I will not have us become savages. He died within the walls of this village." He paused, his face set. His eyes hardened. "We will bury him according to our customs, but none shall weep for his passing."

As Ghazi spoke, I heard a new strength in his voice, a power I had heard in our father's.

"Send word through the village," he told Ali. "I want everyone here in one hour. I will tell them what has happened."

Ali and Braheem nodded and went to do his bidding. Ghazi turned to me, eyes bright and face resolute. "Let us go and weep for our family, Noor," he said, as a tear rolled down his cheek. "We have one hour for our own grief before we go to comfort our people."

I took his hand, and we walked across the courtyard toward our father's house. We passed Rullah, still holding Amira. She put out her hand to Ghazi, and he took it, gripping it in his. He choked back a sob and bent his head to kiss her cheek. He touched Amira's head.

"Where are our children?" he whispered.

"With their Sittu," she said. "Don't worry about them. Go and do what you need to do. You too, Noor. Amira and I will be with her cousins in my mother's house until you come for us."

We walked away and entered the house. Father and Jibran lay side by side on blankets on the ground. Ghazi and I knelt beside them. "We should send word to Sawdah," he said.

I nodded. We had received only a few messages from my sister these many years. She had not yet replied to the news of our mother's death. Still, any travelers who came to us from her city only said that Sheikh Ruhi was happy with his wife and children. They told us his wife rarely ventured outside the palace walls, so content was she with her life within the palace.

"There will be a caravan heading that way soon enough," I told Ghazi. "They can tell her then." I saw no need to rush to give her this terrible news.

"How can I take his place, Noor?" Ghazi asked. "I am not like him." He looked at our father's body. "I don't have his passion or his strength. I am not a warrior."

"You have wisdom, Ghazi," I told him. "And you are strong. You will keep us safe."

"Our world is changing. We have chosen our side, and we will be asked to defend it." He shook his head. "Why do the gods insist that we kill one another in their names?"

"They do not," I said. "They ask that we love one another and honor them with our faith. Men choose to kill and use the names of the gods to justify their killing."

"Then may the gods have mercy on us all." He brushed back the curls of Jibran's thick hair. "We are alone now, Noor."

"I know." Tears fell down my face. "Do you remember how he used to make you climb to the top of the fig tree?"

Ghazi laughed softly. "He would dare me to climb higher, then leave me trapped at the top while he walked away to get his dinner."

"I used to get so mad at him," I said. "When we were little and got into fights, I remember shrieking at him while he stood there speaking in the softest voice possible just to vex me."

"I remember that," Ghazi said. "He used to bet me that he could make you yell loud enough that I would hear you from across the road."

I laughed. "I will miss him. I will miss them both."

We looked at the two men we both loved and wept for them until a soft knock at the door made us dry our faces and stand. Ali was there to remind us of the time. Ghazi splashed water on his face and dried it with a cloth.

"Sameer has returned," Ali said.

"Did he find the other man?"

Ali nodded. "All our men returned unharmed."

"Ali, I need a word with your father. Take me to him." Ghazi turned to me. "Noor, I will be just a moment. Please stand with me when I return to speak to the village."

"I will be there, Ghazi," I said.

I washed my face after they had gone and walked out into the courtyard. The people of our village had gathered around the well. A few minutes later, Ghazi returned with Bassam and Ali. The crowd looked up when Ghazi approached. Everyone fell silent as he stood before them at my side.

"*Allahu Akbar*," he began.

"*Allahu Akbar*," came the reply from the crowd.

"Death came to us this day and took the life of our beloved leader," Ghazi said. "My brother, Jibran, sought vengeance, and he too died at the hands of the nonbelievers."

There was a murmur in the crowd. Word of our father's death had already spread, but many had not yet heard about Jibran. Ghazi continued speaking. The crowd fell silent once more.

"They died because of their faith in *Allah*," Ghazi said. "They died because of fools who think they can stop Al-Islam by killing *Allah*'s faithful."

Ghazi looked over the crowd. "Al-Islam is the way of the truth. The truth will prevail. But I will not lead our village to war. We will not repay these terrible acts with more violence."

I looked at the faces in the crowd. Some of the younger men shook their heads. They were angry at the loss of their beloved leader and wanted to fight back.

Ghazi went on. "One day, we may be forced to fight. On that day, we will take up arms with our brothers and fight in the name of *Allah*. But until that day comes, and I hope it never does, we will remain a sanctuary for travelers and a shelter for those seeking refuge from the fight."

He looked at the young men in the front of the crowd and shook his head. "I feel your anger. My blood boils at what was done this day, but we must be strong. We must overcome the desire for vengeance." He paused to collect himself. "We will not be fools," he said. "We will guard our village and keep it safe. We will ask any travelers who pass through our gates to lay down their arms until they leave our village and accept the guard we give them. We will teach the men and women of this village how to defend themselves and their families." He paused. "And we will pray every day that they shall never have need of that knowledge."

Ghazi looked at Sameer. "You have defended well the honor of my family. I ask that you now defend this village by leading the men who wish to guard her."

Sameer bowed his head. "It will be my honor."

"Bassam," Ghazi said, "you stood at my father's side all his life. You are my other father, and I love you."

Ghazi embraced Bassam and kissed his cheek. "Thank you for all you have done for our people."

Ghazi turned back to the crowd. "I have asked Bassam if he wishes to stand with me as he did with my father. He asked me to give him leave to be with his family now and let another man take his place."

Ghazi turned to Braheem who had been his friend since childhood. "Will you stand with me and be my high advisor as Bassam stood with my father as his?"

Braheem nodded solemnly but said nothing. I saw tears in his eyes.

Ghazi spoke once more. "I cannot hope to take my father's place. I can only hope to honor his memory by giving my life to the service of our people. I ask that you now honor his memory and Jibran's by honoring the word of *Allah*. Let us pray together."

Ghazi led the village in prayer and called out to the heavens, asking *Allah* to bring us peace.

We buried Father and Jibran before sundown per the dictates of Mohammed. The entire village joined us as we laid their bodies to rest. The other man was buried separately, far from the graves of our beloved ones.

The old caravan leader brought his people to honor the memory of my father and brother. His caravan remained with us for three days. After they left our village, Ali discovered four horses and three camels, including one pregnant female, tethered at the southern gate where Jibran had met his end.

وَمَنْ لَا يُصَانِعْ فِى أُمُورٍ كَثِيرَةٍ
يُضَرَّسْ بِأَنْيَابٍ وَيُوطَأْ بِمَنْسِمِ

He who is not agreeable with others will be crushed by sharp teeth
And ground beneath the foot of a camel.
-Zuhair

CHAPTER 22
SAWDAH: MECCA

I could see the palace walls from the door of Ahmed's house, yet never once did I attempt to reach them. Never once did I seek the protection of those walls and the man who dwelt within them.

After two years, Ahmed no longer needed his strap to keep me in line. He had long since abandoned his threats of pain or death, favoring instead a torrent of insults and belittlements that ate away at my already wounded soul. Not once did he touch me or even look at me. He took away my pride. He took away my beauty. But he could not take away my faith.

Allah was my strength and my shield. I knelt in prayer each day in the hope that one day I would meet my Creator and live in His house free of the shame that tormented me.

Ahmed had allowed me none of my possessions. I had only two dresses to clothe my body, two scarves to cover my face and the hidden parchments that were my salvation. Ahmed gave me old blankets for my bed and some castoffs from the palace when my clothes began to show wear.

One night, in the first year of my imprisonment, Ahmed returned from the palace with some scraps of old rugs. The threads were worn and bare in many places. He threw them on the ground and told me they were mine to sleep on. The next day, after my work was finished, I took those rugs and found one whose backing was still sound. I picked all the threads off it and separated the good from the bad. I hid the backing and threads under the other rugs and blankets which made up my bed. Over time, I collected enough silk from those and other rugs that came my way, to make a prayer rug like the one Nadia had given me to use in the palace.

I worked on it when I could, and in the hours I sat selecting and knotting threads, I could pretend I was back home safe in the palace. I learned to anticipate Ahmed's return, so I could hide my work. Rarely did he return before dark, but I was vigilant nonetheless. My greatest fear was that he would one day discover my secret and take from me my only joy.

I knelt for my mid-day prayers then brought it out from where I had hidden it beneath my bed. The carpet was nearly complete. I had perhaps one quarter of it left to fill. It was clearly the work of an amateur, but still that small rug was a treasure to me. Before I could place one thread upon it though, I heard Ahmed's footsteps on the gravel outside. I stuffed the rug under a pile of cushions and stood up.

"Prepare my horse!" Ahmed demanded as he walked through the door. Living this close to the palace, he did not often have need to ride except when he was sent to meet dignitaries as they approached the city.

"Move, woman," Ahmed said. "There's no time to spare. I have to get to the eastern wall."

"As you wish." I bowed my head. Ahmed walked into his room to change his clothes while I walked through the door that led to the stable outside.

Inside the barn, I gave the horse a pat on the head and pulled down his saddle. "You're going for a ride, Karim," I whispered in his ear. He whinnied. Over these years, I had come to love this horse. On the days when he was in the stable, and I was free to care for him, I brushed his coat and sang to him.

This horse was all I had left of my family. I knew the men who had raised and trained him. When I looked at Karim, I remembered the fields and orchards of our simple village and the people who lived there. My face burned when I thought of their shame if ever they learned what had become of me.

I placed a blanket on Karim's back and saddled him. I gave him a handful of barley and turned when I heard Ahmed enter the stable. He had changed his clothes and was now dressed in the black and gold robes he wore when greeting the most powerful visitors.

"Out of my way!" He pushed past me to mount the horse. "Open the door!"

With some difficulty, I pulled open the heavy stable door. Ahmed gave the horse a hard kick and rode out into the street.

Before I could close the door, I heard a cry and a shout. I looked out into the street. As if in a dream, I saw the horse rear up, flinging Ahmed to the hard ground. Men ran to where his body lay. I saw a small boy run crying into his father's arms. Two men ran to the door of Ahmed's house and beat upon it. I walked out from the shadow of the stable and met them at the door.

The men bowed toward me as I approached. Only then did I realize that my face was uncovered. In my haste to hide my work, I had forgotten to put the scarf over my head. In his hurry, Ahmed had not remembered to command me to shroud my face.

"What happened?" I asked them. "Is he alright?"

They walked with me to where Ahmed's body lay still upon the ground. I knelt beside him and put my hand above his mouth but felt no breath. A man sitting on the ground at Ahmed's side put his ear to Ahmed's chest. "He is dead," he said.

I nodded my head.

"Do you know why he was riding so fast?" the man asked me.

"I think he had some business for Sheikh Ruhi," I said.

Just then, one of the men recognized Ahmed. "This is the palace vizier!" he cried. He looked at me. "Should we take him to the palace?"

I nodded. "Take him to Sheikh Ruhi. He will know what to do."

"What about his horse?" Another man pulled hard on Karim's reins as he snorted and pawed the ground, clearly unsettled by what had occurred.

I walked to Karim's side and held my hand out to him. He stopped moving, and I stroked his long face. "This horse is mine," I said. "I will take him." The man put the reins in my hand, and I stood with Karim, watching as two men picked up Ahmed's body between them and carried him toward the palace while the others followed behind.

I was alone.

"Pardon me, Say'yadah."

I turned to see a man holding the hand of a small boy. The boy looked at me with large, sad eyes. I was surprised at the term of respect the man had used toward me. I had forgotten what it felt like to be honored as a lady. I bowed my head. "Yes, Say'yed. How can I help you?"

I looked up. The man's face was bowed low. "My boy, Mohammed, it was he who," his voice drifted off. "I am so sorry." He took a long breath and looked at me. "I am to blame for your husband's death. Please forgive me. I cried out for my son. I meant no harm."

I tried to speak, to stop him, but he went on. "I am a man of some means. Sheikh Ruhi has been generous to me." He paused and scanned my face. "Forgive me, but your face seems familiar. Do I know you?"

I recognized him then. This was the artist whose work had so pleased Sheikh Ruhi on the day he had divorced me and sent me from the palace. The day Ahmed had abducted me. The memory and shame of that terrible day returned as though it had all happened yesterday. I shook my head. "I don't think so," I lied. "I have not lived here very long."

He nodded. "Forgive me." He held out a bag. "Please accept this small token from me. It will not restore your husband, but it may help you."

He pushed a bag into my hands and walked away before I could respond. I looked down at the soft cloth bag. It was deep blue with a golden cord at its mouth. I led Karim into the barn. Only then did I open the bag. Inside were enough gold coins to live modestly for some months. They seemed a fortune to my eyes. No, praise *Allah*, these coins would not bring Ahmed back, but they might buy my freedom!

I knew suddenly what I must do. I set a handful of barley before Karim and tied his reins to a post then went back inside the house. In Ahmed's room, I found clean, white robes. I changed into them and put a white cloth over my head and face in the fashion of Bedouin men. I tied the cloth across my forehead with a woven cord of blue silk. I found a long, thin leather strap and used it to tie the purse of money around my neck, concealing it beneath the folds of my robe.

I went to the next room and collected what things I might need for a journey. I took some loaves of bread, a few handfuls of dates and some skins of water. I put these into a sack. I retrieved Nadia's package and my unfinished prayer rug and threads, wrapping the rug carefully in a large cloth, the corners of which I tied tightly. Parcels in hand, I walked back to the stable.

I tied the bag of provisions to Karim's saddle. I took a sack of barley from the floor and tied it on as well. The prayer rug and parchments, I tied to the front of the saddle. I climbed onto Karim's back with a prayer of thanks for my father who had taught all his children to ride. I checked that the road was clear then rode as fast as Karim could go across the city and out through the gate at the western wall.

I did not know where I was going. I only knew I could not be in that house when Sheikh Ruhi discovered Ahmed was dead. I was terrified that if he found me there, he would learn my shame. That was a thing I could not bear. I knew I had to escape this city forever.

I rode out into the desert as the sun began to set. Even as night fell,

I rode on, keeping my eyes on the stars, suddenly remembering the lessons my father and others had taught me in my childhood, and using them to guide my way. I was not afraid. Indeed, what could anyone do to me that Ahmed had not already done? Even if I met someone along the road, my body was well-concealed under these robes. I would be taken for a youth or small man.

I knew I had to rest Karim, so I stopped under the protection of a grove of palms. I tied his reins to one of the trees near a small pool of water. I pulled some barley from the sack and fed him. I ate a few dates and took a few sips of water. Afterwards, I washed my hands and face then knelt in the sand and thanked *Allah* for my safety and my life, seeking only His will. Afraid to leave Karim, I sat on his back as he stood tethered. I rested my head on the unfinished prayer rug and slept.

I woke with a start and looked up at the black sky. Remembering where I was, I lifted my head and stretched my aching body. I dismounted and bathed my face and hands quickly in the pool as Karim drank and ate. Before long, I was astride my steed again, heading back out across the desert. I knew the direction of a small village in the hills outside the bounds of Sheikh Ruhi's lands. We had visited it together in the first year of our marriage. With only the stars and then the dawning sun as my guide, I turned south and rode toward that village.

I arrived at mid-day. I spoke to no one, stopping only to eat and pray. I found their marketplace and used a few coins to buy a blanket and a brush for Karim. Even then, I did not speak, lest my voice betray my gender. When I saw what I wanted, I pointed at it, and the shopkeeper understood. He must have thought me very strange, deaf or mute, but he took my gold and asked no questions.

I found other travelers in a campsite just outside the village. They nodded to me in greeting. I responded in kind. I found an open spot and tethered Karim to a large fig tree. I watered and fed him, then removed his saddle. I loosened the rope that held him and led him out to a clear patch of sand where he fell to his knees and rolled the aches out of his strong body. When he stood and came to me again, I brushed him, singing softly to him as was my habit. I saw an old man staring at me and remembered my disguise. I stopped singing and applied myself to braiding Karim's tail, hoping no one had heard my voice.

That afternoon, I made myself a bed on the ground at Karim's side, with only his saddle for a pillow. I rested my body but could not sleep. Under a palm tree some distance from me, I could see two men talking. One was a tall, dark man who seemed powerful and intimidating. He reminded me a bit of Sheikh Ruhi. The other was much older and quite short. It was the man who had seen me singing. He had a kind face and did not frighten me as much. When I heard the words "Mecca" and "Mohammed," I could not help but listen to their conversation.

The tall man spoke, "He has taken the city, Uncle. We must join him in this holiest of times."

The older man nodded. "What an honor to be living now in the service of *Allah*, to have a chance to see His Prophet, to hear from his lips the words of *Allah. Allahu Akbar!*"

At sunset, after making my prayers and saddling Karim, I saw the older man again. He was alone now, saddling his own horse. I approached him and spoke in as deep a voice as I could muster. "Excuse me, but is it true that Mohammed is in Mecca?"

He nodded. "He has conquered the city and claimed the Kaaba for *Allah*."

"Can you tell me how to get to Mecca?"

The old man looked deep into my eyes. I wore no kohl, and the rest of my face was completely covered by the white cloth. He tilted his head to one side and spoke. "Child, it is almost two weeks' journey from here. Are you traveling alone?"

I said nothing. He nodded. "From this place, Mecca is due south." He looked around at the bustling campsite. "You will meet other pilgrims on your road. Mohammed has called to all believers to join him in Mecca. There is a caravan just leaving. Perhaps you can join them. May *Allah* direct your steps."

I thanked him for his help, this time forgetting to lower my voice. He only smiled and spoke very softly. "Go with *Allah*, Daughter. I will pray for your safe journey. *Insha'Allah*, if *Allah* is willing, you will find in Mecca that which you seek."

I bowed my head and returned to Karim. I untied his bridle and climbed into the saddle. I rode around the campsite until I spied the caravan. A few quiet words with one of their riders gained me an escort. Karim and I joined the caravan, and we rode south along the road to Mecca.

وَضَيْفٍ طَارِقٍ أَوْ مُسْتَجِيرٍ
يُرَوِّعُ قَلْبَهُ مِنْ كُلِّ جَرْسِ

نَمَا أَكْرَمَهُ وَآمَنَهُ فَأَمْسَى
حَلِيفًا بِالَهِ مِنْ كُلِّ بُؤْسِ

Visitors arrived at night, asking for sanctuary.
He gave them shelter and freed them from their fears and wants.
-Al Khansa

CHAPTER 23
NOOR: HAJJ

In the years after our father's death, my brother Ghazi established himself as leader of our people. Young as he was, he had earned the faith of Bassam and the other men of the village. They understood that war was coming, indeed had already begun, between Mohammed's followers and those whom the Prophet called the unbelievers. These dangerous times would demand a young, strong leadership were we to keep our people safe.

Ghazi brought a new vision to his role. Where our father had enjoyed a more casual role as leader, only intervening in the lives of his people when absolutely necessary and trusting the village to run itself even in his absence, Ghazi took a more active approach. He established a council that at first included me, Braheem, and Sameer as well as Bassam and Ali. We met weekly to discuss the needs of the village and resolve any disputes that had arisen.

Our village was growing. Several young families, devoted to *Allah* and seeking a quiet life outside of the city, had come from Damascus asking to settle within our walls. Ghazi welcomed them and gave them plots of land on which to build their homes. In a gesture of trust and goodwill, which secured their loyalty forever, Ghazi included one of their men on his council.

Ghazi knew his own strengths and accepted his own shortcomings. He knew how to ask for help and from whom. Like our father before him, Ghazi maintained a strong face for the public while allowing his closest advisors and his wife to support him from within.

Ghazi did not love travel as my father had and preferred to remain in the village. There were plenty of young men eager for the road who were happy to set off in his name. For Ghazi's part, he wanted to make our humble village a gathering place for travelers. He expanded our campsites and marketplace and warmly welcomed those who passed through his lands. He continued our father's tradition of lighting torches along the village walls, so travelers would know there was safe harbor within them. Ghazi loved nothing more than to sit with visitors, hearing their news and listening to their poetry.

Jaleel, Ghazi's eldest son, had a gift for recitation. He had listened carefully to my father and Abdullah, and now knew the Prophet's words by heart. Though he was but a child, our people called on him to speak of their faith. When he spoke the words, his eyes lit up as though with flame. Even my skeptical heart could see that this child was truly a gift to our people. I did not always agree with the words I heard, but I knew he stirred souls with his beautiful voice.

As he grew, so did his wisdom and insight into the Prophet Mohammed's teachings. The dearest wish of his heart was to meet the Prophet himself.

A young man, who could also recite the words of Mohammed from memory, stopped in our village with his caravan and stayed when he fell in love with Bassam's niece, Miriam. His name was Adib. He became our Imam, and it was his job to call our people to prayer and instruct them in the faith of Al-Islam. He took Jaleel as his student and schooled him in the faith.

The faith of Al-Islam continued to flourish in our village. Travelers and settlers brought us news of Mohammed and the word of *Allah*. I continued to do my part as best I could. Where I could not believe, I acted as though I did.

In all those years, I had spoken to no one about my conflicted faith. I shared with Amira the routine and ritual of my mother's faith, but these were to her as steps in a dance. She had learned to embrace Al-Islam, and her prayers to *Allah* came unchallenged from her heart.

As the faith of Al-Islam grew around us, we learned of more requirements handed down by Mohammed in the name of *Allah*. We set our calendar by the Prophet's and observed the month of Ramadan by fasting in the daylight hours and feasting in the night.

The women of our village covered their hair in public and whenever men were present, but the men and women of our village shared responsibility for all things. Men and women cooked and washed, tended to their flocks and crops, and worked together to educate our children. We continued traditions my father and his father had established well before the time of the Prophet, working, eating, fasting, and praying side by side.

Ten years after the journey that had claimed my husband and given me my daughter, we received news that Mohammed had finally captured the holy city of Mecca. I shuddered inside when I heard how he had desecrated the idols that lined the walls of the Kaaba. Even as all the village rejoiced, I wept alone in the house of healing, surrounded by everything my mother had held sacred. After Abdullah had cast aside the icon of Manat, I had retrieved it and brought the stone to this place, where I kept it wrapped safely in a corner. With the Priestess Stone, this was all I had left of the faith Mother had entrusted to me.

Mohammed decreed that all believers who were able should join him in Mecca for a Hajj, a pilgrimage, to honor *Allah*. He wanted to show the unbelievers the power of *Allah* and Al-Islam and unite his people in anticipation of the wars that Mohammed said would spread the word of *Allah* and claim this land for His faithful.

The whole village prepared for the Hajj. As had been the case even in the years before Mohammed, a small number of our people chose not to risk the grueling desert journey. These were either the very old or those responsible for the care of the very young. Ghazi assembled an interim council to maintain the village during our three-month absence.

We prepared for the Hajj as Mohammed had decreed we must. Those of our village who were skilled in the weaver's arts made our white pilgrim's garb. These were long robes of seamless white cloth that covered our arms and legs. The women would wear their regular clothing underneath, but men would wear only the cloths of *Al-Ihram*. We fasted and prayed together in preparation for the journey. Everyone seemed excited to make this pilgrimage for the glory of God.

I did not want to go to Mecca, but I could not remain behind. Amira was old enough to make the journey, and I could not allow her to travel alone, nor would I abandon my brother in this critical time. I wore the robes of *Al-Ihram*, mindful that my heart had not truly surrendered to *Allah*. I prayed that whatever god or gods may be would forgive me my ambivalence.

We traveled many long and weary nights across the hot sands to Mecca. Ghazi followed the tradition our father had established, meeting our grandfather's party in Al-Jawl and joining them for the remainder of the journey. Our grandfather was very old now and could not make the trip to Mecca himself. Some of his people, old or ill, who had yet insisted on joining in the Hajj, died during that passage. We buried their bodies in the desert, invoking *Allah*'s blessings upon their souls that they died in service to Him.

At long last, we arrived in the Holy City at the appointed time and made camp. Then did our pilgrimage begin in earnest. Mohammed taught his followers that the Hajj is a time of atonement and redemption. It is a time of setting right the wrong and basking in the light of God's love and forgiveness. It is also a time for reflection.

I had wept much as we traveled the long road to Mecca. I had wept for my beloved Hassan even as I held our daughter in front of me as we rode Shihab across the desert. My heart ached as though I had just touched his face and heard him whisper "I will wait for you." I had wept for my mother and yearned to hear her soft voice teach me what god in which to put my faith, to hear her assure me that I could indeed fill her role for my people. And I had wept for my father and brother who died that their faith might live.

As I braided Amira's ebony hair in our camp one morning, I thought of my sister, Sawdah. I had not seen her in these ten years. In the time since her marriage, I had thought of her often and prayed for her happiness but knew little of her welfare. Travelers who passed through her city told us Sheikh Ruhi's family continued to thrive, but I received no message directly from my sister. After she left our family to join his, it seemed she had not wished to look back.

When I thought of Sawdah, it was with a heavy heart. She had made her choice, forsaking our simple ways as was her right. Still, I felt an emptiness, feeling as though I had lost my sister forever. I prayed that she was content in her choice and that whatever god or gods she now believed in might protect her on the road she had chosen.

Such were my reveries during my pilgrimage. These thoughts did not leave my mind as I followed Mohammed's footsteps through the holy city. The names of those I had loved and lost forever were ever on my lips as I asked the gods for their blessings and mercy upon us all.

As I have said, the road to Mecca is long, and many people died before we reached the Holy Land. There were those, however, who clung to life, determined to fulfill their duty to *Allah*. Hassan's mother, Selma, was one such woman. She had traveled with us to Mecca, despite the grief she too relived with every step of the journey. As she walked to visit the Kaaba, she fell and could no longer stand. Ali carried her back to her tent where she wept, knowing she could not fulfill her obligation to her faith.

My people do all things side by side. They were no less united now. We promised Selma her pilgrimage would not go unfinished. We had no precedent to follow and did not know what Mohammed would ask of us on this pilgrimage, so we followed our hearts.

"I will perform the Hajj for you," Ali told his mother as we sat with her in her tent. "If *Allah* wills it, I can return in another year for my own pilgrimage."

"You will not do this alone," I told Ali.

Bassam's niece, Miriam, agreed, and her husband said, "We will do it together." Adib held out his hand to Ali. "We will return together."

Ali took his hand. "Thank you, my brother."

Amira asked to join us, and the five of us took responsibility for Selma's Hajj. Selma had tears in her eyes as she lay in her bed surrounded by her family and listened to the plans we were making on her behalf.

Bassam wanted to do his part as well. Ali said, "Baba, walk with us and make your Hajj. *Allah* will smile upon us all."

The next morning, Ali, Bassam, Miriam, Adib, Amira and I walked together as we stood waiting to follow the path that Mohammed would prescribe. We each carried a small bedroll and small bag of provisions such as we might need for several days' journey. Hundreds of people stood with us, all in white, all carrying the same supplies.

Surrounded by these devoted followers, intent on completing my part in service for a woman dear to my heart, I could not help but be swept up in the celebratory atmosphere. The air was alive with anticipation as we waited to take our direction from this man who claimed to speak for his God.

"Has this been done before?" I asked Adib.

He nodded. "The Prophet performed the Hajj for many years before his exile to Medina, but it was always in secret until now." His eyes were shining.

A hush fell over the crowd. We were too far behind the crowd to see much, but whispers reached our ears of what was happening. We heard a call to prayer, and everyone knelt, reciting the prayers in unison.

Adib gathered our people together. "It is time to go to the Kaaba. We will follow the footsteps of the Prophet as he makes his pilgrimage."

Adib led us to the Kaaba and showed us what to do. As he entered, he put his right foot on the threshold of the building and asked for the blessings of *Allah*, for forgiveness of his sins and refuge from the evils of Shaitan. Everyone who entered the Kaaba copied his actions and his words.

Inside the Kaaba, we followed the line of people as they walked along the inside wall and stopped to kiss the Black Stone. My heart broke when I saw the empty spaces where our idols had once stood.

We walked seven circuits around the Kaaba, always keeping its walls to our left side. Each time we passed the Black Stone we said *"Allahu Akbar."*

Later, the crowd gathered again before the stone wall. We could not hear what was said, but Adib told us the story of Ishmael, the man said to be the father of our people. He said we were to follow the steps of Ishmael's mother, Hagar, as she ran through the hills of Safa and Marwa, desperately seeking water for her infant son. The angel of God had spoken to her, telling her to stop running and trust in the mercy of *Allah*. Water came from the ground under her baby's feet. On that spot, Ibrahim, the boy's father, later dug a well which the angel promised would flow for all the ages of men.

"The Prophet Mohammed teaches that it was Ibrahim who built the square building of the Kaaba around the sacred black rock near the well *Allah* gave to save the life of his son." Our people huddled around Adib, anxious to learn what he knew.

We traced the footsteps of Hagar, running together between the hills seven times then stopping at the well to drink deeply of the sweet, cool water that flowed from it. I thought of Selma waiting in camp and was saddened by the fact that I had no skin or bowl I could use to take the water back for her.

When all had performed the ritual, we gathered in prayer. We prayed together for seven days, only returning to our camps in the evening for rest before coming together again the next morning.

On the eighth day, we walked out of the city through a valley into Minah where we again gathered in prayer. We were to camp there for the night. It was springtime, and the evenings were mild. We slept under the stars.

At sunrise, we went on to Arafat, where we were to stand and pray silently from noon until sunset. Those who could not stand, knelt or sat. My heart swelled with pride as my daughter stood with us for all those hours on that long day of prayer. Not once did she cease from her vigil.

From that place, we walked to Muzdalifah, arriving at night. We prayed again and slept. At dawn, we returned to Minah where we learned we would remain for three days. Adib instructed us to pick up small white stones along the way. At Minah, we saw stone pillars said to represent Shaitan. We threw the small white stones at the pillars as a symbol of casting Shaitan's evil from our hearts. At the end of the third day of stoning, animals were sacrificed to *Allah*. The meat was cooked then shared among the faithful.

After mid-day on that day, the men were told to trim the hair from their heads. By sundown, all the men had close shorn hair. The women asked if they should cut their hair as well, but we were told we had no need to cut our hair, that we showed our devotion to *Allah* simply by covering our heads.

We returned to Mecca and walked together to Selma's tent. She kissed our faces when she saw us, knowing her promise to *Allah* was being fulfilled by those who loved her.

I returned to the well of Zam-Zam that evening with Amira after we removed the white cloths we had worn over our usual clothing. We walked together, bringing with us a skin to fill for Selma. As the well appeared before us, we saw a small figure kneeling at its side. She still wore the garments of Al-Ihram and bent her head as if praying, but her shoulders shook as though she were weeping. She had still not moved when we arrived at the sacred place. Standing behind her, I saw that she was crying. My heart ached for her, and I put my hand out to touch her shoulder.

PART THREE

دَلِيلٌ لِمَوْجِ البَحْرِ أَرْضَى سُدُولَهُ
عَلَيَّ بِأَنْوَاعِ الرُّسُومِ لِيَبْتَلِي

My nights try me, as a rough sea of woes
Falling like a shroud upon me.
-Umr Ul Quais

CHAPTER 24
SAWDAH: HAJJ

I stayed among the riders at the rear of the caravan as it made its way toward Mecca. I felt less afraid now that I was more certain of my route. I had no plan except that I would go to Mecca and end my days there in supplication to *Allah*. I did not know what would become of me in Mecca, and in truth, I did not much care. The years of servitude in Ahmed's house and the years of sorrow before them had worn my spirit and my body. I sometimes saw my face in a pool and shuddered at the gaunt and stricken creature I beheld. I had been beautiful once but no longer. My body was wasting away. If *Allah* willed it, I would live to see the face of His Prophet. This now was my only wish.

I had the pouch of gold still around my neck and the small unfinished carpet on my saddle. I had my beautiful horse, Karim. These, with my faith and the pages Nadia had given me, were my only possessions. I put my fate completely in the hands of my God. I imagined myself held in His cupped hands as gently and safely as one might hold a baby bird. I would want for nothing in this life or the next so long as I remained in His care and gave myself completely to His will.

When at last I reached the gates of Mecca, I walked through the streets for a time, leading Karim by the reins, not certain what I should do next. With no tent and no real companions, I could not stay in the caravan camps. I had to find shelter in the city itself. I walked down a small street where simple houses stood crumbling from disrepair. This was a poor neighborhood, and I felt ashamed for thinking myself wretched when I still had a horse and some gold in my purse. I saw an old woman sweeping the path in front of a small house. She looked up at me and smiled. She had a kind face, so I approached her.

"I'm sorry to trouble you," I said, "but do you know where I might find a small room and perhaps a place to stable my horse for a few nights?" She looked at me for a time without speaking. I suspected she was examining my appearance in order to assess my means. "I have some money. It is not much, but I can pay."

"*Allah* is indeed great," the woman said at last. She pointed to the house behind her. "This was my sister's house. She died not one month ago. She has no children." She looked down at the ground, sighed and looked back at me. "I had hoped someone might buy it, but it is so small no one will even look at it."

"How much do you want for the house?" I asked, afraid even this small property would fetch too dear a price for me.

She gave a number much lower than I had expected. The gold in my purse would easily pay for this house, leaving me enough to live on for a time. "I will take it," I said.

"Please," she said, "look inside before you decide."

I tethered Karim to a palm tree outside the door and followed her into the small building. It appeared to be a stable that had been altered for use as a home. A wall divided the room in two, and I could see the large doors still set in the back wall of the second room as well as an empty divided trough. We walked back outside, and the old woman looked at me as though expecting me to laugh in her face.

"It is perfect," I said. I touched Karim's long face. "There is room inside for us both."

"May *Allah* bless you a million-fold." She smiled as I emptied some coins into her hand.

She left me the broom, and I used it to sweep the floors of both rooms. I found a clean pile of straw outside and spread it out in the back room for Karim. I led him in through the large back doors and removed the parcels from his saddle, setting them on the floor. I found a hook on the wall and used it for his saddle. I led him out behind the house and smiled as he rolled his body in the sand, grateful to be free of the saddle's confinements. Afterwards, I used his blanket to rub his long strong legs and back.

"I'm sorry I have no apples for you," I told him, "but we still have some barley."

I picked up the sack we had brought with us and poured grain into one side of the trough. I took a sip of water from the skin I carried and poured the last of it into the other side. Leaving Karim to his dinner, I carried my few belongings into the front room. The floor was clean there, so I set the parcels on the ground.

I looked around the room and smiled, realizing for the first time that this space was truly my own. I was alone and safe. The front door still stood open. When I went to shut it, I saw two blankets and some old clean rags at the threshold. The stack had been neatly folded. I looked around for the old woman who was certainly my benefactor but could not see her.

I spread one blanket on the ground and knelt there, giving thanks to *Allah* for His bounty. I unwound my head scarf and set it aside, then removed the last loaf of bread from my small sack of food and chewed it slowly. I wanted to go outside to find a well but found I was too tired to stand, so I lay on the hard floor and soon fell asleep.

The next day, I rose at dawn to the cry of the Imam calling the people to prayer. I knelt and prayed, then covered my hair and face with my scarf and went into the other room to see Karim. He had drunk all his water, and his food was gone as well. I patted his face.

"I will bring water for us both," I told him. I put some more barley in the trough and walked out through my room to the street outside.

I carried the empty water skin in my hand and the pouch of gold around my neck as I walked. I encountered some people gathered around a well. "May I have some water?" I asked.

A man turned to look at me. He smiled. "Let me fill it for you." He filled the skin and gave it back to me.

A woman at his side nudged him, and I heard her whisper, "Give her the pot, Abdu. We have another at home." I shook my head when he gave me an old cooking pot full of water, but his wife insisted.

"Take it, Sister. *Allah* is great. Mohammed teaches us to share with those in need. Please let us help you."

I realized that from my tattered and disheveled appearance, she had taken me for a pauper. I was overwhelmed by her generosity.

"May *Allah* bless your house," I said, taking the pot from her husband's hands. He offered to carry it for me, but I shook my head, and he let me walk alone. I held the skin under my arm and brought the water back to the house.

When I left the house again, I followed another road and found the marketplace. My robes, once gleaming white, were now stained and worn from long travel. I had to buy another garment, so I could wash what I was wearing.

I found some simple white robes and bought them. At another stall, I found crude bowls and bought two. There was an old, wooden box on the floor of the stall. "Are you selling this?" I asked the shopkeeper.

The merchant looked down at the battered box. "If you need it, take it."

"Thank you." I put my purchases in the box and walked to another stall where I bought some bread and another bag of barley for Karim.

I returned to my humble room and set the box on the floor like a table next to the old pot of water. I put one bowl on the box to use for my foodstuffs and set the other, larger one aside to use as a washbasin.

I took the barley into Karim's stall and set it against the wall. With a long stick, I moved soiled straw out from beneath his legs, pushing some clean straw in its place. I stroked his head when I finished and went back across to my room.

I poured some water from the old pot into the washbasin. I removed my robes and cleaned my body with the water and some of the old rags. The water was cold, and I shivered when it touched my skin, but I had no means with which to build a fire. When I was clean, I dressed in the new robes. I poured the water out onto the palm tree outside then filled the basin again with clean water. I used it now to wash my soiled clothes. When the clothes were as clean as I could make them with cold water and no soap, I wrung them out, smoothed them flat and hung them on top of the open door.

I took up the parcel that held my prayer rug. Sitting on my blanket, I opened it, careful not to let any of the loose threads fall onto the floor. I set to work knotting threads and this way passed the better part of the day, stopping only when I heard the calls to prayer.

I tied the last knot just before the sunset call to prayer. I stood, stretched and went outside to care for Karim. When I heard the voice of the Imam, I returned to my room, spread my finished rug before me and knelt upon it for the first time, praising *Allah*.

I knelt on that small carpet for a long while, even after I had completed my prayers. This rug had been my only task, and now it was done. I had nothing left to occupy me, no journey to undertake, no furnishings or food to purchase. I was left with only my thoughts.

What was to become of me? I had my small purse of gold, but it would not last forever. Even if I could do without, my horse needed care. Barley did not come cheap. I could sell Karim if it came to that, but my heart shuddered at the thought of managing without him. That horse was my only friend now, my only link to a family and history that seemed now the dreams of a child.

I thought of the small house in which Ahmed had made me his servant. I thought of the palace, the rich abundance in which I had lived for so long. Then I thought of the village in which I had been raised, of my mother and father, my sister and brothers. I thought of all

I had so carelessly abandoned in my haste to embrace Sheikh Ruhi and his riches. It was then that my grief overtook me.

I woke hours later, having cried myself to sleep. It was very dark in the room. I was still on my knees. I did not rise. I did the one thing that could sustain me. I bowed again and beseeched *Allah* to help me know what to do.

In my heart, I heard a voice. It spoke but one word. *Hajj.*

I knew this word meant pilgrimage, but I was already in the holy city. I had some vague recollection of a series of rituals my mother had taught me to expect when we had first journeyed toward Mecca more than ten years before, but these were ceremonies in service to our pagan gods. Perhaps there was a task I could undertake in service to *Allah*. I lay upon my blanket, determined to seek answers in the morning and fell asleep with another prayer upon my lips.

As the morning call of the Imam rang in my ears, I knelt again. I cleaned the floor of the stable and fed Karim then dressed in the clean clothes I had put away the night before. I walked outside with no clear purpose. In my heart, I asked *Allah* to guide my steps as He always had.

At the end of the street, I saw a woman rocking a baby in her arms. I greeted her, and she smiled.

"Welcome, neighbor," she said.

"Good morning." I smiled at the baby. "How old is he?"

"Three months." She beamed. "He is my angel."

We introduced ourselves. Her name was Saffiyah. "You are new here. Have you come for the Hajj?"

I stared at her a moment, my mind struggling to comprehend what I had heard. *Hajj.* "H-Hajj?" I said aloud. "What is that?"

Her face lit up the way Nadia's always did when given a chance to talk about *Allah* or Mohammed.

"It would be my honor to share what I know," she said. The baby had fallen asleep in her arms. "Would you take tea with me while we talk?"

"Thank you," I said. "That would be wonderful."

I followed her into her modest home and watched as she set the baby down in a small cradle.

"Please sit." She motioned toward a large pile of cushions.

I made myself comfortable and watched as she walked to a courtyard behind the house where a low fire was already burning under a pot. She poured some liquid into two cups and brought them inside.

Saffiyah sat across from me and handed me my drink. I sipped the hot, strong beverage. "Delicious," I said. "It reminds me of home."

She considered me a moment. "Please, may I offer you some food?"

I shook my head. "The drink is sufficient." I had little appetite and had become accustomed to eating not much more than one small loaf of bread in a day, and perhaps a date if I had it.

We started talking. Only once in our long conversation did she ask anything of my own history. "Have you traveled far?" was her only question.

I replied as much as I could. "Far enough." She asked no more, and from that point on we spoke only of *Allah*.

"Mohammed, praised be his name, has called upon all believers to join him here in Mecca," she began. "He saved our sacred city from the unbelievers nearly one year ago." She looked toward her sleeping baby. "My son was conceived on that blessed day." She clasped a hand to her mouth and blushed. "I'm sorry. I should not have spoken of that."

I smiled. "It is nothing shameful. You have a right to rejoice in the victories of the Prophet."

She thanked me and went on. "*Allah* commands that all Muslims make Hajj at least once in their lifetime."

Saffiyah explained the Prophet had decreed that pilgrims must first observe Al-Ihram, the state of purest thought and deed in preparation for the Hajj, filling their hearts with only love and charitable thoughts, and covering their bodies in seamless white cloth.

"The Prophet has observed the Hajj himself," she said, "but always in secret. This is the first time his faithful will be able to join him without fearing the eyes of the unbelievers."

She glanced at her son. "I am not able to attend this year. My son needs me here." She looked back at me. "It will be a glorious time." She told me the stories she had heard of the Prophet Mohammed's personal pilgrimages. "Always the same," she said. "He begins with the *Tawaf*, where he walks around the sacred mosque, the Kaaba, seven times, kissing the Black Stone in its easternmost corner on each turn."

I took in every word of Saffiyah's story as she described what Mohammed had done in years past. After she had explained the rituals of the Hajj completely, I asked a few questions, but then the baby woke from his nap, crying. He calmed as he suckled at her breast, and we talked about him as he nursed.

When the baby was satisfied, we both stood. "Thank you, Saffiyah," I said. "You have been most kind to share what you know."

"It was my pleasure, Sawdah."

She walked me to the door. "Come visit anytime. We are always here."

Back in my room, I prayed again, remembering all that Saffiyah had taught me. I knew now why I had been called to come to this place. I asked *Allah* to help me perform my duties with honor and humility and prayed for the strength to complete my responsibility to Him before leaving this earth to sleep forever in His warm embrace.

The next morning, I walked to the well and saw the woman who had given me her cooking pot. I returned it to her. "I thank you for its use," I told her, "but I am going on the Hajj and have no more need of it now." She took it from me. I saw a young boy at her side. "Is he your son?"

She nodded. "This is Amr. He will be ten years old next season." I smiled at the boy and thought fondly of my father.

"Do you think he would be willing to care for my horse while I am away?" The boy looked eagerly at his mother. "He would have to feed him and walk him in the city. Perhaps, if you or his father are willing to help, he might even take him for a ride?"

The boy was pulling at his mother's dress now. She smiled. "I think he is willing." She looked at her son. "If you give her your word, you must fulfill your promise. Will you do everything she asks of you?"

He nodded repeatedly.

I smiled at them both. "I have some money I can give you." I handed the gold to Amr who examined the coins carefully.

When he put one between his teeth to bite it, his mother was embarrassed. "Stop that, Amr," she scolded. "Those are real gold."

I laughed. His mother looked at me. "I promise your horse will be well cared for. My husband will help Amr look after him for you."

"Thank you." I showed her which was my house and took leave of them both.

With another of my pieces of gold, I bought new white cloths from the market. At home, I washed my body thoroughly. I put on some garments that covered me completely. Over my clothes, I wrapped one cloth around my waist and draped the other over my shoulders, leaving one arm free. I could not cover my head or face. When explaining the rituals to me, Saffiyah had said it was forbidden. I then began my supplications to *Allah* as Saffiyah had instructed.

The days of Hajj were long and arduous. I followed as closely as I could, but despite my effort, I was not able to see the Prophet. Still, I knew he was near, and that was enough. I spoke to no other of the thousands of men and women who joined him in this pilgrimage. I wept and prayed. I gave *Allah* my soul as He had given me my life.

When the Hajj ended, I walked alone to the well of Zam-Zam and fell to my knees. My duties fulfilled, I knew I could now die in service to *Allah*. I only feared to die alone, yet that too I could do with my God. I felt I had given myself up fully to my Creator. A flood of feeling washed over me.

A moment later, I felt a hand upon my shoulder. I looked up to see God's angel, sent to bring me home.

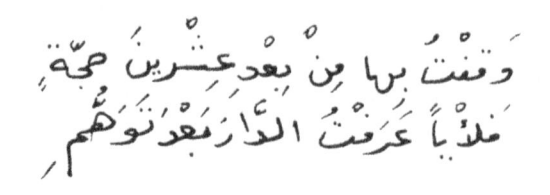

وَقَفْتُ بِهَا مِنْ بَعْدِ عِشْرِينَ حِجَّةً،
مَلِيًّا عَرَفْتُ الدَّارَ بَعْدَ تَوَهُّمِ

After twenty years, each a lifetime, I stood there
Not knowing the home I had so often imagined.
-Zuhair

CHAPTER 25
SAWDAH: HOME

Still on my knees at the side of the well, I looked at the figure standing over me. She had a kind and beautiful face. My eyes filled with tears. She took a step back and looked at me with a surprised expression. My heart felt it might break from joy. This was not the angel of *Allah* come to take me to His side. This was my sister, Noor, come to bring me back to life.

"Noor!" I cried.

She fell to my side and held me. "Sawdah, is it really you?" She touched my face and my hair.

I could not speak for crying. We embraced one another and wept until we had no more tears to weep. She spoke again. "Sawdah, why were you crying? Why are you sitting here alone? What has happened to you?"

I thought of all that had passed in the years since I had looked upon her face. The shame and guilt of those years washed over me once again, and I looked down at the ground. "Noor, I am ashamed even to look upon your face. I do not deserve to be called Sister by one such as you. My sins are many and unforgivable."

She lifted my chin and looked into my eyes. "What is it, Sawdah? What demon thoughts are these telling you such lies? You are my sister, my flesh. Speak no more of such nonsense, but tell me now, what has happened to you?"

I dried my eyes with the hem of my robe. I did not know what to say. After a moment, I looked up and saw a beautiful young girl standing near us. She smiled at me, and I saw Hassan in her smile.

"Is this your daughter?" I asked Noor.

She nodded and held out her hand. The girl came to her mother's side. "Amira, this is your Auntie Sawdah," Noor said. "She is my sister."

Amira beamed. "I know who you are. You are the one who was so beautiful that the most powerful sheikh in the world took you to live in his palace."

I laughed a little. "That is a good story, Amira, but it happened a long time ago."

I tried to stand but had been kneeling too long. I had to support myself against a rock. Noor and Amira took my arms and helped me to my feet. "Can you walk?" Noor asked.

I nodded. "Just give me a moment to gather my strength."

They let me lean against a wall while they filled a skin with water from the well. Noor came to my side while Amira finished the work. My sister had a question upon her lips, but I stopped her and shook my head. "Not now. Please."

She nodded and said nothing. Amira joined us, and we had just started walking when I stopped and turned back. "I've left my prayer rug at the well," I said. "I need to get it."

"I'll go, Auntie." Amira ran off and returned in a moment with the small carpet rolled under her arm.

We walked back through the city. When we reached the road that led to my house, I made to turn down it. Noor and Amira stopped walking. "This is where I live," I said.

Noor looked bemused but asked no questions, only nodded.

"Can we see your house, Auntie?" Amira asked.

I looked at her and smiled. "I suppose so," I said. "It's not very big. I don't live in a palace anymore."

"That doesn't matter," Amira said. "Auntie Rullah says that every house is big if it fits *Allah* inside."

I nodded. "That sounds like something Rullah would say." I looked at Noor. She met my eyes and smiled.

We walked together into my neighborhood. With my sister at my side, I saw how my house must appear to her eyes. It was the house of a pauper. She seemed surprised when I stopped at the door. She must have thought I was stopping to greet a neighbor.

"That's all of it," I said, as I led them into my small room.

Amira saw the door to the stable, and we walked through to where Karim stood. He saw me and whinnied. I had not seen him in all the days of my Hajj. His trough was full. He had been well cared for in my absence. I stroked his mane and whispered a greeting in his ear.

"Your horse," Noor said. "He looks like one of Baba's."

I nodded. "This is Karim. He is the horse Baba gave Sheikh Ruhi ten years ago."

I knew that sentence would speak volumes to my sister. She would know I would have referred to him as my husband if that were still true. She would know, too, that I would not have this horse in my possession except that my dowry had been returned to me.

Amira found an apple and fed it to Karim, stroking his beautiful mane. While she was thus occupied, Noor took my hands. "Sawdah," she said, "whatever trouble has befallen you, know that you are no longer alone. What is in the past cannot be undone, but from here you can go on. Come now, back into your family's loving arms where you shall ever more have a home."

I nodded. "It seems that is the will of *Allah*. Let me just collect my things."

It took me but a few minutes to gather up my belongings into a small pile on the floor. I left the crate and bowls and folded the blankets neatly beside them. "Perhaps someone else will need them now," I said, as I surveyed the space.

Noor brought me my clothes. "Your Hajj is complete, Sawdah. Would you like to change into these?"

I took my traveling clothes from her. "Thank you."

Noor went into the stable to help Amira while I dressed. I put the robes on my body but still wrapped a white cloth around my hair and face. When I was ready, I looked in on them. "Will you excuse me a moment? I want to see the boy who has been caring for Karim." Noor nodded, and I walked outside toward the well.

I found Amr's mother sitting on a chair at the threshold of her house, enjoying the evening air. She stood when she saw me. "He rode that horse nearly every day you were gone," she said. "You've given my son a thrill he will never forget." She laughed. "He says he wants to join the armies of Mohammed and ride with him into battle."

I smiled at her. "Would you give this to Amr?" I asked, taking the money pouch from around my neck.

"But you've paid him already," she said when she saw what was inside.

I nodded. "But perhaps this will help him buy a horse of his own."

"But don't you need this money?"

I shook my head. "I have found a treasure. I don't need that gold anymore." I turned to go but stopped. "I've almost forgotten," I said. "I want you to take my house. It's hardly more than a stable really, but perhaps it will be of use to you."

"Where will you go?" she asked.

"I'm going home." She looked worried, and I knew she was looking at my gaunt figure and thinking the worst. "My sister has come for me," I explained. "I am returning with her to our village."

"Then go with the blessings of *Allah*. I thank you for your most generous gifts."

I walked back to the house where Amira and Noor had already saddled Karim. Amira was carrying what was left of his barley. Noor had found Nadia's package in a corner of the room and held it out to me as I approached. I smiled and took the bundle in my arms, drawing strength from it as we walked away from the small house.

When we neared Saffiyah's house, I stopped. "I want to tell my neighbor I am leaving," I said. I knocked on the next door, and Saffiyah looked out. "You have made your Hajj?" she asked.

I nodded. "And *Allah* has brought my family to me. I am going home."

Saffiyah's face lit up with a smile. She held me in a tight embrace and kissed my cheek. She waved to Noor and Amira.

"*Allahu Akbar!*" she cried.

I lifted the package I had received from Nadia, the parchments upon which were written the word of *Allah*. Every word was etched upon my heart. "Please take this." I gave it to Saffiyah. "*Allah* put you here that I might partake of His mercy. Were it not for the things you taught me, I would have never found my hope."

She looked inside the package and gasped. "I cannot accept this gift, Sawdah. It is too dear."

"Please take it. The words are in my heart. I no longer need to read them."

I rejoined my sister and Amira, and the three of us walked with Karim to the outskirts of the city, toward our family's tents. As we approached the campsite, I stopped once more. "Please, do not tell anyone who I am. Not yet."

Noor nodded. "Of course, Sawdah. As you wish." She spoke softly to Amina who looked up at me with wide eyes and nodded her assent.

When we reached the encampment, I kept my head bowed low. Most of my face was covered, but I did not dare let anyone see even my eyes lest they betray my identity. We passed two men securing a tent with a line. I recognized one of them instantly as Hassan's brother, Ali. The men looked up from their work and nodded in greeting. "Peace be with you all," Ali said to us.

"And with you," I said automatically, then silently cursed my indiscretion. A strange look passed over Ali's face as he looked first at me then at Karim, but he said nothing more.

Noor walked to Ali and gave him the skin of water. "This is for your mother," she said. "Will you give it to her?"

He took the water, and I saw tears welling in his eyes. "Thank you, Noor. I will go now." His companion nodded, and Ali turned toward his mother's tent. He stopped and looked back only once. This time, he spoke directly to me. "Praise *Allah* for your safe return," he said. "If you wish, I can tie your horse here. I will soon return for him and see that he is well cared for." Feeling certain he had mistaken me for someone else, I nodded my head, and Amira handed him the reins.

We walked on to Noor's tent. As we entered, I felt the rich sweet air swirl around me like a warm embrace. This was a sacred space. She kept her healing herbs in this tent and those of our mother's tools that she had brought with her on this journey. I felt that Mother's spirit was here among her things.

I sat on the ground and touched a long, blue cloth Noor had piled loosely in a shallow basin. "I remember this scarf," I said almost to myself. "Do you remember, Noor? Sheikh Ruhi sent this to Mother." My hands were worn and rough from hard use, and I hardly dared to touch the cloth, but I drew it up and saw a deep blue stone hidden beneath its folds. I knew at once that my mother was dead, and tears filled my eyes. I looked at Noor. "When?"

She looked down at the stone. "Four years after you wed. Did you not get my message?"

I shook my head and took in a deep breath. "And Father?"

"It has been two years this spring since we lost him and Jibran. Ghazi is Sheikh now."

I nodded. I had known they were gone from this life, had felt it in my very being, but to hear the truth of it was a blow.

"Can I bring you anything, Sawdah?" Noor asked.

I shook my head. "May I just sit here a while?"

"Of course." Noor looked at her daughter. "Amira, why don't you go and find Jaleel. I know he will be anxious to tell you again what it was like to meet Mohammed's closest followers."

Amira nodded. "See you later, Auntie," she said to me. "I promise I won't tell anyone that you're here. It will be our secret."

"Thank you." I smiled as she left the tent and let the flap fall closed behind her.

"Would you sit with me, Noor?" She did, and for a long while we did not speak. I looked around the tent at the belongings Noor had brought, touching things with my eyes and fitting them carefully in the chambers of my memory.

I touched my finger to the deep blue stone. "Mother's stone," I said. I looked at my sister and asked, "Have you taught Amira the ways of Manat?"

Noor paused before answering. When she finally spoke, it was in guarded tones. "She knows a little."

I smiled. "I am glad of it. I remember your faith in the gods was very strong. It must not have been easy for you to embrace this change. I am glad you have not been entirely alone."

"Can you talk now, Sawdah?" Noor asked, though she seemed afraid to speak the words. "Can you tell me what has happened to you?"

I nodded and related to her the tale of my ordeal. It took but an hour to tell and Noor wept as she listened to my story.

As we sat together afterwards, Amira returned with a small basket of food. "I told Auntie Rullah you had a visitor," she told her mother. She looked at me, "But I did not tell her who it was." I smiled. "She sent dinner for all of us."

I ate a little with them. Noor prepared a bed for me on the floor. I put my head upon it and slept until I heard the voice of the Imam calling us to prayer at dawn.

$$\text{إِنَّ الَّتِي زَعَمَتْ فُؤَادَكَ مَلَّهَا}$$
$$\text{خُلِقَتْ هَوَاكَ كَمَا خُلِقْتَ هَوًى لَهَا}$$

$$\text{فَبِكَ الَّذِي زَعَمَتْ بِهَا وُكِلَتْ كَمَا}$$
$$\text{يُبْدِي لِصَاحِبِهِ الصَّبَابَةَ كُلَّهَا}$$

She claims your heart has wearied of her, though she created your love as you created hers.
She claims this even as you both demonstrate the utmost love.
-Zuhair

CHAPTER 26
SAWDAH: ALI

In Mecca, I sought the shelter of *Allah*'s great love. When I sat alone at the well of Zam-Zam, I wanted to die. I was ready to die. I believed I would die, for I could no longer endure this life. But *Allah* spared me for a better life, and I am forever grateful for His compassionate mercy. He gave me strength and courage and brought my sister to save me.

Noor. The light had indeed reentered my life when she touched my shoulder and revived my despairing heart. As the days passed in her company, I grew strong again. She gave me salves that soothed my chafed skin, food that strengthened my withered frame, and love that healed my broken spirit.

For two days, I stayed in her tent away from the others. On our third morning together, I told my sister I was ready to begin seeing the others of our family. "I told Ghazi and Rullah to expect my visit this afternoon," Noor told me at mid-day. "I did not tell them why."

After the mid-day meal, we walked together to my brother's tent. Noor held the flap for me, and I entered. Ghazi and Rullah stood there, surrounded by their three beautiful children and Amira.

"Ghazi," Noor said, "Our sister has returned to us."

Tears ran down my face, and I removed my headcloth. My brother stood frozen for a moment then rushed to take me in his arms. He held me as we cried and laughed together. Rullah embraced me too, and we stood among their children, who stared at us as though we were madmen. Amira was among them, telling them all who I was and relating the fantastic story of how I had once lived in a glorious palace as the wife of a fabulous sheikh.

I bent to kiss each child and lifted up the smallest, a beautiful little girl who clung to me with her arms and legs as though I were a tree she was trying to climb.

"My name is Leila," she said. I smiled through my tears and hugged her close.

Ghazi and Rullah never asked what had happened to return me to their fold. They were content to be overjoyed at my homecoming. Later that day, Noor took me to see Fatima. She too embraced me and welcomed me home. I wondered how I could have believed Ahmed's words when he told me I could not return to my family. What a fool I had been to think these wonderful, kind people would ever turn me away.

"I want to see Selma," I said to Noor. "Can you take me to her?"

We walked together to the tent where Selma sat propped up in a soft bed. "Who is this?" she asked. "Who is coming to me?" Noor had told me that Selma was not well, and it broke my heart to see her face so frail and lined with age.

I went to her side. "It is Sawdah," I told her. "I've come back."

She reached a hand out and touched my face. "You are so thin," she said. "Your husband, he did not treat you well." She shook her head. "I would spit on him and put a curse upon his house."

I laughed. "They told me you were sick, Auntie. But I can see you are as strong as ever."

She smiled at me and whispered. "I will outlive them all. You will see."

I hugged her, and she kissed my cheek.

I stood to leave. "I want you to rest."

She nodded. "Rest is all I ever do these days. It is good to see your face. Come and visit me again, Sawdah. But eat something in the meantime! You are far too thin!"

"I will. And I will visit again." I promised.

Soon, our days in Mecca ended, and we returned home to the village that had once seemed to me so squalid. I did not think that now. As I walked along the small streets and watched the children playing upon them, I knew that every stone, every small house of that land was precious to me.

From the day of my return, I was blessed to be surrounded by the loving women of my family. Rullah walked with me and talked with me. Fatima cared for me and cooked for me, but I trusted Noor above them all, for I soon saw that we were the same. Noor had shared with me some of the story of her own journey, and I knew that we were both lonely and afraid. We both sought peace. We both yearned to be whole again.

My sister asked nothing of me but that I let myself heal. In time, my body recovered from the years of abuse it had endured. When I was able, Rullah asked me to join her in the village school. We taught and tended to the children together, and I was happy doing it, for I came to love these children. I had wept many nights that I could not bear a child of my own. Now *Allah* had given me many children to love. It did not matter that they were not mine.

One afternoon, when we had been back in the village but two months, I was walking in the orchard when a man approached me. It was Ali. He spoke in a quiet voice I almost did not hear. "Hello, Sawdah."

I looked into his eyes. They were soft and brown. These were eyes that sparkled at me in my first memories. His eyes made the years slip away, and I was a child again. I was happy again. "Hello, Ali."

He smiled and looked down at his feet. "I was afraid you had forgotten me."

I shook my head. "I could never forget you, my friend, though it has been many long years."

Still looking down, he said, "I am glad those years have ended." With those words, he turned and walked away through the trees, leaving me alone with my thoughts.

Ali was five years old when I was born. His mother had attended my own mother in childbirth. Ali had always loved his mother and had spent much of his childhood at her side. He was smaller than the other boys in the village and not as popular as his elder brother.

My birth had not been easy for Mother, and Ali watched over me as Selma saved my mother's life. It was Ali, my father once told me, who had walked outside into the darkness of that day to find him and bring him to me.

I could still hear the words of the poem Ali wrote and sang to me when I was just a little girl.

So beautiful, so rare, on the day she first opened her eyes to the world,
The jealous moon hid herself in the sun's embrace, lest any see her shame.
The sun, afraid to cast his light upon her, lest his light seem dim beside,
Turned away from the land and the sea and from this ebon-eyed beauty
Whose earliest glance could change the skies: Sawdah.

Ali was my first and truest friend. He came with Selma when she visited my mother, bringing me toys to play with that he had carved himself from thick bits of palm wood. He sang to me. He told me stories. He made me laugh.

Ali had no sisters, and his brother, Hassan, was always busy with Noor and the other children. Ali was a quiet, shy boy, uncomfortable in the company of the louder children. As the years passed, and he grew taller and stronger, he helped his father tend the camels and horses. Ali's visits were less frequent, but each time he came, he brought me a toy or told me a funny story. He played the games I wanted to play and cared about what was important to me.

As I grew and my body began to develop into that of a woman, I noticed a change in the way men and the older boys treated me. They stared with lust in their eyes. Ali did not. He continued to look on me with the same gentle eyes I had known when I was a child. Even as he grew into manhood, he never changed his manner or attitude toward me.

I am ashamed to say that I was the one who changed. I began to treat him with contempt. I wanted him to look at me the way the other men did, as though he desired me, so I would have that power over him as I knew I had it over the other men. When he continued to treat me as a precious friend instead of some sweetmeat over which to salivate, I scorned his kindness and thought him weak. I laughed at his dirty hands and dirty clothes. One terrible day, I told him he stank like the camels, and I did not wish to be around him anymore.

When I think on it, I remember that day as vividly as though it had happened yesterday.

"As you wish, fair Sawdah," he had said then. He had cast his eyes on the ground and turned away from me. I thought I was better than him, and for many years afterwards I did not speak to Ali, though I saw him in the village nearly every day.

When I left to marry Sheikh Ruhi, I gave no thought to the welfare of this man who had been my friend. When my fortune changed, and I sat alone in the dark hours of my sorrow and loneliness in that city, I had thought often of Ali's kind eyes, eyes so unlike those of the men around me.

I had forgotten to remember my own eyes as they must have seemed to him. I had forgotten my coldness, my disdain. I felt a burning shame as I remembered it now and wondered at the kindness that still shone from his eyes when he spoke to me.

My thoughts turned, as they sometimes did, to the horror I had endured in Ahmed's house. There was a man about whom I had never had a second thought, and yet his perception of my intentions toward him had been enough for him to revile me, had made him wish to crush me beneath the heel of his boot.

Now here before me was a man whom I had actively mistreated, whose friendship I had trampled upon, whose love I had disdained. And this man praised *Allah* for my safe return. I thought of his words to me when I first set foot in our family camp in Mecca. He had known, even then, only on the strength of a phrase that had escaped my lips, that it was I who had returned.

He should hate me. He should be reveling in my misfortune, filling the air with songs about my cruelty and the justice of the treatment I had received. But he did none of those things. He only smiled and welcomed me home.

I did not have occasion to speak to Ali again for many weeks. I saw him sometimes as I walked from the school. We nodded a greeting and that was all. When I went to visit his mother, as I often did these days, he was never there. I would bring a meal to her side and sit with her, often in silence, until it was time for me to return to my duties. Selma did not ask questions about my past. She only repeated, "*Allah* is merciful, Sawdah. *Allah* is merciful. Put your faith in Him."

I did not speak to anyone of Ali, not even to Noor. Then one evening, as I walked with her through the village to fetch Amira, we passed him as he drew water from the well. When he saw us, he bowed and spoke a simple greeting. I bowed my head, and Noor smiled. We walked on. I found myself trembling and drew a deep sigh to steady my heart.

After we had walked a while, Noor stopped me. She looked into my face. "What is it, Sawdah? What troubles you?"

"It is nothing. I just wonder," my words drifted away.

Noor usually did not press me to speak my feelings, but this time she did. "What do you wonder?"

I looked at her face glowing in the light of the full moon above us. "I wonder why Ali does not hate me. I treated him so badly."

Noor smiled and held my hands. "Sawdah, Ali is a gentle man. It is his nature to forgive. I am certain he bears you no ill will. He is truly kind."

"But Noor, I treated him the way," I stopped. I had been about to say Ahmed and Sheikh Ruhi, but the names stuck in my throat. "The way they treated me. I did not strike Ali with my hands, but I struck him with my words. How can he possibly have forgiven me?"

"He forgives you because there is room in his heart only for love. He has always been a kind man with a generous heart. That is increased now by his strong faith. He believes it is the will of *Allah* that we live in love and not bear grudges."

Noor sighed. "Sawdah, when our father and Jibran were killed, Ali's words helped to hold our people in check. He stood with Ghazi as an example to the other young men and kept them from rushing into war. He helped us teach our people to forgive those who wished us harm and pray for them as we would pray for our own sick and wounded. He is truly a good man, Sawdah. I consider him my brother and my friend." We retrieved Amira and returned home. Noor and I did not speak again of Ali.

On a beautiful clear night that autumn, with the moon shining bright in the sky, Selma slept her last sleep. We all grieved for her, but Noor knew Ali would take it the hardest. During her illness, he had retreated more and more into his own thoughts, barely speaking even to those closest to him. Noor feared for him. I went with Noor and Amira to take a meal to Ali and his father. We sat with them. Noor spoke comforting words, and my heart broke at the sight of their drawn faces and sad eyes.

They had been caring for Selma every day for the past year, never knowing when she would leave this earth or how much longer they had with her. The year of sleepless nights and worried days had taken a toll on them both.

A few days later, Ghazi and Rullah asked us all to dine with their family. I sat with Amira and Leila and the other children, while Noor and Fatima sat with Ali, encouraging him to eat something. Bassam sat with my brother and Rullah. They gave him their undivided attention and encouraged him to speak openly of his feelings and thoughts.

"Come dine with us again tomorrow," my brother said when we stood to go. We all returned the next night and soon began taking meals together every night. Surrounded by my family during those meals, I felt truly happy, even as we all grieved for Selma.

I looked at Ali across the table and thought of the forgiveness he had shown me. Was it possible that I might also forgive? I asked *Allah* for guidance, and in time I came to forgive Sheikh Ruhi. My heart softened toward him, and I came to believe that he had indeed loved me. In forgiving him, I could forgive myself the loss of our baby and my fertility and the toll that tragedy had taken on both our lives. In Ahmed's case, I found forgiveness much more difficult. I prayed for him for many years until my hatred was completely lifted, but even as it first began to pass, I felt an indescribable freedom. No longer burdened by the weight of those terrible years, I could smile again. I began to laugh again. I spoke with Ali again.

He walked me home one night when we had lingered behind to help Rullah tidy up after a meal. I was still living with my sister then and he left me at the door of her house with a simple "Good night." As the days passed, our walks grew longer and soon we were strolling together in the orchard every evening. The others had their children to care for, and Bassam did not like to stay up late. On these walks, Ali and I spoke of *Allah,* and Ali shared with me all that had passed in the village in the ten years I had been away. I marveled at how effortlessly we slipped back into the easy friendship I had forsaken so many years ago. Still I said nothing of my own history. I was afraid to lose this time with him. I had come to treasure these walks and to depend upon them. Ali seemed not to notice my reticence and was content to answer my questions and relate to me the story of his life.

"Why did you never marry?" I asked Ali one night after listening to the tale of how Sameer had wooed and wed his wife.

Ali stopped walking and lowered his gaze. "When Hassan died," he said, "my mother took it very badly. I wanted to be with her, to help her." He looked up and smiled at me. "Your brother tried to marry me off one time." Ali laughed. It was the first time I had heard him laugh since we were children. The sound warmed my heart.

"A caravan passed through from Damascus. The leader's daughter took a fancy to me. She was beautiful, I suppose." His voice drifted away. "But she wasn't you. I knew in my heart that I could not love her." He shook his head. "You must think me a fool waiting so many years with no hope you would ever return."

I said nothing but only took his hand in mine. When I touched his skin, I felt I wanted to hold his hand forever. He lifted my hand to his lips and kissed it. We walked on in silence until he left me at the door to my sister's house.

The next night, we walked again. When we passed a bench that now sat at the base of the enormous fig tree, Ali said, "I built that for Fatima." He smiled. "She has always loved that tree."

"Can we sit there?" I asked. He nodded and we sat together under the spreading branches. "Ali," I began, "I have cherished these walks with you and only fear their end."

"But why should they end?" he asked.

"Because I have never told you of my life in the time I was away from this village."

"I have never asked. You don't need to tell me anything. I am only grateful you returned safely."

"I know. I just want you to know the truth so you may make of it what you will."

Ali took my hand. He never let it go while he listened silently to my story.

"And now you know the truth of it," I said when I was done, my eyes filling with tears. "I will understand if we have to stop our walks together. I know that I am not the worthy companion I might once have been."

Ali took both my hands in his and looked into my eyes. "Sawdah, that evening, when you returned to us, when I heard your voice in Mecca, my heart leapt with joy and cracked for the sorrow I knew must explain your return." His voice broke. "I am so sorry for what you have had to endure."

He touched my face then, wiping a tear from my cheek. "Sawdah, dear Sawdah, whatever has passed, has passed. You remain as you have always been, beloved of me."

He knelt on the ground at my feet and said, "I have loved you all my life. I love you still. I have looked to the stars and longed to be among them that I too might shine in the sky above you and know you are content and safe. These nights we have walked together have been the happiest of my life. I can think of only one thing that would increase the joy I have felt since your return. I ask that you consent to be my wife."

"Oh, Ali. I do love you, and I am honored that you would ask me to be yours, but you know now that I cannot bear children."

"It does not matter. Sawdah, I have nothing to offer you except my heart and the promise that I will spend every day of my life loving only you. Please say that you will be mine."

I fell into his arms. "Yes," I whispered in his ear as he held me tight. Tears fell from my eyes. "Yes, I will."

Eight years I had spent in the palace and two years in the house of Ahmed. One year from the day of my return from Mecca, I stood with Ali before our family and *Allah* and pledged to him my fidelity and faith. I felt truly blessed by *Allah*'s great mercy.

I wanted for nothing so long as I could be with my beloved. Silk sheets were no substitute for his gentle touch. His humble home was a palace to me, grander than any I had seen, for it became our home together, and I knew *Allah* would reside with us always.

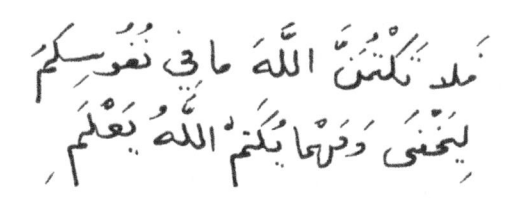

$$\text{لا تَكْتُمَنَّ اللَّهَ ما في نُفُوسِكُمْ}$$
$$\text{لِيَخْفَى وَمَهْما يُكْتَمْ اللَّهُ يَعْلَمُ}$$

Don't keep from God what is in your heart, thinking it will remain secret. Whatever is hidden from Him, God already knows.
-Zuhair

CHAPTER 27
SAWDAH: NOOR

As my happiness increased, I watched my sister's sorrow grow. As we sat alone in her house one afternoon, I asked *Allah* to guide my words that I might be of service to her. "Are you happy, Noor?" I asked.

She looked at me in surprise. "Of course I am. I have Amira. I have my work. I have you. My life is full. Of course I am happy."

"I think you are not," I said. "Tell me, Noor, why do you walk along the path of Al-Islam when *Allah* still does not reside in your heart?"

She gazed at me for a long time without speaking then lowered her head. When she did speak, it was with a malice I had never heard in her voice. "I do it because I must. Because I have no other choice."

I took her hand. "Noor, were you with Mother the day she died?"

She looked up and nodded.

"Will you tell me about that day?"

"I came to her side that morning as she lay resting. She told me her time had come."

"Is that when she gave you the Stone?" I watched Noor's eyes move to glance at the stone that now hung on the front wall of her house.

"Yes." A tear slid slowly down her face, and she brushed it away with a quick sweep of her hand.

"What did she say to you, Noor?"

Noor opened her mouth as if to speak, but no sound came. She coughed and swallowed. "She said, 'Remember who you are.'" The tears fell from her eyes now, falling too fast for her hands to catch them all.

Noor trembled with the sobs that wracked her body. She spoke again in a gasping voice. "We have betrayed her, Sawdah. I have betrayed her."

"No, Noor. You have done what she would have done in your place. You honor her memory."

"No!" Noor cried out in agony. "I betrayed her. I let them kill everything that she believed in. I stood by and let it happen." She shook her head. "I did not have the courage to fight."

"Is this why you hate *Allah*, Noor? Because you believe He betrayed our mother?"

Noor spoke in a hoarse voice. "Yes. And because *Allah* murdered our father and brother."

"Men murdered them, not *Allah*."

"They died because they put their faith in their god, and their god did nothing to save them," she said bitterly.

"The men who killed our father and Jibran were fools, and *Allah* weeps for their folly," I told her.

She shook her head. Fresh tears spilled from her eyes, and she gripped my hands. She crumpled, her strength leaving her, and she lowered her head onto our joined hands.

I let her rest a moment before speaking again. "Have you told *Allah* how angry you are with Him?"

Noor sat up, confused, wiping the tears from her face. "What?"

"Have you told *Allah* how angry you are with Him?" I repeated.

Noor tilted her head to one side. "I don't understand."

I took up her hands again in mine and looked her full in the face. "You must tell *Allah* that you are angry with Him. You must hold Him accountable for the wrongs you believe He has done you."

"What do you mean?"

"A thief is brought before his accuser to atone for his actions. So perhaps you should bring *Allah* before you and state your accusations."

"I cannot."

"Why not? If you neither fear nor love Him, what would be the harm?"

I watched as the hint of a smile stirred on Noor's lips. She burst into laughter. "Indeed, why not?" She laughed out loud. I had not heard my sister laugh like this in all the months since my return. We laughed together at the idea of taking *Allah* to task for His transgressions.

I silently asked *Allah* to forgive my levity. I knew my sister would likely spend her life wrestling between the faith she had known and the faith that had been thrust upon her, but I felt if Noor could give voice to her emotions, she might forgive and might then be able to reconcile herself to *Allah*. At the very least, anger directed at *Allah* meant she had to believe in His existence. It was a place to start. In my heart, I beseeched *Allah* to soften her heart that she might find her way to His warm embrace. I hoped she would find comfort there as I had.

There was a soft knock at the door. I opened it. Amira stood in the doorway, her face flushed. "What's wrong?" I asked.

"I think I am bleeding," she said quietly, looking down at the ground.

I knew at once what she meant, but Noor looked up, frightened. I stopped her with a wave. "Let us go together to the moon tent, Amira. We can play games there and gossip with the other women. You will love it."

I smiled at Noor who was beaming now that she realized what was happening. "Join us when you have time, my sister. We will save some stories to share with you."

I felt I had spoken enough of *Allah*, perhaps said too much. I waited for Noor to broach the subject again, praying to *Allah* as always for guidance.

She did speak again, bringing up *Allah*'s name as we picked grape leaves together one afternoon.

"Sawdah," she began, "Mother and Hassan died never having heard the words of the Prophet Mohammed. Is Paradise denied them? They lived their lives in service to the gods they knew, gods in which they believed."

"I do not think *Allah* would forsake them, Noor."

She went on, "Would embracing Al-Islam have made them more than what they were? Our mother carried a village's faith on her shoulders. She tended the sick and wounded. She birthed their babies. She held their hands on their deathbeds. Would she have loved more, given more had she spoken the words *Allahu Akbar*?"

She set her basket upon the ground and paced as she spoke. "What about Hassan, who gave his life that others might be spared. Would he have been nobler, more courageous? Would he have been any more the man I loved, the man I still love?" She was crying now, and my heart broke for the pain she must still feel every time she spoke his name.

"No," I replied. "Even Al-Islam could not have improved upon him." I held out my hand. "Come, let us sit and talk." We sat in the shade of some fruit trees. "Go on, Noor. Tell me what is troubling you."

She sighed. "I have spent my adult life divided in service." She held out her left hand. "Here, I have the rituals and traditions of our mother. They bring me peace. They keep her memory strong."

She went on, now indicating her right hand. "Here, is the God of my father, whose very existence makes me question everything I have ever learned. I speak His words with my lips and still cannot feel them in my heart."

She looked at me. "What do I do, Sawdah? How do I reconcile these two worlds?" She brought her hands together and clasped them in her lap.

I covered her hands with mine. "When I have been lost, forsaken, *Allah* has sent His angels to guide me and see me through. If you try, even a bit, to put your trust in Him, He will not fail you."

"But what about Mother and all she believed in? Do I say she was ignorant? I cannot do that."

I looked away across the orchard. "Noor, perhaps we all worship the same one God. Perhaps He is a God who wears many faces. In years past, we called him by the wrong name, even believed Him to be multiple beings. We did not know any better. *Allah* is no new god. He is our Creator. He has been with us from the dawn of time and will remain after the last soul has departed this earth. Perhaps, in the end, we shall meet Him and finally understand everything. I think what matters most, Noor, is what we leave behind us in this life, not what we walk toward in the hereafter."

I took her hands in mine. "Can I say I have loved? That I have been loved? I can. Can I say I am living a virtuous life, one that brings honor to my family? I can. Can I say I worship my God with my whole heart? I can."

I watched as a look of peace crept over my sister's face. "What does a name matter?" I asked her. "*Allah* is Great. He may smile at an offering to the four corners of the world or delight at a prayer spoken five times each day. It is my belief that *Allah* can be all things. He is our Creator, our Benefactor, our Savior. He can take for Himself any name and wear upon His visage any face." I paused. I wanted desperately to reconcile Noor's faith with mine and hoped my words were helping. Still, I could not deny what I believed. I added, "Now we have heard His laws, now that we have learned His name, we have a duty to revere them."

A smile played upon her lips. It reached her eyes. Noor spoke. "I may never believe in *Allah* as you believe, but you make me hate the idea less."

I laughed. "That is all I can hope for."

She looked out to the horizon, still smiling. "Let us return, Sawdah." We took up our baskets and headed home.

وَأَنَّ غَدًا وَأَنَّ الْيَوْمَ رَهْنٌ
وَبَعْدَ غَدٍ بِمَا لَا تَعْلَمِينَا

Our todays and tomorrows are collateral
For the days which follow, and a destiny we cannot yet know.
-Amr Ibn Kulthum

CHAPTER 28
SAWDAH: HASSAN

I know I am dying. I feel the sickness envelop my body. I do not begrudge *Allah*. He has been most merciful and just. He has given me but one year with my beloved Ali, but it has been a year of delights I could never have imagined. I have been happy, sharing my life with one who is my equal and my friend. I have known passion in the arms of this man who cherishes me as I cherish him. I would not trade these months we have shared for any number of years without him.

I believe Noor must know I am not well. She says nothing, still I see it in her eyes when we speak. It is a cautious glance, the Healer's glance. These past days, she has kept me from my usual duties, keeping me out of the sun and lightening my burdens. I know she will say nothing directly unless I ask.

I will not approach her. I want no special care. I will not fight the will of *Allah*. He has given me a second life, a most wondrous life. I will not fight in a vain attempt to postpone my meeting with Him.

Ali will grieve, I think. We have been so happy. My heart aches at the thought of him alone again. And yet, he has spent a lifetime alone. I must trust that *Allah* will be with him.

"Noor, come quickly!"

I opened my eyes to find my husband kneeling at my side as I lay on the floor of our house. He helped me to my feet, and my sister ran through the open door.

"What happened to her?" Noor's eyes scanned me as she spoke breathlessly to Ali.

I heard their voices through a thick fog as they both helped me onto the bed.

"We were talking. She had just returned from a walk with Leila. Suddenly she was on the floor." He looked anxiously at Noor. "What can have happened?"

Noor put her hand to my face. It felt warm against my cold skin. Ali brought a cloth and wiped the sweat from my brow.

"Sawdah, have you fallen before?"

I shook my head. "I have felt weak and dizzy, but I have never fallen."

Noor nodded. "Have you eaten today?"

"A little. I have not had much appetite for many months now."

Ali took my hand. "I beg her to eat. She is so small as it is."

"Not anymore," I said, trying to lighten the mood. "I am growing fat like an old man."

They did not laugh.

"May I examine you, Sister?"

I turned to Ali. He looked so worried that I consented for his sake. He made as though to leave us, but I grabbed his hand. "Please, stay with me." If I was to hear the worst, I wanted him at my side. Much as it would pain him to hear the truth, still I needed his strength.

Noor reassured him. "You can stay, Ali. There is no shame in it."

He took his place at my side and stroked my hair. "I'm sure everything will be fine. You have just been in the sun too long." His eyes were bright. I knew he was frightened. I asked *Allah* to give him strength to endure what Noor was about to tell us.

Noor touched my abdomen through my robes. "Do you feel discomfort when you eat?" she asked.

I nodded. "My stomach seems to burn sometimes."

She put her hands on the side of my waist. "Do you have any pain here?"

"Yes, sometimes at night. There have been some nights I could not sleep."

Ali looked shocked. "Why did you not wake me?"

I touched his face. "I did not want to worry you."

"And now? How do you feel now?" Noor asked.

I put a hand to my stomach. "There is pressure here. It is not painful, but sometimes it is difficult to breathe."

I heard Noor sigh. I knew she would tell him now. I knew she would confirm what I had long suspected. Our mother had not lingered long in the end. I only hoped that would be my fate as well, for my own sake, and for the sake of my beloved Ali.

Noor's face was solemn, and she put a hand to her heart as she spoke. "I have long suspected your illness, Sawdah. I only wish you had confided this in me sooner. I could have made it easier for you to bear."

I felt Ali tighten his grip. "What do you mean, Noor? What is wrong with her?"

"My dear Ali," Noor said, "you must prepare yourself." She swallowed and her voice broke. "You are going to be a father."

"A father?" he exclaimed, "But how has this happened?"

Noor smiled, "In the usual way, I suspect."

Ali laughed and kissed me. I had not fully grasped the situation and still lay frozen in shocked silence.

Noor looked at me, a twinkle in her smiling eyes. "Sawdah," she spoke slowly, as though to a small child. "You are not ill. You are not dying. You are with child. If I am any judge, you will be a mother before spring returns."

Ali spoke in stunned amazement. "Only four months more? How can it be so soon? How can this be true?"

"It can be true because my sister is obstinate and independent and does not trouble others with her discomforts."

Noor rose, and as she did, the fog seemed to lift from my mind. I finally understood what she was saying to me. "But Noor, it can't be. I am barren. I was sure I was dying."

Noor's face broke into a beaming smile. "I suppose your *Allah* had other plans."

She and Ali laughed.

"*Allahu Akbar!*" Ali cried.

As the reality of Noor's words reached my heart, I too began to smile. Finally, I laughed with them. Me, a mother? After all these years? I found myself awed once again by the grace and glory of *Allah*.

I spent the next four months under my sister's watchful eye. I ate what she told me to eat, took exercise or rested as she instructed. As the sun rose in the East, Ali held my hand, and Noor helped our son into the world.

My life has been a tapestry of sorrow and joy, fear and hope, hate and love. Yet nothing I have experienced can compare to the day I became a mother. In the hours before my son's birth, I felt pain mingled with a joy I could not have believed possible. And in those hours, I felt healed. I felt truly new and alive. I was young again.

We named our son Hassan. He is a strong and vibrant child. He has my black eyes and his father's powerful hands, Noor's kind face and his namesake's boundless spirit of adventure. They are the best parts of us all.

EPILOGUE

We have seen the sun rise and fall upon our people. God's blessings be upon you, friend. You have seen our world, and you have heard our tale. We pray that you look upon us with kindness that our world might live again in you.

We fear for our people, for we have seen the coming of the *Jihad*. We have heard the cries of the lost souls and the wails of the grieving mothers. We sit helplessly in the care of our One God, while He weeps at the sight of His children killing one another in His name.

Our time has passed, but yours has just begun. Remember our words as you move forward on your own journey. We are all God's children, and He dwells in all our houses.

God's love and peace be upon you.

Insha'Allah we will meet again.

ACKNOWLEDGEMENTS

The author wishes to thank the gentle readers who cried and laughed in all the right places. And thank you, Ernie, for the beautiful cover. You brought a dream to life and gave it wings.

ABOUT THE AUTHOR

A. Afaf was raised by a father who loved the history of his native country, Syria. The stories he told and history he taught her, kindled her desire to bring that world to life. This is her first novel.

Connect with A. Afaf

https://intheshadowoftheprophet.com/
facebook.com/people/A-Afaf/61550728840770
instagram.com/intheshadowoftheprophet/
tiktok.com/@intheshadowoftheprophet